Resounding praise for *New York Times* **Bestselling** author

STUART WOODS
and
THE RUN

"**A** straight-ahead, damn-the-torpedoes
storyteller."
Washington Post

"**W**oods is off and running in this political thriller that includes assassination attempts by
right-wing extremists, sexual tension from an
old flame, and handshaking the hordes along
the campaign trail. . . . Whichever party you
belong to, you may find yourself rooting for
Will Lee and his honest approach to
politics and the presidency."
San Antonio Express-News

"**W**oods tosses in twists from the get-go. . . .
[His] intriguing plot carries us along with plenty
of action. . . . The main character is heroic,
someone we can identify with, someone we
wistfully would wish really existed."
Florida Times-Union

"**S**tuart Woods is a wonderful storyteller
who could teach Robert Ludlum and
Tom Clancy a thing or two."
The State (SC)

Books by Stuart Woods

THE RUN

STUART WOODS

HARPER

An Imprint of HarperCollinsPublishers

This is a work of fiction. Names, characters, places, and incidents are drawn from the author's imagination or are used fictitiously and are not to be construed as real. Any resemblance to actual events, locales, organizations, or persons, living or dead, is entirely coincidental.

HARPER

An Imprint of HarperCollins*Publishers*
10 East 53rd Street
New York, New York 10022-5299

Copyright © 2000 by Stuart Woods
ISBN 978-0-06-171157-2

First Harper Premium paperback printing: January 2009
First HarperTorch paperback printing: March 2001
First HarperCollins hardcover printing: June 2000

This book is for Melody Miller

THE RUN

1

United States Senator William Henry Lee IV and his wife, Katharine Rule Lee, drove away from their Georgetown house in their Chevrolet Suburban early on a December morning. There was the promise of snow in the air.

Kate sipped coffee from an insulated mug and yawned. "Tell me again why we drive this enormous fucking car," she said.

Will laughed. "I keep forgetting you're not a politician," he said. "We drive it because it is, by my reckoning, the least offensive motor vehicle manufactured in the state of Georgia, and because Georgia car workers and their union have shown the great wisdom to support your husband's candidacy in two elections."

"Oh," she said. "Now I remember."

"Good. I'm glad I won't have to put you in a home right before Christmas." He looked in the rearview mirror and saw another Suburban following them. "They're there," he said.

"They're supposed to be."

"How did they know?"

"Because I called them last night and gave them our schedule."

The week before there had been a terrorist attack on CIA employees as they had left the Agency's building in McLean, Virginia, and certain Agency officials had been given personal protection for a time; Kate Rule was the deputy director for Intelligence, chief of all the CIA's analysts, and was, therefore, entitled.

"Oh," Will replied, sipping his own coffee and heading north toward College Park, Maryland, and its airport. "They're not going to follow us all the way to Georgia, are they?"

"I persuaded them that wouldn't be necessary."

"Good."

"It's a little like having Secret Service protection, isn't it?" she nudged. "Does it make you feel presidential?"

"Nothing is going to make me feel presidential, at least for another nine years."

"What about the cabinet? If Joe Adams is elected and wants you for Defense or State or something, will you leave the Senate?"

Joseph Adams was vice president of the United States and the way-out-in-front leader for the Democratic Party's nomination for president the following year. "Joe and I have already talked about that. He says I can have anything I want, but he doesn't really mean it."

"I always thought Joe was a pretty sincere guy," Kate said.

"Oh, he is, and he was sincere with the half-dozen other guys he told the same thing. But I don't really have the foreign-policy credentials for State, and while I think I really could have Defense, I don't want it. I don't want to spend eight or even four years doing battle with both the military and Congress; the job killed James Forrestal and Les Aspin, and it's ground up a lot of others."

"What about Justice? Your work on the Senate Judiciary Committee should stand you in good stead for that."

"I think I could have Justice, if I were willing to fight for it tooth and nail, and there's a real opportunity to do some good work there."

"Well?"

"I think I'll stay in the Senate. Georgia's got a Republican governor at the moment, and if I left, he'd get to appoint my replacement, and we don't want that. Also, if Joe's elected, three or four top senators will leave to join the administration, among them the minority leader, and I'd have a real good shot at that job. And if we can win the Senate back, then the job would be *majority* leader, and that is very inviting."

"It's the kind of job you could keep for the rest of your career," she said.

"It is."

"But you don't want to spend the rest of your career in the Senate, do you?"

"You know I love the Senate."

"Will, you've been awfully closemouthed about

this, but I know damned well you want to be president."

"One of these days, sure," Will replied.

"You mean after Joe has served for eight years?"

"I'd only be fifty-seven. Why not? I might even appoint you director of Central Intelligence."

"Yeah, sure," she said. "The world would fall on you."

"If Jack Kennedy could appoint Bobby attorney general, why couldn't I appoint my wife to be head of the CIA?"

"Well, it's a nice thought, anyway," she said.

"Listen, here's a thought; Joe's going to owe me after the election, and if I'm not going to ask him for a cabinet job, I could ask him to appoint you DCI."

"Would you really do that?"

"Let's just say that I know the candidate well and have the highest confidence in her. It's not as though you're not supremely well qualified."

"Mmmmm. I like the sound of it."

"Of course, I'd want my back scratched *a lot* if I pull this off, and I mean that in the literal, not the figurative sense."

"I'll start growing my nails now." She laughed.

"Promises, promises."

"I think about it sometimes," she said.

"Scratching my back? Less thought, more action!"

"No, I mean your being president."

"And what do you think when you think about it?"

"Mostly about what a huge pain in the ass being first lady would be."

"Oh, it might have its up side—weekends at Camp David, travel on Air Force One, that sort of thing."

"I'd have to make a lot of speeches, and you know how I hate doing that."

"Well, how about this? If Joe has already appointed you DCI, I could reappoint you. Then I could *hire* a first lady."

"Just run an ad, you mean?"

"Why not?"

"Well, I must admit, the idea of being appointed and then reappointed has its appeal, but the substitute wife doesn't."

"I'm glad to hear it." Will turned into the entrance of the little airport at College Park, which had been founded by the Wright Brothers and was located on the grounds of the University of Maryland. He drove down the taxiway to where his airplane was tied down, got out of the car, and unlocked the cabin door. The airplane was new, a Piper Malibu-Mirage, a six-seat, pressurized single-engine aircraft, loaded with the latest equipment. Will had traded his elderly Cessna for it a couple of months before, and it made trips back to Georgia a lot faster and more comfortable.

He climbed in and lowered the rear seat backs, then stowed the luggage Kate handed him. She drove the Suburban back to the little office and parked it there.

Will had nearly finished his preflight inspection

when Kate returned. She started to say some-thing, but her voice was drowned out by the noise of a large helicopter setting down on the grass nearby. Will recognized it immediately.

So did Kate. "I thought the president had al-ready gone home to California for Christmas," she said.

"I thought so, too," Will said.

The airstair door of the helicopter was low-ered, but the engines were kept running. A young Marine officer in a crisp uniform left the craft and came jogging toward where Will and Kate stood.

He ran up to them and saluted smartly. "Sena-tor, Mrs. Lee."

"Good morning, Lieutenant," Will said.

"The vice president and Mrs. Adams would be honored if you would join them for breakfast at Camp David," the officer said.

Will and Kate looked at each other. "We were just about to take off for Georgia," Will said.

"The vice president instructed me to *insist*," the Marine replied. "We'll have you back here before noon, and our people will get you an expedited clearance to Georgia."

"We'll need to change clothes," Will said. There was no telling who might be there.

"That won't be necessary, sir; it will be just the two of you and Vice President and Mrs. Adams."

Will looked at Kate and shrugged. She shrugged back. He locked up the Mirage and followed the Marine back to the idling helicopter. A moment

later they had taken off and were headed northwest across the Maryland landscape.

Kate leaned over and spoke into Will's ear. "You
have any idea what this is all about?"

Will shook his head. "Not a clue," he said.

2

As they approached Camp David, it began to snow, and they could see nothing from the helicopter except whiteness. Kate squeezed Will's hand.

"I don't like this," she said. "How are they going to land?"

"Don't worry, they'll get us in safely."

He was right. At around five hundred feet they could see the interstate highway, then a deep forest, and then the big chopper alit gently on the pad. Will had been to Camp David only once before, in summer, and the contrast was startling. The trees were bereft of leaves, and the summer golf-cart transportation had been replaced by a Secret Service Ford Expedition. It had not been snowing long, but already a broom machine was sweeping the roads and paths ahead of them. They drove past a number of buildings, then stopped before a large structure of timber and stone.

"This is Aspen Lodge," Will said, as they got out of the car. "It's the president's residence here."

A Secret Service agent escorted them up the path to the door, on which hung the seal of the vice president. He opened the door for them and ushered them in. Past the foyer they emerged into a large, luxuriously furnished living room, with deep sofas and chairs scattered artfully about. The walls were hung with fine paintings, mostly American landscapes, chosen by the president and first lady from the collection of the National Gallery of Art.

"Vice President and Mrs. Adams will be with you shortly," the agent said, then left them alone in the room.

A Filipino butler entered. "Good morning, Senator, Mrs. Lee," he said. "May I get you some refreshment?"

"A V-8, please," Kate replied.

"Orange juice," Will said.

The man disappeared and returned with the juices. They stood in front of the huge fireplace and warmed their backsides while they waited.

"This is quite a place," Kate said. "No wonder presidents love it so much."

"If you were first lady, it would be yours," Will whispered.

"It's too early in the game to start tempting me, Will; there's plenty of time for that."

"Tempting you has always been one of my chief pleasures," Will said.

"I wonder what's keeping Joe and Sue?"

"They're entitled."

As if on cue, the vice president and his wife entered the room from a rear hallway. "Will!"

Adams said, ignoring the outstretched hand and embracing him. "It's good to see you!"

The women, who were less well acquainted than their husbands, touched cheeks and exchanged pleasantries.

"Have you had breakfast?" the vice president asked.

"Not really," Will replied.

"Neither have we." Adams nodded at the waiter. "Tell Carlos what you'd like."

"An egg white omelet, dry toast, and coffee," Kate said.

"Scrambled eggs and smoked salmon, home fries, English muffin, and more orange juice," Will said, ignoring a sharp glance from his wife. "Coffee later."

The Adamses ordered, then joined Will and Kate before the fire. "I love this place in winter," Adams said, "and the president was kind enough to offer us the lodge. Where is Peter? I thought he'd be with you."

"It's his dad's turn to have him for Christmas," Kate said of her son. "He's going to Boston."

"And how old is he now?"

"Sixteen. A sophomore at Choate, his father's school."

"I know you're proud of him."

"I certainly am. He's doing very well in school; sports, too. Where are your children, Mr. Vice President?"

"It's Joe and Sue, please," Adams said. "They're already at my folks' place in Florida. We're flying down to join them this afternoon."

"How was New York?" Will asked. The vice president's trip had been in the news—he'd made some speeches while his wife Christmas shopped.

"Just lovely this time of the year," Adams replied. "We got to the theater a couple of times. It was almost a vacation."

"Have you got your shopping all done, Kate?" Sue Adams asked.

"I'm relieved to say I have," Kate replied. "We sent Peter's gifts to Boston earlier in the week, and I found a very nice lump of coal for my husband."

The Adamses laughed, then the food arrived, and everyone dug in, keeping up an animated conversation. Will knew Joe Adams very well—Adams had been the first senator to befriend him as an equal, when Will had arrived on the Hill as a senator, instead of as a senatorial aide, and he had known him through committee work before that. While their conversation was the chat of good friends, Will thought he caught something strained in Adams's behavior, and in his wife's, too.

Finally, the dishes were cleared away, and a pot of coffee was set on the table. Sue Adams poured for everyone, then sat down. There was a moment of complete silence, then the butler came back.

"Would you and your guests like anything else at all, Mr. Vice President?" he asked.

"Thank you, Carlos, no. Would you tell the Secret Service man at the door and your own staff that we don't wish to be disturbed for a while?"

"Of course, Mr. Vice President." Carlos bowed and left the room.

The silence came back. Will waited for someone to break it.

Joe Adams finally did. "Will, Kate," he said, "we've asked you up here to give you some news personally." He paused and cleared his throat. Sue Adams stared out a window at the snow.

He's not going to run, Will thought. *Is he insane? The office is his for the taking. Has he had an affair? A stroke? What the hell is going on?*

"First of all, I want you to know that this room is not bugged, and our conversation is not being recorded. I had the Secret Service double-check that earlier today. What I'm about to tell you and Kate I intend to tell *only* you and Kate—you, Will, because, more than anyone else besides Sue, you have a right to know. You're as close a friend as I have, and you've put more into my presidential effort than anyone else. Kate, I want you to know, because I don't want Will to have to keep this from you. I know that I don't even have to ask you both to keep this in the strictest confidence."

Will and Kate nodded. The atmosphere in the room had become somber. Sue Adams got up and went to the window, turning her back to them. She produced a tissue and dabbed at her face.

"Our trip to New York wasn't just for speeches, the theater, and shopping," Joe Adams said. "There was another reason."

Oh, God, Will thought. *I don't know what this is, but I know I'm going to hate it.*

Joe Adams took out a handkerchief, blew his nose, returned the handkerchief to his pocket, then continued.

3

The vice president took a sip of his coffee and began to speak. "The week before last I had my annual physical at Walter Reed Hospital. It went beautifully, and I got a clean bill of health. Ironically, it was the first time I can remember when everything—weight, cholesterol, blood pressure, the works—was right on the money." He took another sip of his coffee. "But I wasn't entirely frank with the staff at Walter Reed."

Will shifted uncomfortably in his seat. If his friend had a clean bill of health from Walter Reed, what the hell could be the matter?

"There was something they didn't pick up on at the hospital," Joe Adams said, "something they wouldn't have detected unless they had been looking for and tested for it specifically. I'd had some symptoms that only Sue and I knew about; that's why we arranged the New York trip. My old college roommate is now one of the two or three top neurologists in the country, and he put together a very thorough series of tests, some of them quite new. Those things that had to be accomplished at a hospital were done in the middle of the night, and under an assumed name, with a minimum of trusted staff present. The other tests were conducted in a suite at the Waldorf Towers, adjacent to our own quarters. The results of all this testing, by the top experts in the field, were conclusive." He looked at Kate, then back at Will. "I'm in the early stages of Alzheimer's disease."

Will had been holding his breath; he let it out in a rush. "Joe . . ." he began.

Adams held up a hand. "Please; let me tell you everything. I know your first question will be, shouldn't I get a second opinion. My testing encompassed *three* opinions, independently arrived at. They were all in complete agreement. I have it; it's going to get worse; and, unless I get lucky and have a coronary, I'm eventually going to die from it."

Sue Adams returned from the window and took her seat. Her eyes were red.

Kate put her hand on Sue's.

"Joe and I have a hard road ahead of us," Sue Adams said, "and we're going to need your help."

Adams continued. "Your next question is going to be, I know, will I resign? The answer is no, and I'll tell you why. I talked with the president yesterday, before he left for California, and I told him I was thinking of resigning my office in order to pursue my presidential campaign full-time. He neither encouraged nor discouraged that action. As you know, he hasn't made any promise to support my candidacy. We weren't the best of friends or the closest of colleagues before we were elected—he picked me as his running mate for purely pragmatic reasons—and we've disagreed as often as we've agreed on issues. So I asked him, frankly, who he would appoint as my successor if I resigned."

Given what he had heard so far, Will was very anxious to hear the president's answer to this question.

"To my surprise," Adams continued, "the president told me he had anticipated my thoughts about resigning. He knew that not being vice president would allow me to disagree with his policies more often. As a result, he said he had given a lot of consideration to whom he might appoint. I half expected him to ask for my recommendation, and I was going to recommend you, Will."

"Why thank you, Joe," Will managed to say.

"But he didn't ask. Instead he told me he had decided not to appoint a new vice president. He's under no constitutional obligation to do so, of course, and he said that, with barely more than a year left to serve, he thought that the speculation surrounding the appointment and the jockeying for advantage by various groups would create too much distraction from the important issues he wants to resolve before he leaves office. As it happens, I think he's right, but if I resigned, his failure to appoint a successor would leave us with an unacceptable situation: It would put the Speaker of the House in line to succeed the president, if he should die before his term ends."

Will nodded his understanding.

"Now, I've always made a great effort to have good relations with the Speaker, and I've tried to consider his position on various issues, but I have to tell you that his positions are so bizarre, sometimes, and always so self-serving and partisan, at the expense of the country, that I swear, if he became president, I'd have to shoot him myself."

Will and Kate both laughed.

"But rather than entertain that possibility," the vice president continued, "it seemed simpler just not to resign my office and continue to campaign for the presidency as vice president."

Will blinked. *"Continue to campaign?"* he asked incredulously.

Adams held up a hand. "Easy, Will; I'm not crazy yet. In my condition, I'd never try to be elected president. There'll come a right moment to leave the race, and when it happens, I'll recognize it, but it's not now. The best medical advice I can get is that the progress of my disease will be slow, and that there's no reason why I shouldn't serve out my term. I'd like to do that, especially because I know now that I can never be president. I think that I can have a positive influence on events and, particularly, on the next session of Congress, if I remain in office."

Will conceded to himself that that was so.

"However, I don't want my medical condition to become public knowledge as long as I can lead a fairly normal life. That would keep me from having any influence on events, and I don't want that while I can be a positive force in national affairs. I announced for the presidency early on, in order to discourage some other potential candidates, and if I withdraw now, I'll have to explain why, and I can't think of an explanation that would ring true. I'd have the press all over me, probing into my life for the real reason, and eventually they'd find it."

"That's true enough," Will said.

"So I plan to continue as if nothing were wrong," Adams said. "I'll do my job as vice president, I'll do the minimum necessary in the way of campaign appearances, and I'll continue to raise money."

"Joe," Will said, "that troubles me, because when you finally do withdraw from the race it will be apparent that you will have been accepting campaign donations under what amounts to false pretenses. I don't think you can do that."

"I've already addressed that problem," Adams said. "What I plan to do is to make an offer to every campaign contributor at the time of my withdrawal. I'll give them a choice: I'll refund their donation; I'll direct it to the campaign of any candidate they designate; or I'll turn it over to the Democratic Party. I'll mail a form to every contributor that they can fill out, sign, and return, and I'll act on those wishes."

"Have you given any thought as to when you might withdraw?"

"Early on, but after the Iowa caucuses and the earliest primaries, like New Hampshire."

Will nodded. "Are you sure you're doing the right thing, Joe?"

"No, I'm not. I'm just making the best decision I can in the circumstances. If I announce my condition and resign now, then all I can do is go home to Florida, sit on the beach, and wait to go crazy and die. If I stay on, I can have some real influence on the president's legislative program and on next year's congressional elections. The Republican majority in both houses is razor-thin, and I want to win back both the Senate and the House, as well as a great many governorships. If I'm out of office, I'll leave a vacuum, and I don't want that."

"I can understand your position, Joe," Will said.

"Sue supports me in this," Adams said. "She's always been my closest advisor, and she's going to stick close to me to be sure that I don't do the wrong thing because of a memory lapse—which, by the way, is my principal symptom so far—short-term memory loss. I'd like to stress that I am *not* delusional. I plan to deal with my memory lapses by having notes taken at every opportunity, so that nothing will get by me. I'll depend a lot on Sue for that."

"That's a good idea," Will said.

"There's something else, Will," Adams said. "When I withdraw, I'm going to do so in your favor. I'm going to ask my contributors to assign their contributions to your campaign."

Will had not yet given any thought to his own position, and he was stunned. "That's incredibly generous of you, Joe," he managed to say. "But Kate and I are going to have to talk about this."

"Of course you will," Adams replied. "Fortunately, you have the holidays ahead of you, and there'll be time before you announce."

"Announce?" Will said.

"I want you to announce for the presidency right after New Year's; I want you to have established yourself as a candidate independent of me in the minds of the electorate before I withdraw."

"I'll have to give that a lot of thought, Joe."

Sue Adams spoke up. "Will, speaking for myself, I think you're now the Democrat who is best qualified for the presidency. You're well established at the center, as well as at the heart of the party, and Joe and I want to see you elected next November."

"We certainly do," Adams said. "You are superbly qualified by temperament, training, and intellect. As far as I'm concerned, nobody in *either* party comes close."

Will warmed to the praise, but he was being sucked into this little conspiracy, and he wasn't entirely comfortable with it.

Adams seemed to sense his disquiet. "Will, all I'm asking you to do is to help me make a graceful exit from public life, while accomplishing as much as I can in the time remaining to me. Is that too much to ask of a close friend?"

"No, certainly not," Will replied.

"Good," Adams said. "Call me when you've made a decision about announcing."

4

Will took off from College Park Airport and called Washington Center for his clearance, as the Marine lieutenant had instructed him to do. To his surprise, he was cleared direct to his home airport in Warm Springs, Georgia, instead of being routed on airways. He climbed to his assigned altitude of 18,000 feet, leaned the engine, punched the identifier for Warm Springs into his GPS computer, switched on the autopilot, and sat back, doing an instrument scan every minute or so.

Hardly a word had passed between him and Kate on the helicopter ride back to College Park, and until now, he had been too busy flying to talk. He wanted to talk.

"This whole thing scares me to death," Will said.

"You? Scared of running for president?"

"Not that, so much; it's Joe's situation. It's like a bomb that may or may not go off."

"Do you really think he's doing the right thing?"

Will shrugged. "I'm not sure there's only one

right thing," he said. "It would be right if he announced his condition publicly and resigned, but who's to say that what he's doing is wrong? He has some very good points about his usefulness to the party and the country over the next months. I certainly wouldn't deny him that."

"You understand that, if the bomb goes off, it's going to hurt you, as well as Joe."

"Maybe; that's entirely unpredictable. I've been thinking back over the history of the presidency, and the only thing I can think of that resembles this situation is Woodrow Wilson's illness in office, and his wife's acting for him. Of course, it's not quite the same thing; Joe's not president. If he were, I think he'd have to resign, regardless of the consequences."

"Do you think Reagan was in the early stages of Alzheimer's during his last term?"

"I don't know; it's possible, I guess, and it's also possible that nobody really noticed. After all, he was the oldest president, and you'd expect some slowing down at that age."

"Remember when he had to testify in court? He said 'I don't recall' dozens of times. At the time I thought he was dissembling, but maybe he really didn't remember."

"Maybe not."

Kate was quiet for a while, then she spoke. "If you do this, it's going to play hell with our lives."

"That's true of everybody who ever ran for the office," Will replied. "Do you not want me to do it?"

"Oh, Will, I think you'd make a superb president, you know that."

"I'm glad you think so. What we have to get clear between us is what your role is going to be."

"What do you want my role to be?"

"We have two choices, I think: One is that you resign from the Agency and play the campaign wife. I know you don't want to do that, and I don't expect you to. The other is for you to remain at the Agency and do your job. I can say, in campaigning, that my wife and I are both public servants and that we decided, together, that the country would be best served by your remaining at the Agency."

"Sounds good to me," Kate said.

"Understand, though, that there are times when I'll want you at my side: at the convention, for instance, and, if I get the nomination, on election night."

"At the whole convention, or just for the smiling and waving at the end?"

"At the whole convention, I think. There has to be *some* time when the party and the press get to feel that you're a real person and not just a cardboard cutout that's set up for photo ops."

"All right, I can take vacation time for the convention."

"Also, when I make evening appearances in or around Washington, I'd like you on the platform, work permitting."

"Work permitting, okay. What about Peter?"

"The last night of the convention and election

night only; that's all I'll ask of him. I don't want to interfere with his schooling or with his relationship with his father."

"Yes, that would *really* set Simon off."

"I don't want you to press Peter to do this; I'd rather not have him there than have him think I'm imposing on our relationship."

"Peter loves you, Will; you know that. He'll be glad to help."

"You're going to have to warn him about the press, too, and . . ." Will stopped.

"Tell him to stay out of trouble?"

"Well, yes. He's a normal kid, and I want him to stay that way, but I don't want him getting busted for smoking pot, or anything like that."

"I think that's a reasonable request"—she laughed—"and I think he'll think so, too."

"I'll need to talk about this with my folks, of course," Will said.

Kate laughed. "You think they're going to discourage you? It's their dream come true!"

"Well, yes."

"Who else should you talk to?"

"I wish Ben Carr were still alive; I'd sure like to talk to him."

"Who else?"

"Tom Black, of course; I'd want him to run the advertising and to advise, in general. I'll want Kitty Conroy and Tim Coleman on board right away." Conroy was the chief of his Senate staff, and Coleman, his press secretary.

"You need a top politician to be campaign manager," Kate said. "Maybe another senator, to do for you what you were going to do for Joe Adams."

"I'll have to think about that," Will replied. "Nobody jumps to mind, and a third of them will be running for reelection."

"Thank God you don't have to make that decision—whether to run for president or for reelection to the Senate. At least, if you lose, you'll still be in the Senate."

"There is that."

"All in all, Senator, I'd say you were in pretty good shape."

"Sure, all I have to do is beat a big field in the primaries and a Republican in November and, along the way, raise sixty or seventy million dollars."

"Oops, forgot about that."

"I'm not president yet. Of course, in the event that I actually get elected, the problem of your role is going to be a thorny one."

"Will, I cannot be Nancy Reagan or Rosalyn Carter or Eleanor Roosevelt."

"I understand that, but even if you stay at the Agency, there'll be a lot of times when you'll have to be at the White House—interviews, events, state dinners, and receptions—and probably some foreign travel."

"I know the situation is different now than when we talked this morning," she said, "but do you really think that, if you were president, you could appoint me head of Central Intelligence?"

"I think a better thing would be for me to appoint a group to evaluate candidates and make a recommendation. If you were among the recommended, it would be a lot easier to appoint you. Certainly, there's no precedent for a first lady holding down a top government job. Not even Bobby Kennedy's appointment as attorney general was as sensitive as that. Can we leave it that I'll do the very best I can?"

"I suppose we'll have to leave it that way."

"At worst, you could stay in your present job. And anyway, if I'm *not* elected, you have no guarantee of ever having the top job. The fact that you're my wife would probably weigh against you with almost any president, certainly with a Republican."

"You mean, my best shot is having my husband in the White House?"

Will laughed. "You said that; I didn't."

"All right, I'll accept that: Nepotism is my best hope. But how am I going to hold down a full-time job at the Agency and still attend all these state dinners and receptions?"

"Listen, I'd have to hold down a job as president, while attending them."

"Touché," she said.

5

They were met at the Warm Springs airport by Henry, the African-American retainer and factotum who had served the Lee family for decades. Will shook Henry's hand, inquired after his health and that of his wife, Marie, and got a satisfactory reply. Henry looked little older than he had ten years before.

Henry dropped them at Will's lakeside cottage and drove on to the main house. Will and Kate showered and rested a while, then walked up to the main house for dinner. The house, a brick-and-granite Georgian structure, had been copied from Will's mother's family home in County Cork, Ireland, and Patricia Lee had acted as the general contractor, supervising every detail of the building. It was fifty years old, and had a patina of maturity about it, wearing its age well.

Henry brought them drinks in the library, and a moment later Billy and Patricia Lee entered. Patricia was nearly eighty and her husband five years older, but they both looked remarkably well, Will thought whenever he saw them. Billy had had two heart attacks during the past twenty years and walked with a cane, but he was pink-faced and healthy-looking. There was an exchange of embraces and kisses, more drinks were brought, and they settled in to catch up.

"We were so sorry Peter couldn't be with us," Patricia said, "but we know it's his father's turn. How is the boy?"

"Thriving," Kate replied.

"Will he come back to us this summer?"

"For at least a month," Kate said. "I'm not sure there are enough girls in Delano to suit him."

"I'll see what I can do," Patricia replied, smiling.

Will's father spoke up. "How come you were so late, Will? We were expecting you for lunch."

"I'm sorry about that, Dad," Will replied, "but we were diverted before we could take off. The vice president invited us to Camp David for brunch."

Billy cocked his head. "That's a little odd, isn't it, right at the beginning of the Christmas holiday?"

Will and Kate exchanged a glance, which was not lost on Billy Lee.

"What's up?" Billy asked.

"I can't tell you all of it," Will said, "and what I do tell you can't go any farther."

"Shoot."

"It looks as though Joe won't run for president."

Everybody in the room sat stock-still for a long moment.

"He's ill, then," Billy said with finality.

"I didn't say that."

"You didn't need to. Heart? Cancer?"

"Nothing like that. I can't tell you more at the moment."

Billy nodded. "Then you'll be running." It wasn't a question.

"Very likely. I haven't made a final decision."

"What decision? There's no decision to make. If Joe Adams is out, you *have* to be in."

Will didn't quarrel with his father. "I haven't decided when to announce. Joe wants me to come out the first of the year."

"He's right; time is short. Who else knows about this?"

"Just Joe and Sue."

"That's what he told you, anyway. Joe's a pretty sly politician."

"I believe him," Will said.

"Believe him, if you like, but don't act on that belief."

"You're not getting cynical on me, are you, Dad?"

"Just realistic."

It wasn't bad advice, Will knew. He nodded.

"We'll have a lot to talk about over this holiday," Billy said.

"Let's not rush it, Dad."

"At my age, I have to rush everything. I wouldn't want to kick off next month without having given you the benefit of my wisdom."

"Well, you've never denied me that." Will laughed.

His mother laughed with him. "It's been pretty good wisdom, hasn't it?"

"It has."

"I still know a few people around the country who could help," Billy said. "Of course, there are fewer of them than there used to be."

"I'm going to need all the help I can get," Will said.

Billy nodded. "Just be careful what you have to give for it."

Henry came in to call them to dinner.

For the first time he could remember, sex did not render Will unconscious. He and Kate made love in their usual slow, caring way, and soon Kate was snoring softly and Will was staring at the ceiling. He got out of bed as quietly as he could, went to the kitchen, and poured himself a glass of milk. He took it into the living room and sat in his leather recliner.

Normally, decisions came easily to Will; he had an orderly mind, and he organized and considered alternatives quickly. But this situation resisted resolution. Try as he might, he could not arrange the problem in a way that suggested a course of action. There were too many variables— Joe Adams's illness, its current state and its rate of progression; the president's preferences with regard to the Democratic nomination; other potential candidates; his own loyalty to Joe. If Joe had simply resigned and gone home to Florida, it would be easier, but he wasn't going to do that. He was going to hang on to what power he had,

Will thought, for as long as he could. What would he, himself, do in the same situation? Maybe the same thing. He could hardly urge Joe to get out and make way for him.

He sat for a good two hours thinking about all this before he got sleepy. Finally, he crawled into bed beside his sleeping wife and drifted off. Sleeping on it would help, he knew. And when he woke up, he had made a decision.

They brought muffins and coffee to the bed and propped themselves up, watching the *Today* show.

"Why do they allow all those people in the street to make such fools of themselves?" Kate asked.

"Careful," Will replied. "Those people are voters."

"I've never understood why Americans go nuts in front of a TV camera," she said, shaking her head. "And even less, why a television network would inflict them on us."

"I'm not going to do it," Will said suddenly.

Kate turned and stared at him wide-eyed. "You're not going to run?"

The phone rang.

Kate looked at the bedside clock. "It's not seven-thirty yet; your parents would never call this early."

Will picked up the phone. "Hello?"

"Senator Lee?"

"Yes."

"This is the White House operator. Will you speak to the vice president?"

"Of course."

There was a click. "Hello, Will?"

"Good morning, Joe."

"I hope I'm not calling too early."

"No; I was about to call you."

"I wanted to have your views on our conversation of yesterday, after you'd slept on it."

"Joe, I understand what you're doing and why you're doing it. In your place, I might very well do the same thing."

"Is there a 'but' at the end of that sentence?"

"There is."

"Give me your best advice, Will."

"I'll try, Joe, but you have to consider that my advice may be colored by my own interests."

"I doubt it, but I'll take that into account."

"Joe, I think you should wait until after the holidays, then resign." There was a long silence before Adams spoke, and when he did, Will caught a hint of hurt in his voice.

"Give me your reasons," he said.

"Whatever the state of your illness and its progression, the public perception of it is one of decline and delusion. You couldn't continue in office if the country knew, and I don't think you should keep this from the country."

"Are you worried about how I might behave if I continue in office?"

"No, I think you and Sue together could figure out if you got to the point where you couldn't make good decisions. But you can't predict accurately if or when that might happen. There's also the danger of this getting out."

"I believe I have it contained," Adams said.

"Still, there are a number of people who know,

and if there were a leak, you wouldn't be able to control the situation."

"That's possible but not likely."

"Joe, I tell you this as your friend and admirer: The only way you can control this situation is to announce it and resign. If you don't, control will eventually pass to someone else, perhaps not someone of your choosing. If you leave office, you can still have influence. People will judge you by the quality of your reasoning and your statements. If you keep this quiet, and it becomes known, then doubt will be cast on your every action and utterance during the time it was a secret. You must see that."

"I certainly see that as a possibility. It's a question of how much risk I'm willing to assume."

"I suppose it is," Will replied. "But I wouldn't be your friend if I didn't tell you exactly how I felt."

"I thank you for your advice, Will, and for your honesty and candor," the vice president said. "I'll be in touch. Merry Christmas to you and your family."

"And Merry Christmas to you and yours, Joe."

The line went dead. Will turned to Kate. "I'm not going to announce while he's still a candidate; people would think I'm crazy if I did. And when Joe finally did pull out, they'd think that he and I had somehow colluded to get me the nomination, and they'd be right. They'd think I was using Joe's illness to my own advantage."

"That's not true; you'd never do that."

"The appearance would be there." Will sighed.

"I wish I didn't know about this; I wish Joe hadn't called us up there and told us. I'd rather have found out at the same time as everybody else."

"In my business," Kate said, "there's no such thing as too much information. At the very least, Joe has given you time to think and plan. That's a great gift."

"It's one I'd rather not have."

"Nevertheless, you're stuck with it."

6

By midmorning they were up and dressed and had stopped talking about Joe Adams. There didn't seem to be anything else to say. Will was trying to read a novel, a pleasure denied him except when he was at home in Georgia, and Kate was rummaging through the *Atlanta Constitution*, looking for international news. There was a knock on the door, and Henry entered.

"Morning, Senator, Mrs. Lee," he said, handing them each packages. Will's office was already sending him papers to read, and Kate got a daily pouch from the Agency that was, somehow, hand-delivered each morning, even when they were in Delano.

Will noticed that Kate also got an ordinary letter through the U.S. mail, which surprised him, since she never got any mail there, except from Peter. The letter was not on the stationery that they had given the boy. She went through the pouch first, then made a call to her office on the secure line that the CIA had provided, leaving Will wondering about the letter. Finally, she opened it, read it more than once, returned it to its envelope, and put the envelope in her purse.

Kate looked at her watch. "I need to take the car," she said. "I'll be gone for several hours."

"What?" Will asked, surprised. Kate never went off on her own when they were in Georgia.

"It's business," she said.

That ended the discussion. They had long ago agreed that Kate would not discuss her work. "Sure," he said. "What time will you be back?"

In plenty of time for dinner," she said. "Probably in time for a long walk, if you're up to it." She was always at him about his lack of exercise.

"I'll borrow Dad's cane," Will said.

She pecked him on the cheek, took the car keys, and left the house.

Will tried not to be curious about Kate's work, but she had never had business in rural Georgia before, and he couldn't help wondering about it.

After Kate had gotten onto the interstate and headed north toward Atlanta, she took out the letter and read it again. It was written in a hand she had not seen for many years.

Dear Kate,

I know about J.A.'s problem. It is most important that you and I meet without delay. You can come anonymously anytime between eleven and two, weekdays. Any other time, you'll have to show some official ID. This is important to Will's future.

E.R.

Kate felt sick to her stomach.

Atlanta Federal Penitentiary was on the map and easy to find. She found a visitor's parking space, went to the main gate, and made her request. After half an hour's wait she was taken into the main building, down a series of corridors and to a small room, divided by a heavy wire mesh, with a door at each end. After another ten minutes a man in a suit arrived.

"My name is Hill," he said. "I'm an assistant warden. May I see some identification?"

Kate showed him her D.C. driver's license.

He handed it back to her. "You're going to have to do better than that."

She gave him her Agency ID. "I don't want an official record of this visit," she said.

"It will have to be entered in his record," Hill replied, "but I doubt if anyone will ever look at it."

She nodded. "Is the room wired?"

The man shrugged. "Would you rather see him outside? It's pretty cold."

"Yes, I don't mind."

"Do you have any problem with not being physically separated from him?"

"No."

"Please wait." The man left, then returned five minutes later. "Follow me." He led her to a door that opened into a small courtyard that had been planted as a garden, now dormant in winter. Ed Rawls stood up from a teak bench; he was wearing civilian clothes and a warm jacket.

"Hello, Kate," he said, opening his arms wide.

Kate ignored the gesture. "Hello, Ed," she said. "You're looking well. Prison must agree with you."

"I've lost a few pounds, I guess. Please, come sit down." He beckoned her to the bench.

It was the only place in the courtyard to sit, so she joined him.

"Did he make you show Company ID?"

"Yes. You knew he would. That means I'll have to write a report on this meeting."

Rawls nodded. "Can I have the letter back? That way, you won't have to turn it in." He handed her another letter. "This one reads better, I think."

Kate glanced at it. It was a more conventional note, saying that he missed seeing her and wanted to apologize in person. She removed his original note from its envelope, handed it to him, then replaced it with the second letter. "All right, Ed, what is it?" She had not seen him for twelve years, not since he had pleaded to a single charge of espionage and been sentenced to life without the possibility of parole. She had been entirely responsible for putting him in prison. Once, they had been friends, confidants; he had been her mentor in the Agency. After the passage of so much time, she felt no anger toward him any-more, but she was determined to be cold and busi-nesslike.

"This is a funny place these days," he said, looking around. "It was closed some years back, then parts of it were reopened for various popu-lations. It's still more than three-quarters empty."

Kate said nothing.

"Millie remarried, you know."

"I heard."

"Pete Warburton, one of the old crowd. After so many years, she didn't know anybody that wasn't Company."

"I suppose not." She wished he'd get on with it, but he had the upper hand, and she couldn't rush him too much.

"I'm seventy-one, you know," Rawls continued. "I gave Millie pretty much everything, but I hung on to an old family place in Maine, at Dark Har-bor, on the island of Islesboro. Do you know it?"

"I visited you and Millie there, once."

Rawls chuckled. "I'd forgotten. An old school chum of mine rents it for me, keeps a roof on it and the garden weeded. Puts what little profit there is in the bank for me. I still have some sav-ings; I pleaded guilty so I wouldn't have to spend it on lawyers. I'd like to spend the rest of my years in Dark Harbor, winter and summer. I always loved the Maine winter."

"Would anybody speak to you?" she asked.

"A few people would," he replied. "Fewer each year."

"It sounds as though you have a plan to get out of here."

"Just the beginning of one," he said. "I want a presidential pardon. That's where you come in."

"Ed, be realistic; the Agency would oppose a pardon, and they wouldn't let me do anything to further one."

"I know about Joe Adams," Rawls said.

"What are you talking about, Ed?" This was why she had come, to ask this question.

"I know he's ill."

Kate was stunned. She and Will had only found out about it the day before; how could a federal prisoner know it even sooner? The postmark on Ed's letter was three days old. "Ed . . ."

"You wouldn't be here if you and Will didn't know about it, would you? It was all I had to get you here. It's all I have, period."

"Ed, what do you want of me?"

"This is how I see it playing out," Rawls said. "Adams drops out of the race, Will runs, Will gets elected." He turned and looked at her. "Will pardons me."

"Do you *really* think you can blackmail Will through me?"

Rawls shook his head vehemently. "I don't want to *blackmail* him; I want to *help* him. I think Will's a good man and a fine senator; I want to see him be president. I can help put him there."

"Ed, you're delusional."

"One Republican politician already knows about Joe," he said.

Kate could not prevent a sharp intake of breath.

"Exactly. He's holding his peace, at the moment, but he may decide to move. Let's say he's having a little tussle with his conscience."

"How the hell could you possibly know all this?"

Rawls chuckled. "Everybody thinks when you're in prison, you're out of it. I know a guy in here who's built a substantial fortune in the stock market from a laptop in his cell; I know another one who knows about fixed horse races, who makes big bets. I know guys with cell phones in their pockets. There are all kinds of people in here, Kate; they're smart, they're bored, and they're on the make, just like people on the outside. Just like me."

"What are you proposing, Ed?"

"I can tip you early to some events, possibly even influence them. I may even be able to prevent this Republican politician from revealing what he's learned about Joe Adams."

"I can't be a party to this, Ed," Kate said, "and neither can Will. I'm not going to trade you my influence with my husband for your help; I'm just not."

Rawls smiled. "I didn't expect you to, Kate. You don't have to be a party to anything. I'm going to do whatever I can to help Will get elected, and if he is elected, and if I helped get him there, then all I want from you is a word in his ear when he's in office."

Kate started to speak, but he held up a hand.

"You don't have to make me any promises; I'll rely on your sense of fairness and your good heart.

You and I have no deals—I'm not proposing any. Will's conscience will be clear, and so will yours."

Kate stood up. "I have to go, Ed. As far as I'm concerned, this conversation never took place. We just chatted for a few minutes. I'll send in my report, and I won't mention the pardon business."

Rawls stood up, too. "That's fine. You'll hear from me from time to time—untraceable messages, nothing that could possibly get you into trouble. I'll use a code name: Jonah." He grinned. "In the belly of the beast."

Kate held up a hand. "Don't, Ed, please don't."

"And when it's all over, I know you'll do the right thing."

"How do I get out of here?"

Rawls walked to the door through which Kate had entered and rapped on it sharply. A moment later, Assistant Warden Hill opened it and beckoned for Kate to follow him.

Kate didn't say good-bye to Rawls, didn't even look back.

She ran the meeting over and over in her mind as she drove back to Delano. She could fudge her report on the meeting; Ed's second letter would help with that. Somebody would interview her about it; she could handle that part. What she couldn't handle was Ed Rawls. He was smart as a whip and as skilled in intelligence work as any man alive. He would do what he was going to do, and she couldn't stop him. Even if she called the warden and had him locked down until after the election, he would find a way. But how much did he know? He had said that Joe Adams was "ill," but did he know the nature of the illness?

She would not tell Will any of this. That she could not do.

7

Will left the farm and drove into Delano, to his and his father's law office. The firm of Lee & Lee had been central to the family's life since Billy had founded it after his return from World War II. It provided a business center for the family and outside income from cases, local and statewide, which had helped the Lees build a comfortable life. Now the firm was called Lee, Lee & Robertson, to include their partner of recent years, Tim Robertson, who, since Billy's virtual retirement and Will's election to the Senate, had essentially run the firm.

Will was stopped half a dozen times between his parking place and the front door of the little office building they had erected years before. Everyone in town knew him, of course, and he knew practically everyone. Small talk of families and friends was exchanged, and, finally, he made it into the building. His office was neat and dusted, and a stack of mail and telephone messages was

waiting for him. He went through it quickly.
Apart from a personal letter or two from old
friends, most of it was requests for constituent
services. He stuffed those into a large envelope
and marked it for forwarding to his Atlanta con-
stituency office, then turned to the phone messages, answering a couple and scribbling notes for
Tim Robertson or his secretary to answer the others. The last message in the pile gave him pause.
It read, "Charlene Joiner would like to speak with
you urgently," and the return number was in the
310 area code.

Will stared at the message, and a flood of mem-
ories came back. He remembered defending her
boyfriend, one Larry Eugene Moody, against
charges of rape and murder in a trial that fell in
the middle of his first campaign for the Senate; he
remembered losing the trial; and, most of all, he remembered a hot summer's afternoon spent, naked,
with the beautiful Charlene in the little lake beside his cottage and in his bed. He and Kate had
not yet been married, or even engaged, and they
had been estranged at the moment when Charlene turned up at the cottage. He remembered the
flurry that the brief affair had caused in his campaign, and how it had probably worked out to his
benefit in the election. But most of all, he remembered Charlene, naked, uninhibited, and imagi-
native. He felt a married man's guilt for the stirring
that came with the memory.

After a moment's thought, he dialed the
number.

"Hello?" she said after the fourth ring. Her voice was sleepy, husky.

"Charlene? It's Will Lee."

"Will? How are you?" She was suddenly wide-awake.

"I'm very well. I'm sorry to call so early; I forgot about the time difference between here and L.A."

"It's all right; I've got a ten o'clock call today; I'd have to get up anyway."

"I saw one of your movies on TV not long ago—the one about the singer."

"*Country Blues*? Oh, yeah; I got a nomination for that."

"I thought you were terrific; I'm glad about the way your career has worked out."

"Thank you, Will; that's nice to hear."

"You're living in L.A. all the time, then?"

"In Malibu; that's where I am now. Keep the number, so if you're out here, maybe we can get together."

Will didn't want to reply to that. "What are you doing next?"

"I've just signed to do a film with Vance Calder next summer," she said.

"Movie stars don't get any bigger than that," he said.

"It's a wonderful script; my agent thinks it's going to do a lot for me. I'll be doing an English accent, if you can believe that."

"I think you can do anything you want to." He stopped talking; it was time to find out why she had called.

"Ah, Will," she said, somewhat hesitantly, "the reason I called is about Larry Moody."

The mention of the name soured Will's stomach. "What about him?" he asked cautiously.

"I'm going to finance an appeal for Larry; I'd hoped you might represent him again."

Will resisted the temptation to respond with anger. "Charlene, I've been in the Senate for nine years now; I don't try cases anymore, and I was never an appeals lawyer."

"I just thought that since you originally represented him, you might consider it."

"The only conceivable grounds for appeal I can think of is that he was inadequately represented by his lawyer, and you can hardly expect me to argue that before an appeals court."

"Oh, well, I just wish you would represent him."

"I'm afraid I can't."

"Can you recommend somebody?"

"I'm sorry, but I'm so outside the loop on appeals of criminal cases that I couldn't even do that. Do you have an L.A. attorney?"

"Yes, but he's an entertainment lawyer."

"He'll have some networking connection with a good appeals man. Talk to him and get him to research it for you."

"All right, I'll do that."

"Charlene, hasn't Larry already been through the appeals process?"

"Yes, but he wants to try again. He's looking at the electric chair, you know, and sooner rather than later."

"I know." He was silent again.

"Well, I won't keep you, Will. I really would love to see you, though; it's lovely out here in Malibu, the beach and all." She paused. "We'd be discreet, of course," she breathed.

"Thanks, Charlene, but I rarely get to L.A. I'll look forward to the new film with Vance Calder, though. What's the title?"

"It's called *Spin*; it's a political thriller."

"I can't wait. You take care of yourself, now."

"You too, Will. And I hope you'll call."

"Bye." He hung up, and he was sweating a little. His phone buzzed, and he picked it up. "Yes?"

"Tom Black is on the line for you," Betty, the office manager said. "Will you speak to him?"

"Yes," Will said, but he paused a moment before pushing the button. Tom Black was the political consultant who had run both of Will's Senate campaigns. When he was ready to announce for the presidency, Tom would be the first person he would call, but he wasn't ready for that yet. He wondered why Tom would be calling at this time, when they hadn't spoken for months. He pressed the button. "Tom?"

"Will, how are you?"

"I'm extremely well; and you?"

"Just great. And Kate?"

"She's wonderful; what are you up to?"

"Oh, I'm just getting some ducks in a row for next year," Tom said. "I'm afraid Joe Adams's candidacy has squelched a lot of others. Nobody wants to oppose him for the nomination, and that's not good for my business."

"You'll stay busy, Tom; I'm sure you've already

got half a dozen congressional and Senate candidates lined up." Black's business was big now.

"Oh, we'll be well represented next fall, I guess. I wish you were running."

"One of these days," Will replied. He was on thin ice here, and he wanted to head off any direct questions from Tom.

"Will," Tom said, "I'm trying to set my house in order for 2000, and I want to ask you a question."

Will winced. How could he head this off? "As long as you don't expect an honest answer," he said. Would Tom get that?

He got it. "Let's make this a purely hypothetical question," he said.

"Okay, hypothetical is all right, I suppose."

"Okay, here it is: Will, if Joe Adams, for some hypothetical reason, decided to pull out of the race, would you, hypothetically, consider a run?"

Will phrased his answer as slowly and carefully as he could. "Well, hypothetically speaking, if Joe were, hypothetically, out of it, I might consider a purely hypothetical run. You understand, don't you, Tom, that right now, my first obligation is to Joe, and that I would never oppose him? That, apart from my friendship with Joe, I would be cutting my own throat in the party if I opposed him?"

"I understand that completely, Will, and I agree with you. You certainly should not oppose Joe."

"I'm glad you grasp that, Tom."

"One more question, then I'll let you off the hook."

"A hypothetical question?"

"Absolutely."

"Shoot."

"If you should make this hypothetical run, would you want me in on it?"

"Hypothetically? You bet your ass, I would."

"I was hoping you'd say that."

"Who else would put up with me?"

Tom laughed. He seemed about to say something, then stopped.

"You have a great holiday, Tom," Will said.

"Sure, Will; you too. We'll talk again after New Year's?"

"I'm sure we will, Tom. Good-bye." He hung up.

Tom Black knew something, Will was sure of that. But what did he know? And who else knew?

8

Christmas dinner at the Lee farm was much the same as Christmases past, with Billy and Patricia Lee, Will and Kate and Will's Aunt Eloise, Billy's younger sister. They ate goose, which Kate preferred to turkey, and they drank a sturdy California Cabernet. Will reflected that theirs might be the only Christmas table in Meriwether County with a wine bottle on it.

After lunch and coffee in the library, Billy took Will's arm and led him out in back of the house. It was an uncharacteristically warm day for late December, with the temperature in the mid-sixties, and they took seats on some teak chairs beside the swimming pool, which had been covered for the winter. A light breeze played through the bare oak trees around the backyard of the house, but the sun was warm on their faces.

"I want to talk to you," Billy said.

"Sure, Dad."

"I've reached a peculiar time in my life," Billy said. "My political career is over; my legal career is over; my health is less than perfect. Still, I'm well enough to enjoy the comfortable life your mother and I have built for ourselves." He paused and looked out over the little lake beside Will's cottage. "But I'm not enjoying it very much."

"What's the problem, Dad?"

"I thought I had just explained that. I miss the action. I miss problems to solve. I miss the give-and-take of politics and the courtroom. I miss *doing* something."

"I'm sorry if I was dense; I understand."

Billy held up a hand. "Now don't suggest that I take up a hobby. I read a lot, and that's enough hobby for me. I wish that, when I was in office, I had read what I've read now. I'd have been a better governor, and maybe more."

"What can I do to help, Dad?"

"You can run for president, that's what you can do. That'll keep me going for a few more years."

"Dad, I'd love to run, but . . ."

"All right, all right. Now, I know something's wrong with Joe Adams, and I know you can't tell me about it. I'd be disappointed in you if you breached a confidence, even to me."

"I'm glad you understand."

"I take it that whatever is wrong with Joe isn't going to be revealed immediately. I remember that, a week or two ago, he had his annual physical at Walter Reed, and that his office released the results in a routine manner. So whatever's happened has happened since then."

Will didn't say anything.

"What I'm trying to say to you is that you have

to make the most of the period between right now and the time Joe drops out."

"How can I do that?"

"Without breaching a confidence? Come on, boy, you're a better politician than that. You've got to put together a core of people to get a campaign organized. It's late, Will, very late to be starting from scratch, and you're going to have to find a way to let your key people know what's coming. If you wait and let them be surprised when Joe pulls out, they'll be insulted, because you didn't trust them."

"I see your point," Will said. "Tom Black called me yesterday and asked a lot of hypothetical questions, and I gave him a lot of hypothetical answers."

"That's good enough," Billy said. "Now you've got to start talking hypothetically with some other people. How much money have you got at this moment in time?"

"I've got a little over three-quarters of a million dollars in my campaign fund."

"That'll get you started while you get a fundraising campaign under way."

"I can't spend any of that on a presidential bid right now," Will said.

"You can spend it on your next Senate race, can't you?"

"Well, sure, but that's three years off."

"Listen, you can turn a Senate race into a presidential race in the blinking of an eye."

"I suppose so. What do you think I should do right now?"

"Pick people for your key campaign slots and tell them to start putting together a plan right now, something that can be put into immediate effect when the moment comes."

"I guess I can do that, if I do it carefully."

"Also, I think you should start accepting speaking engagements in states with large blocks of electoral votes—California, New York, Illinois, and so on. And New Hampshire, of course. I've still got a few friends around the country; I'll see if I can arrange a few speaking invitations."

"Dad, we can't let it get out that you're doing this."

"Of course not," Billy snorted. "And you shouldn't be giving blatant political speeches. What you should do is select topics that are important to your audiences and give good, common-sense speeches on those issues. Your goal is not to win votes right now, but to impress the people you're talking to. That way, when you announce, you'll have people out there who'll remember that they liked what you said or the way you said it. You should include statements in each speech that will be quoted prominently in the press, too."

"I suppose you have some topics in mind."

"Oh, I guess so." Billy laughed. "I think the situation in Russia and our relationship to that regime would be a good one. It's a dangerous situation, and it's not getting the attention it should either in the press or in Congress. It's not too hard to envision circumstances that could lead to a nuclear incident."

"You're right about that. What else?"

"Start suggesting solutions to some big problems—saving social security, better health care, that sort of thing. If you show people now that you have some ideas for solving these problems, they'll remember that when you're a candidate."

"Dad, will you write me a long memo on all this?"

"Sure I will; give me something to do. Lately, I've been thinking too much about dying. Be nice to have something else to think about."

"Have you been feeling ill, Dad?"

"No, just more tired than I want to feel."

"Have you talked to your doctor?"

"He said there's nothing much wrong with me except the two heart attacks I've had. He told me to get a hobby." Billy smiled. "You're going to be my hobby, Will. I can't think of anything more fun than getting you elected president. I'm beginning to understand how Joe Kennedy must have felt when he was out to elect Jack. I only wish I could *buy* you an election, the way he did."

Will laughed. "I wish you could, too."

9

Will and Kate returned to Washington after Christmas, and Kate returned to work at the Central Intelligence Agency the following morning. Kate, as deputy director for Intelligence, or DDI, was in charge of all the Agency's analysts. She had risen through the ranks on the Soviet Union desk and had distinguished herself throughout her career. She arrived in her large, corner office at 8 A.M., and was surprised to find a note on her desk asking her to report to Elliot Baskin, deputy director, the number-two man at the Agency. She went up to the executive floor and was admitted to his office.

"Good morning, Kate, welcome back," Baskin said, rising to shake her hand.

"Good morning, Elliot," she replied.

"Hey, Kate," said a voice from the other side of the room.

Kate turned to find Hugh English sitting on the

sofa before the fireplace, where a cheery blaze was burning. English was deputy director for Operations, DDO, head of the spy department.

"Morning, Hugh," she said.

Baskin waved her toward the fireplace. "Take a pew; let's talk."

Kate walked over and sat in a leather armchair, while Baskin took a seat beside Hugh English. She wondered why he had done that; he could have taken the other chair. The seating arrangement seemed, somehow, adversarial.

"Good holiday?" Baskin asked.

"A quiet one," she replied. "We spent it with Will's parents in Georgia."

"So I hear," English said.

"Why, Hugh," Kate said, smiling, "I thought you were barred from conducting domestic intelligence operations." Something was up.

"Just an ear to the ground," English said, waving a hand.

Baskin spoke up. "I hear you visited Ed Rawls in Atlanta," he said.

Kate nodded. "Yes, I did."

"You should have reported it, Kate."

"You haven't been reading your mail, Elliot; I did report it."

Baskin reddened slightly. "I haven't caught up after the holiday. Tell us about it."

"The day after I arrived in Delano, a letter from Ed came for me, asking me to visit him. I enclosed his letter with my report."

"What did he want?"

Kate shrugged. "I think he was lonely. He seemed apologetic about his crimes, though he didn't quite apologize."

"How many times have you seen Rawls since his conviction?"

"This was the first."

"Heard from him? Written to him?"

"No."

"Why do you think he *really* wanted to see you, Kate?"

Kate had already decided to stick strictly to her report. "If he had a *real* reason, he never got around to it. He talked about his place in Maine, said he'd like to finish out his days there."

"Is he planning an escape?" Hugh English asked, chuckling.

"I got the impression he hopes for a pardon."

"From whom?" Baskin asked.

"I suppose from the president, since no one else can pardon him."

"I'd certainly oppose that," Baskin said. "The director would, too, I think."

"I expressed that opinion to Ed," she said.

"The son of a bitch," English said heatedly. "He cost me half a dozen good agents."

Kate turned to him. "My recollection, Hugh, is that you were working in the Bangkok station when Ed was caught."

"I meant Ops. He cost Ops some good men."

"And women."

"Yeah. All because he couldn't keep his dick in his pants."

"So gracefully expressed, Hugh," Kate said.

"All right, you two," Baskin interjected, "let's not get off the subject."

"What exactly *is* the subject, Elliot?" Kate asked.

"Your visit to Rawls."

"I don't see how you could even sit in the same room with the bastard," English said.

"We were once good friends," Kate said. "You may have heard that he was one of the best people the Agency ever produced, and that, at the time he was arrested, he was the leading candidate for your job."

English squirmed a little. "You might remember what he did."

"And you might remember that I put him out of business," she said. "I don't like him for what he did, but I don't hate him for it, either." She turned to Baskin. "If you don't want me to see him again, all you have to do is say so." She saw Baskin and English exchange a quick glance, and she wondered what it meant.

"Oh, no," Baskin said. "See him anytime you like, just report the content of your conversation."

"I don't have any plans to visit him again." She looked at both men. "I don't get this. Ed is no longer a threat to anybody. Why are you two so exercised by my visit?"

"Kate," Baskin said, "I want to ask you a very serious question."

"Shoot."

"Your marriage has always been something of a concern to me, and to the director."

"And why is that?"

"Do you ever discuss Agency business with your husband?"

"No," she said immediately. "When Will and I got married, we agreed that we would not talk about my work."

"You talked about it *before* you were married?"

"Elliot, you might remember that, before we were married, and before Will was elected to the Senate, he was the counsel to the Senate Intelligence Committee. We had occasion to discuss business—always, I think, to the benefit of the Agency."

Baskin nodded. "Does he know about your visit to Rawls?"

"No. When he asked me where I was going, I told him it was business, and he dropped it, just as he always does."

"You're sure about that?"

"I am. I'd be pleased to take a polygraph, if you like."

"Oh, no, no," Baskin said. "That won't be necessary."

English spoke up. "*I'd* like her to take a polygraph."

"I said it wouldn't be necessary," Baskin said sharply.

"I'd be happy to take a polygraph and have you administer it personally, Hugh," she said. "Now, either do it or never question my word again."

"I'll question your word whenever I feel like it," English said.

"Now, people," Baskin interjected. "This is unnecessary."

"Apparently it *is* necessary," Kate said. "I *insist* on a polygraph, and I want it done before lunch." She stood up. "I'll be in my office; call me when you're ready."

"I'm ready right now," English said, getting to his feet.

"Both of you, shut up!" Baskin barked. "I'm not going to have this sort of childish display at the upper levels of the Agency."

Kate wheeled on him. "*Childish?* You haul me in here and accuse me of an unreported visit to a jailed officer, when my report is already on your desk; then Hugh as much as accuses me of some sort of treasonous behavior. Then you imply that I'm discussing Agency business with my husband. If you think I'm going to put up with it for a minute, you're very, very wrong."

"Kate, I apologize if it seemed that way, and I'm sorry I didn't look for your report before calling you in." He turned to English. "Hugh, I think you owe Kate an apology, too."

"Sorry," English said, not looking at her.

"Will that be all?" Kate asked.

"Yes, of course. Again, I'm sorry about the tone of this meeting, and I fully accept your representations both about your meeting with Rawls and about your conversations with your husband."

"Thank you," Kate said, then walked out of the office. All the way back to her floor and her own office she fumed inside, while greeting people pleasantly in the hallways. Back at her desk she took deep breaths and tried to cool down. She wished she'd never gone to see Ed Rawls.

10

On New Year's Eve Will and Kate threw a dinner party, a nearly annual event, with a guest list of fifty. At the time of their marriage they had each owned a small town house in Georgetown; they had sold them both and bought a bigger house with a wider facade and three stories and a garage in the basement. It was perfect for entertaining, which they did fairly often, ranging from intimate dinners of eight or twelve to the New Year's bash. They had it down to a science, and, except for work on the guest list, it had become an almost effortless exercise. A perfectly trained caterer took over the house; all Will and Kate had to do was get dressed.

Guests were due at seven, and at six-thirty, the doorbell rang. Joe and Susan Adams had been invited to come early. To Will's surprise, they were accompanied by Senator Frederick Wallace of South Carolina and his wife, Betty Jane. Will tried not to seem annoyed; he had wanted a few minutes alone with Joe and Sue.

"Come in, come in," Will said, kissing the women and shaking the men's hands. "How are you, Freddie?" he asked the elderly senator.

"Better than can be expected," Wallace rumbled. An ancient tuxedo covered his bulk, and his wife was dressed in a lace gown. They looked like something out of the forties, Will thought. "Kate will be down momentarily," he said. "Everybody have a seat, and we'll get you a drink. Anybody want champagne?"

Nobody spoke. A moment later, each guest had been served with his usual—bourbon for the men, white wine for the women.

"Freddie and Betty Jane were on the way, so we gave them a lift," Joe Adams said.

"I don't get to ride in many limousines," Wallace said. "Couldn't turn it down."

"Come on, Freddie," Adams said, "half the lobbyists in Washington have limousines. You could have one at your door on command."

"Wouldn't seem seemly to South Carolina's voters," Wallace said, looking cherubic, with his shock of white hair and his pink face. "I might get my picture taken in one, and we couldn't have that, could we?"

"I'm surprised you aren't riding around town in a BMW," Will said, "since they opened that factory in South Carolina."

"We're happy to have them there," Wallace said, "but they make *German* cars."

"My limo is a Cadillac," Adams said.

"And you're looking for an even bigger one next election, aren't you?" Wallace asked, chuckling.

"I'll ride in whatever comes with the territory, Freddie," Adams replied.

"The territory ain't yours yet." Wallace grinned.

"Tell me, Freddie," Will said, "if you could choose the next president, who would it be?"

Wallace lowered his chin and peered at Will over the gold half glasses that seemed permanently attached to his nose. "Jefferson Davis," he rumbled.

Everybody laughed.

"Old Jeff would know how to handle you liberals," Wallace said, grinning.

"I'll accept the characterization as a comparative one," Will replied. "Next to you, Freddie, Jesse Helms was a liberal."

"He was a goddamned socialist!" Wallace laughed.

Joe Adams spoke up. "I was hoping to get Freddie to cross party lines and support me."

Wallace snorted.

"I don't think you could afford to lose that many votes, Joe," Will said, getting a laugh. He looked up to see Kate coming down the stairs, stunning in a black Ralph Lauren dress. The men got to their feet, and she greeted everyone. A waiter brought her a glass of champagne on a silver tray.

"I hope that ain't French," Wallace said.

"It's Schramsberg," Kate replied.

"*German*?"

"Californian."

"Damn near as foreign," Wallace replied.

"Californians are your countrymen, Freddie," Kate said.

"Not *my* countrymen," Wallace said blandly. "You know, there's something you two fellows have never figured out." He nodded at Will and Joe. "A senator can have nearly about as much power as a president, if he's smart, and he don't have to please anybody from California or New York or anywhere but his home state, and he only has to please fifty-one percent of the actual voters there!"

"You've got a point there, Freddie," Adams agreed.

"You fellows don't know when you're well-off," Wallace said. "Look what you got up on the Hill: You got a nice big office with a loyal staff who does your bidding; you got a nice place to have lunch every day; you got somebody to cut your hair when you need it and a girl to massage you, whether you need it or not; you got free medical care, free parking, and free trips to nice places overseas; and on top of all that, you get paid pretty good money!"

"Yeah, Freddie," Adams said, "but if you're president, you get all that, *plus* a very nice house with a swimming pool, a putting green, and a movie theater; a bulletproof limousine to ride around in, a helicopter and a 747 to take you wherever you want to go—and no waiting for your luggage. Plus you get Camp David for weekends and you can play golf anywhere in the world you want to."

Wallace snorted. "I can play at Burning Tree anytime, and in my underwear, if I've a mind to, and that's good enough for me."

"I'm trying to summon up that image," Kate said, "but the mind boggles."

"And," Joe Adams said, "when you've served your eight years—or even if you're kicked out after four—you get a great big presidential library to hold all the documents that make you look good in the eyes of the world. And when you finally pack it in, you get a free plot in Robert E. Lee's front yard and a very nice funeral."

Wallace raised his hands in mock surrender. "Well, I guess we know what's important to *you*, Joe."

"What's *really* important," Will said, "and what separates the big guy from all the pretty big guys in the Senate is the veto."

"Yeah," Wallace agreed, "and if the Supreme Court had just let it get by, the line-item veto. Somebody once said that if Lyndon Johnson had had that, he'd have been a Nero. Shit, if I had it, I'd be *God!*"

Will got up to answer the doorbell. Now, the deluge.

They began arriving in clumps, now—three or four senators from each party, plus a few congressmen; columnists, TV reporters, cabinet members, a couple of sports figures, and a movie star. Will's press secretary made up the guest list, and few people were invited in successive years, except the president and the vice president, and the president had never shown.

Champagne was poured, scotch was dispensed, canapés were distributed, and rumors were exchanged, but no news was made. Will extracted a moratorium from all the journalists invited.

Dinner was served—racks of lamb, haricots verts, pureed carrots, and a huge spinach soufflé for the vegetarians. The wine was a California Cabernet, not for patriotic reasons, but because Will preferred California wines to French. People sat everywhere—on sofas and chairs, on the stairs, on the floor. The talk was high-spirited without being raucous.

Will was waiting for someone in the powder room under the stairs to finish when he was joined by Paul Epstein, the Washington bureau chief for the *New York Times*.

"Good party, Will."

"Thanks, Paul; we're glad you could come."

"Will, while I've got you here, there's something I need to ask. Certainly, I won't quote you on your answer."

Will said nothing, to show disapproval that a journalist would question him in his own home.

"One of my people heard that Joe Adams might not be well. Anything to that?"

"Jesus, Paul." Will sighed. "Walter Reed published the result of his last physical less than a month ago. You want to know his cholesterol count? His triglycerides? I'm sure Joe's office would be happy to send you a copy of all the results. And I happen to know that Joe played squash this afternoon with somebody twenty years his junior, and Joe cleaned his clock. You ever played squash?"

"No."

"The game is a man killer; I wouldn't touch a squash racquet with a fork."

"Will, we hear it might not be physical."

Will pointed to the living room. "He's sitting right over there; go talk to him and tell me if you think he's nuts."

"Well . . ."

To Will's relief, the powder-room door opened and an undersecretary of state vacated. "See you later, Paul," Will said, closing the door behind him. He used the toilet, noticing that his pulse rate was up. He splashed some cold water on his face and looked at himself in the mirror. The face that stared back at him looked worried. "Come on, boy," he said to his reflection. "Go back out there looking happy."

11

On New Year's morning, Will arrived at his hideaway office in the Capitol at ten. Tim Coleman, his chief of staff, and Kitty Conroy, his press secretary, were waiting for him.

"Happy New Millennium!" Will cried, eliciting flinches from both people.

"Senator, I hope this isn't your idea of a joke," Tim groaned. "I was out until four."

"I haven't even been to bed," Kitty said.

"Sorry about that; my last guests didn't leave until after two, so I'm a little fuzzy around the edges myself."

"So what's up?" Kitty asked. She was the less patient of the two.

"I wanted to talk to you today, because the building is pretty much empty, and I didn't want anybody around."

"You firing us?" Tim asked.

"No, I'm doubling your workload."

"Swell," Tim replied.

"This stays among the three of us, until I say differently, agreed?"

"Agreed," the two said in chorus.

"No spouses or lovers to know."

"Agreed," they said again.

"I want you two to start—today, right now—to put together a plan for a run for the presidency."

"The presidency of what?" Tim asked, looking blank.

"The United States of America."

Tim's expression didn't change, and Kitty looked just as blank.

Will sat there and let it sink in.

"Okay," Kitty said finally, "I'll bite. What's the punch line?"

"I started with the punch line," Will said.

"Senator," Tim said slowly, "don't you think it's a little early to start planning a campaign for eight years hence?"

"I'm running *this* year," Will said.

Kitty piped up. "I didn't see the *Post* this morning; did Joe Adams drop dead last night?"

"I saw him at midnight, and he looked fairly alive to me."

"Let me get this straight," Tim said. "*You*, of all people, are going to run against *Joe Adams?*"

Will took a deep breath. "I can't answer many questions," he said. "Just take my word for it."

Tim and Kitty exchanged a long look.

"Well," Tim said, "can we assume that you know something we don't?"

"Tim, Kitty, it's not inconceivable that someday someone may ask you for an account of this conversation. I'd like you to be able to answer, truthfully, that I didn't tell you anything, except that I intended to make the run, and that you took my word for it."

"All right," Tim said, "you're running, and I'm going to do everything I can to help."

"Me too," Kitty echoed.

"But we can't tell anybody we're helping?"

"Not for the moment."

"Then how can we organize a campaign?"

"I want you to put together a structure that will serve us from the day I announce until the second Tuesday in November—everything from issues to fund-raising. Make a chart. Next to every box I want you to write a name—more than one—we won't get everybody we want. There should be a campaign manager at the top, and I don't want a figurehead; I want a working manager. You know what the other boxes will be; they won't be all that different from the senatorial campaigns."

"Are we going to get Tom Black in on this?" Kitty asked.

"Not yet. Tom's on hold; he won't commit to anybody else. I want to keep this as close as the three of us and Kate—and Kate, although she knows, will be at arm's length throughout, for obvious reasons. She's not going to quit her job.

"Back to your chart: On the day we're ready, I want to be able to call everybody we need very quickly. When this happens, it's going to happen fast; I doubt if we'll have a week between the moment of the final decision to go and the announcement, and I want to have everybody who's really important to us aboard during that week. I want to hit the ground running so fast that nobody will ever be able to catch us. Right now, our only advantage is that my eventual opponents don't know *they're* running."

"How much time do we have before you make the absolutely final decision? I mean, when is go day?" Tim asked.

"I can only guess, but I should think it will happen this month."

"How much can we spend?"

"Nothing. We've got about three-quarters of a million in my campaign fund, but we can't touch it yet. One of the first things we'll have to do on go day is round up enough people in enough states to get enough signatures on petitions to qualify for federal campaign funding. Pay particular attention to that."

"Of course," Tim said.

"Forgive me for stating the obvious, but I want every base covered. Kitty, of course you'll pay particular attention to the press operation, but I want you also to concentrate on finding us the right person to assemble and train a staff of advance people. We'll want someone who can pick up the phone and recruit at least a dozen experienced people on day one."

"We're going to need a campaign headquarters in Washington," Tim said.

"Put that at the top of your list."

"Can I feel out some people on real estate?"

"Absolutely not. Your effort has got to be completely secret until we go, and I'll tell you how secret: I gave you both briefcases for Christmas?"

"Yes, thanks very much," Kitty said.

"Me too," Tim echoed.

"They have locks on them. I don't want you to create a piece of paper that won't fit into those briefcases, and I want you to be practically handcuffed to them. In the unlikely event that you have time to go out to dinner or to the movies, I want those briefcases securely locked in a safe. You are to talk to no one, not even each other, about this on the telephone. You are to create no computer files, not so much as a memo on this subject. You are not to talk to each other about this anywhere except in this room, in your offices or homes, or in my office, and then only behind a locked door.

"You're going to have to keep regular office hours and do your regular work. I don't want anyone on the staff to know or even suspect what you're doing. Don't say anything to anybody that might make them think you're working on anything special."

"Whew!" Kitty said. "This is going to be tough."

"It won't have to be secret for all that long; just in this initial organizing phase. We ought to be able to get a lot done today, since nobody is going to come looking for us until dinnertime."

They both nodded.

"And I want you to find me a Holy Man."

Tim's eyes narrowed. "*What*?"

"I don't mean a guru or a television evangelist;

I mean a man or a woman—a lawyer—who is so clean, so upright, that no one would ever believe him capable of doing a wrong thing. I want this person to be in charge of two things: one, to see that we strictly conform to both the letter and the spirit of the campaign-finance laws; and two, to serve as a sounding board on ethics, so that if anyone on the campaign has the slightest doubt that what he is about to do comes close to the line, he can call the Holy Man and get advice. The Holy Man's opinion will be final."

"Someone from academia," Tim said.

"Or a retired federal appeals court judge," Kitty chimed in.

"You're getting the picture. If Oliver Wendell Holmes could be resurrected, he'd be ideal."

"How are Kitty and I going to divide our time between the office and the campaign, once we're under way?" Tim asked.

"You're not. It has to be one job or the other; I don't want anyone to be able to say that I'm using Senate staff to run my campaign. Frankly, I'd like you both on the campaign, but I'll leave the final decision to you."

"I want the campaign," Kitty said.

"Me too," said Tim.

"Fine with me. Start thinking about finding your replacements, and think about who else from the staff we'll want on the campaign."

"You know," Kitty said wonderingly, "until a few minutes ago, I had a hangover; now it's gone."

Will laughed. "Me too. Now let's get to work."

12

Kate looked at him across the kitchen table. "How do you feel now that you've started?" she asked. She had whipped up a dinner of leftovers from their New Year's party and had opened a bottle of merlot.

"Strange," he said. "Exhilarated; tired; a little scared."

"I don't blame you, on any of those counts."

The phone rang.

Will picked it up. "Hello?"

"Will, it's Susan Adams; how are you?"

"Great, Sue; let me put you on the speaker so Kate can hear." He pressed the speaker button. "Okay, we're here."

"First of all, I want to thank you for such a wonderful evening on New Year's Eve. It was a great way to finish out the millennium."

"We were delighted to have you both," Kate said. "How's Joe?"

As you saw the other night, he's doing well.

Which brings me to my point. I have some good news, some bad news, and some good news."

"Shoot," Will said.

"First, the good news: Joe is going to make his withdrawal announcement next Friday."

That took Will's breath away; he hadn't expected Joe to move so soon.

"We both felt we should get it over with and give the other candidates as much time as we can."

"I expect you're right," Will said.

"I know this won't give you as much time as you'd like to prepare, Will, but at least, you're getting most of a week."

"I can't complain, Sue."

"Now the bad news: I'm going into Walter Reed tomorrow for a lumpectomy."

"Oh, Sue," Kate said, "I'm so sorry. I assume it's contained, if you're not having a radical mastectomy."

"That's what my doctor assumes, too. I'm not real exercised about it; I'm sure everything is going to be okay. The other good news is that Joe is going to have an excuse to drop out of the race: more time with me, and all that, and it won't be a lie. We've both become very conscious that our time together will be a lot shorter than we'd planned."

"I see your point," Will said. "It's going to be a shock any way you put it, but—"

"We're going to let a rumor out starting on Wednesday," Sue said, "just to give some sort of media transition. By Thursday night, it'll probably make the news. Joe thinks you should announce on Saturday; that'll give you a shot at the Sunday-morning TV shows."

"That makes sense, I guess," Will said.

"You can say that I told you today. Let's not refer to our meeting at Camp David; it would hurt a lot of feelings around town, if people thought you knew that far in advance."

"Good point."

"You won't have to lie, Will; I know how you feel about that. After all, I *did* tell you today, just now."

"I'm okay with that," Will said.

"Oh, I'm being called to dinner," Sue said. "I'd better run."

"Thank you, Sue, and thank Joe for the warning. And our prayers will be with you tomorrow." They both hung up.

"Well, it's really on, I guess," Kate said.

"Looks that way."

"I'll tell you the truth," she said, "I'd half suspected that Joe would have second thoughts and let the clock run out through the campaign before he pulled out. That would have made him more the kingmaker."

"That wouldn't be like Joe," Will said.

"I know, and I feel guilty about thinking that."

The phone rang again, and Will picked it up.

"Hello?"

"Will, it's Joe."

Will punched the speaker button. "Hi, Joe; Kate can hear you, too. We were both sorry to hear about Sue's illness."

"It's going to be okay; don't worry. The reason I called is that Sue forgot to tell you something."

"What's that?"

"I'm going to wait a while after my announcement on Friday before I make an endorsement. I'm not sure just how long."

This was a blow, but Will took it as well as he could. "I understand, Joe."

"I think my endorsement will mean more after all the candidates have had an opportunity to establish a presence in the campaign and had an opportunity to have their positions on the issues known."

"You have a point, Joe," Will said.

"Don't worry, Will; I still think you're the best man for the job, and I'm sure I'll still think so closer to the convention."

"Thanks, Joe."

"They're holding dinner for me, so I'll say good night, and thanks again for the great evening."

"Good night, Joe." Will hung up.

"Well," Kate said, "now I don't feel so guilty about thinking Joe wanted to be a kingmaker."

"Oh, I don't know; this might be the best thing. The endorsement might mean a lot more later, when he can say he's considered everybody."

"You noticed, didn't you, that he didn't exactly say he was going to endorse *you*?"

Will poked at his food. "Yeah, I noticed that."

"He's playing his cards close to his chest; he's going to want something when the time comes."

"He already knows he can have anything in my gift."

"So, how do you feel now?"

"A little deflated, and more scared than ever. Somehow I thought I was going to have most of January to plan. I guess not."

"Six days is better than nothing, which is what the other candidates will have."

"Don't worry about them; when the rumor hits the streets, people all over town are going to start making plans." He punched the speaker phone and started dialing. "Excuse me." It took less than a minute to conference Tim Coleman and Kitty Conroy. "You both listening?"

"Yes," they said simultaneously.

"I'm going to announce on Saturday," he said.

"*This coming Saturday?*" Tim said, aghast.

"It can't wait; you'll know why later in the week. We'll start calling the people on our list on Friday. Kitty, wait until then to stake out the Capitol steps for the announcement."

"This is all very strange," Kitty said.

"It'll make a lot more sense by the end of the week," Will said.

"Will," Tim said, "I think our first calls on Friday should be to your Atlanta office. You've got a hard core of supporters there who'll volunteer to man a campaign office until we can get up and running. Let's get a couple dozen people on a chartered bus Saturday morning and have the office open on Monday."

"Sounds good, but we're going to have to find a headquarters, and we can't start looking until Friday."

"Can't we fudge the date just a little?"

Will thought about it. "All right, you can start on Wednesday morning, but do it through a third party. I'll see what I can do, as well."

"Okay," Tim said.

"Kitty, start working on a draft of a two-minute announcement speech, with the appropriate built-in sound bites."

"Right. I've got an idea for Saturday."

"Shoot."

"Let's get that bus started up here from Atlanta on Friday night and have you surrounded by supporters for the announcement."

"Good idea. Call the Atlanta office and tell them to book the bus, but don't tell them why. Book some hotel rooms around town for these folks to stay in."

"Consider it done."

"Okay, people, I want to see you both in my hideaway at 7 A.M., so get a good night's sleep. It might be your last for a while." He hung up.

Kate put a hand on his cheek. "I think maybe you've had your last good night's sleep for a while, too."

13

Will had already made coffee in his hideaway office when Tim and Kitty arrived. "First things first," Will said. "I want each of you to write a campaign manager's name on a piece of paper; I'll do the same."

They each did so.

"Let's see yours, Tim," Will said.

Tim held up a sheet that read Sam Meriwether.

Kitty held up hers: Sam Meriwether.

Will grinned and showed them his: Sam Meriwether. "It's unanimous. You both realize, you're going to be working for him, as well as me."

They both nodded.

Sam Meriwether was Will's own congressman, representing Georgia's fourth district, which included Delano. He was in his late thirties, smart, energetic, and supremely well organized.

"Kitty, call Sam at home and ask him to come and see me here as soon as he can."

Kitty went to the other side of the room and

picked up a phone. She came back a moment later. "He's on his way; he was already in his office."

"Good. Now, tell me: Who did you two come up with for the Holy Man?"

"Mason Rutledge," Tim said, "known as Rut to his friends."

"I know him vaguely," Will replied. "Bring me up-to-date on him."

Tim read from a sheet of paper. "Harvard Law, class of '52; private practice with Woodman & Weld in New York for thirty years, with occasional leave for public service; worked for Archibald Cox when he was independent counsel, during the Watergate investigations; was axed with Cox during the Saturday Night Massacre; an assistant attorney general under Griffin Bell during the Carter years, responsible for, among other things, campaign-law violations; said to have turned down the AG job when Clinton offered it to him. Clinton appointed him to the Court of Appeals. Rumor had it he would have appointed him to the Supreme Court, but the Republicans on the Senate Judiciary Committee would have obstructed, so he walked away from that. Last year he retired from the court, and he now holds a chair in constitutional law and legal ethics at Harvard Law. Married forty years, two sons—one an assistant AG, the other at Woodman & Weld. Old New England stock, spotless character, only a little pompous."

"Will he do it?"

Kitty spoke up. "I know the son, Arthur, who's at Justice. We had lunch a couple of weeks ago, and Artie said his father missed public life a little. My impression is he'll do it, if he can stay in Cambridge."

"No reason why he couldn't do it with a phone and a fax machine, is there?"

"Not that I can see. I don't think Harvard Law would require him to take a leave if he's just a consultant on campaign law and ethics."

"Put him high on the list to call on Friday." Will consulted his notes. "Who to run the advance operation?"

Tim shuffled some papers. "We think Leo Berg would be good."

"Secret Service guy?"

"Retired. He ran the White House detail for four years; before that he was their top advance man. He'd be good for liaison with the Secret Service detail, too. He's well liked in the Service."

"Good choice; I would never have thought of him. Tim, you call him Friday afternoon."

"Right." Tim made a note. "Kitty and I both think that Mimi Todd would be good to run Issues. She's done a great job in the Senate office, and she's already trained an assistant."

"I agree. On Wednesday, have her start rewriting everything, removing references to Georgia and putting a national cast. I want us all to review each issue before anything is carved in stone."

There was a rap at the door, and Will pressed the button under his desk that released the lock. Sam

Meriwether walked in. Tall, shambling, always slightly disheveled, he gave an almost opposite impression of the man he really was.

"You're up early, Sam," Will said.

"Shoot, I've been at my desk for at least two hours." Sam grinned.

"Come sit down," Will said. "I've got some good news for you."

Sam folded his length into a chair. "Always like getting good news."

Sam," Will said, "I've decided to make you a United States senator."

Sam smiled broadly. "Well, I guess I could choke that down." He half rose. "You want to switch seats now?"

"Sit down, Sam." Will laughed. "I didn't say I was going to do it today."

"How long do I have to wait?"

"A little over three years, if you're lucky."

"What do I have to do to get lucky?"

"You have to get me elected president of the United States."

"Is *that* all?"

"It's the only way you're going to pry me out of my Senate seat."

"Well, shoot, it might be worth it to get you out of the state of Georgia. How am I supposed to help you?"

"I want you to manage my campaign."

Sam looked at Will narrowly. "You're still drunk from New Year's Eve, aren't you?"

"I'm as sober as a Supreme Court justice."

Sam looked around at his companions. "Are you

three planning to assassinate Joe Adams? 'Cause, if so, I'm calling the Secret Service right now."

"I can't tell you all the details until Friday, but around noon on Saturday, on the Capitol steps, surrounded by friends and supporters, I'm going to announce."

Sam stared at him, speechless.

"Sam," Tim said, "it's all right; he's not crazy. Say yes."

"Hell, yes," Sam said. "You want me to resign from the House?"

"No, keep your seat. You're going to be based in Washington, anyway, so you can make all your votes. If you get me elected, you can come to the White House with me, and after two years, you can run for my seat against whoever the next governor of Georgia appoints to replace me."

Sam frowned a little. "If our Democratic colleague gets elected to that office, who do you think he might appoint to fill your term?"

Will laughed. "Okay, Sam, if I get elected, and you want my seat right away, I'll do everything I can to get you appointed. If he won't do it, or if the Republican beats him, then you stick with me?"

"Jesus," Sam said, "I don't think I can get a better deal than that." He leaned over and shook Will's hand.

"Welcome aboard," Will said. "Your first job is to find us a national campaign headquarters without letting on to anybody that it's for me." Will scribbled a name on paper and handed it to Sam. "This guy just built a new office building downtown that's renting. I think there's some storefront space available, and we'll need a floor for offices, too. Feel him out."

"I know him a little," Sam said. "I don't think he'll figure out that I'm doing it for you."

"Good. You've got to play this very closely until, say, Friday afternoon. If we can really get rolling this week, we'll have at least a few days' jump on the competition."

"Who else knows about this?" Sam asked.

"Just the people in this room and Kate."

"Does Joe Adams know about it?"

"I can't answer that right now, Sam. You're going to have to trust me to do the right thing."

"Shoot, Will, I trust you, and I'll keep my mouth shut."

"As soon as I announce, you're going to have to get your own office organized to run pretty much without you. I'm going to keep you real busy."

"Whooeee!" Sam said. "Sometimes your life just changes in the blinking of an eye!"

14

Will and his little core of a campaign staff worked steadily at adding names to their list of campaign people. They had now added, from Will's computer files, possible state chairmen in each of the fifty states, and they were working on county chairmen in large municipalities. They divided the names among themselves, each with a list to telephone before the announcement—Will's made up of those people who would be insulted if not asked directly by him, Sam's of people just below that level, and Tim or Kitty to call the rest.

Late Tuesday afternoon, the vice president's office announced that Mrs. Joseph Adams had undergone a lumpectomy at Walter Reed Hospital. In Wednesday morning's *Washington Post* a columnist reported that Vice President Adams, the leading candidate for the Democratic nomination, was considering not running in 2000 because of his wife's illness. The story was all over the evening network news shows, and the vice president's press secretary had declined comment. Adams was said to be spending a lot of time at Walter Reed with his wife.

On the day of the surgery, Will had dispatched two dozen yellow roses to the hospital in advance of the announcement, and early in the afternoon on Wednesday he called the vice president at Walter Reed.

"How'd it go, Joe?"

"Perfectly, Will; she's already recovering beautifully, and her doctor is pretty confident that she won't need further surgery."

"I'm glad to hear it, and so is Kate."

"How are you coming on your campaign plans?"

"Well, we've been mostly confined to making lists of people we want, but Sam Meriwether has signed on as campaign manager."

"A great choice."

"I'm going to want some of your people, as soon as you cut them loose," Will said. "When can I start talking to them?"

"Not until after my announcement on Friday," Adams said. "And, at this stage, there are only a couple who aren't already on my current staff. I hope you won't steal too many of those."

"You tell me if there's someone you don't want me to ask."

"I'll leave it up to them, Will, but you have to realize that this is going to come as a great disappointment for all of them. They've been looking forward to the campaign. Maybe you should give them a few days to get used to the idea."

"Sure, I will."

"I'd better get back to Sue; I'll tell her you called."

"Give her my love." Will hung up and went back to work. Ten minutes later, the phone rang.

"It's Senator Kiel," his secretary said.

Will picked up the phone and spoke to the minority leader of the Senate. "Afternoon, George," he said.

"You okay, Will?"

"You bet. What's up?"

"I was a little annoyed that I didn't know Susan Adams was having surgery, until I saw it on CNN."

"I don't think she wanted anybody to know until she was sure it went well."

"But you knew." Kiel sounded a little peeved, but then he usually did.

"Sue called us over the weekend. She and Kate are . . ." Will let his voice trail off; he had been about to say that they were close, and that wasn't exactly true. He knew what was coming next.

"What about this thing in the *Post* this morning?"

"I haven't read all the *Post* yet. Which thing?"

"The thing about Joe might be dropping out."

Now Will was stuck. "I heard about that," he said.

"Is it true?"

"If it is, I'm sure you'll be hearing directly from Joe," Will said.

"If it's true, are you going to run?"

Will knew that Kiel would likely be his biggest opposition. "Tempting, isn't it?"

"Sure is. You know damn well *I'll* run. What about you, no kidding?"

"You never know," Will said. "But if I do, you'll be among the first to know."

"I like you, Will," Kiel said, "and I'd hate to have to clean your clock in the primaries." He chuckled unconvincingly.

"I'd hate that, too, George." Will laughed.

"Who do you figure for the Republican nomination?"

"Eft Efton, Hale Roberts, or Mike Knowles." Howard "Eft" Efton, congressman from Texas, was Speaker of the House, Hale Roberts was governor of Ohio, and Michael Knowles was senator from Kansas.

"That's what I figure, too. You reckon either you or I could beat one of them?"

"Why not?" Will replied. "Of course, I'd rather have been vice president for the past seven years, like Joe."

"Joe won't give it up," Kiel said. "He's wanted this for a long time, and it's his for the taking. Nobody just walks away from the presidency."

"That would certainly be unlike Joe," Will said.

"Okay, see you later," Kiel said, and hung up. Will punched a button and called Tim Coleman into his office. "I want you to call Moss Mallet and commission a nationwide poll of likely Democratic voters and find out who they'd vote for in the primaries with Joe Adams out of the race."

"That's going to cost."

"We're going to have to have it anyway, and I'd like to have it before Joe withdraws and muddies the waters. Don't tell Moss anything, and swear him to secrecy on who ordered the poll. Tell him we might let him release the results as his own poll—*if* we like the results."

"And if we don't?"

"He can reveal all in his memoirs."

"I'm on it."

"And I want it no later than noon Friday. Tell him to make sure there are half a dozen names on the list, not just George Kiel and me."

"Done." Tim went back to his office.

Will realized he had been reluctant to commission the poll, because he might not really want to know the results. George Kiel was on television three or four nights a week, and he was a lot better known than Will.

Thursday morning, Sam Meriwether called. "I think I got that real estate I was interested in," he said guardedly.

"How much?"

"More than I want to pay, but it's a prime location."

"Nail it down."

"I can't write a personal check for this, Will; I'm not a senator, you know."

"Nail it down with your personal word of Southern honor, instead of money."

Sam laughed. "Yeah, that ought to do it."

"Tell him he can have a check on Saturday."

"Okay—hang on a minute, Will." Sam covered the telephone.

Will waited impatiently; he had a lot to do.

Sam came back on. "Turn on CNN," he said. "I'll hang on."

Will took the remote control from a desk drawer and switched on the TV, which was already tuned to CNN. A reporter was standing on the White House lawn.

". . . unusual for this president to cancel all his appointments without some sort of announcement from the White House press secretary," he was saying. "The Israeli ambassador was told only after he had arrived for a meeting with the president. We'll keep you posted."

"What is that about?" Sam asked.

"I don't have a clue; he canceled his morning appointments?"

"All his appointments for the day, apparently."

Tim Coleman and Kitty Conroy walked into Will's office, and he pointed at the TV.

"We heard," Tim said. "What's going on?"

"Maybe we're at war, or something," Sam said over the phone.

"With whom?" Will asked. "We're not that mad at anybody, are we?"

"I don't know," Sam said. "Wait a minute, here comes more."

Will turned back to the TV. The anchorwoman was being handed a sheet of paper.

"We're going to the White House, now, for some sort of announcement by the president's press secretary." The camera switched to the White House briefing room, where the press secretary was approaching the podium.

"I have an announcement," he said, "and I will not take *any*—repeat—*any* questions. This morning, before dawn, the president's valet found the president on the floor of his bathroom in the White House family quarters, unconscious. He had apparently fallen and struck his head. He was seen by his doctor a few minutes later, and as a precaution, he was taken by helicopter to Walter Reed Hospital, where he is undergoing tests. I do not expect to have any further announcement about the president's condition until around three o'clock this afternoon, when the test results are expected. The vice president has been informed and is meeting with the White House staff as I speak. I stress that this is a normal procedure, in the event of the president's illness or temporary incapacitation. I will speak to you again around three o'clock." He turned and walked off the stage and through a door as a chorus of questions was shouted at him.

"Holy shit," Sam Meriwether said.

15

Will picked up the phone and called the vice president's private office number. The phone rang six times before someone picked it up, but no one spoke into the phone, although he could hear voices at the other end. "Hello?" Will said repeatedly. Finally he recognized the VP's secretary's voice.

"Yes?" she said.

"Catherine, it's Will Lee; is the vice president available?"

"Hello, Senator," she replied. "I'm sorry, he's over at the White House. He's asked me to tell everyone calling this line that he won't return any calls today, and probably not tomorrow, but I'll add your name to the list. I'm sure he'll get back to you as soon as possible."

"I understand, Catherine, and thank you. Can you tell me what's going on over there?"

"I'm afraid I don't know any more than was said at the news conference. All I know is that the

congressional leadership and some others are
meeting with the vice president now."

"Thank you, Catherine; good-bye." Will hung
up and looked at Tim and Kitty. "Joe is meeting
with the congressional leadership now, and he
won't be calling me back today."

"Sounds bad," Kitty said.

"Not necessarily," Tim said. "This is all standard operating procedure when the president is
ill."

"Yes," Will agreed, "and we don't know how
ill. It might just be a bump on the head."

CNN had another report. Trading had been
halted on all the stock exchanges for the remainder of the day after stocks had taken a steep dive.

"Tim, Kitty, start calling your contacts at the
White House," Will said. "See if you can get any
information at all."

They left the room, and as they did, Will suddenly remembered something: at their meeting at
Camp David, Joe Adams had said that, if he resigned the vice presidency, he would recommend
to the president that Will be appointed in his
place. Now it occurred to him that, should the
president die, Joe might very well wish to appoint
him vice president. And that was an earthshak-
ing thought.

Kitty came back into the room. "Nobody I know
at the White House is taking calls. In some cases,
the switchboard wouldn't even put calls through
to their offices."

Tim joined them and gave the same report.

"Senator," he said, "has it occurred to you that, if the president dies, Joe Adams might appoint you vice president?"

"It crossed my mind," Will said.

"That would certainly change everything to do with our plans," Tim said.

"None of our planning would be wasted; I'd still be running this year."

Tim looked at him oddly. "Do you really think that, if Adams became president, he'd decline to run?"

Will shrugged. "I can't get into that. Just continue to work on the campaign as if nothing has happened."

Tim and Kitty looked at each other, then at Will, askance.

"Don't ask," Will said.

At three o'clock they gathered around the TV set and waited for the press conference. The White House press secretary strode onto the platform and took his place at the podium. A hush fell over the room. "Same rules as this morning," the man said. "Absolutely no questions." He took a sheet of paper from his inside coat pocket and read from it. "Tests being conducted on the president at Walter Reed Hospital are not yet conclusive. The press office will issue bulletins as information comes in. The vice president will address the nation on television at six o'clock this evening, eastern time. I will be making no further statements between now and then." He turned and walked from the stage.

An uproar ensued. "Is the president conscious?" someone screamed, but the press secretary left the briefing room and closed the door behind him.

"This doesn't look good," Tim said.

"We've no way of knowing that," Will replied. "We don't know what's happening." He picked up the phone and called a couple of people close to the president, but got nowhere. He hung up. "Everybody is just shutting down," he said. "We're just going to have to wait."

The phone rang, and Will picked it up. "Hello?"

"It's Kate; I gather you're going to be late for dinner this evening."

"Quite possibly."

"Have you heard anything?"

"Nothing. Nobody's talking."

"Neither have I. I'll see you when I see you."

They both hung up.

Will, Tim, Kitty, and Sam Meriwether were gathered in Will's office at six o'clock. An announcer intoned, "Ladies and gentlemen, the vice president of the United States."

Joe Adams came on screen looking calm and confident. He was sitting at a desk, but it looked like a studio set, not a real office. "Good evening," he said. "As you have, no doubt, already heard, the president suffered a fall early this morning and was taken to Walter Reed Hospital, where he underwent a battery of tests. The doctors there have determined that his fall was very likely the result of a stroke, and the concussion resulting from his fall has complicated his condition. As of this time, the president has not regained consciousness, and the prognosis is guarded. The first lady is with him in the hospital.

"Upon receiving this news, I convened meetings with the leaders of both parties in Congress, the members of the cabinet, the national security advisor, and the Joint Chiefs of Staff. At that time, since the president has been at least temporarily incapacitated, all the necessary steps were taken to have the vice president assume the role of acting president, with all the powers of that office. This is a day that I hoped would never come, but I have always worked to keep myself ready for the possibility. I will act as president until such time as his doctors feel the president is ready to assume his proper role again.

"I want to assure you that the business of government will continue without pause, and that the interests of the American people are being looked after in the same way as they were yesterday. I intend, during my stewardship, to continue the policies of this administration as they have been formulated over the past seven years.

"Effective immediately, I will move into the Oval Office, bringing only a few of my vice-presidential staff with me. The remainder of the vice-presidential staff will remain at their desks in the Executive Office Building, to do their work as before. All the members of the president's staff have agreed to continue their work as usual, for which I am very grateful. The first lady will continue to live in the White House, and my wife and I will continue to live in the vice-presidential residence at the Naval Observatory."

Adams paused, then continued. "Now I must tell you of a personal decision which was speeded by the events of today. As you will have heard, my wife underwent surgery yesterday at Walter Reed. The surgery was a success, and she is doing well. Her full recovery and her continued enjoyment of our life together is, of course, very important to me. Last year I let it be known that I would be a candidate for my party's nomination for the presidency, and many of you have been kind enough to offer your support. However, my wife's illness, combined with the incapacitation of the president, has caused me to make the irrevocable decision to withdraw from the race. I shall not be a candidate for my party's nomination. I shall, instead, devote myself to the work of acting president until the president recovers, and to my wife's full recovery and future happiness.

"I know that there are other able men and women of my party who may have been kept from the presidential race because of my presence in it. I now leave the field open to them, and I encourage them to take their ideas to the American electorate with enthusiasm and without delay. In order to have the fullest and widest-ranging discussion of the issues by all the qualified candidates, I have decided that I will not endorse another candidate before the Democratic convention in August. At that time, depending on the circumstances, I may or may not choose to do so. I ask all members of my party to respect my wishes in this matter.

"Now, it remains only for all of us to extend our heartfelt sympathies to the first lady, to pray for the president's full and speedy recovery and return to office, and for me to ask for your prayers in my execution of the work ahead.

"Thank you, and good night."

Will stared blankly at the TV screen.

"That went very well," Tim said. "I think everybody is going to be reassured."

"Will," Kitty said, "what's wrong?"

Will's consciousness returned to his surroundings. "Nothing," he said. "Joe's speech was good." And now, he thought, we have a president of the United States who has Alzheimer's disease.

16

Will was discussing Joe Adams's TV address with Tim, Kitty, and Sam Meriwether, when his phone buzzed. He picked it up. "Yes?"

"Senator," his secretary said, "the president is on line one."

"*What*?" Could he have dreamed all this?

She repeated herself.

Will picked up the phone. "Hello?"

"Will," Joe Adams's voice said, "I'm sorry I couldn't call you before now, but you've no idea what it's been like around here today."

"Mr. President," Will replied, "that's quite all right; I understand perfectly."

"You've got a scrambler on that phone, haven't you?"

Will had a scrambler because of his membership on the Senate Armed Services Committee. "Yes, sir."

"Turn it on."

Will pressed the button. "It's on," he said.

"Good; I don't want this to go any further."

Adams took a deep breath. "The president is in a deep coma; he may well be dying."

"I see," Will said, conscious that others were in the room.

"I took his doctor aside and had a frank talk with him. The president's chances of survival are poor, in the short term."

"I see," Will repeated.

"That means that I have to start planning right now. I want you to know that, if the president dies, I'll appoint you as vice president. I would expect the Senate to confirm you without delay."

"I see," Will said.

"Will, are you alone?"

"Not exactly."

"Oh. I was wondering about your reaction. Don't say anything else, except yes, you'll accept."

"Yes, of course I will."

"Good. My first impulse was to install you in my EOB office right away, so we could get your feet on the ground as soon as possible, but on reflection, I think it would be better to wait until we have more word on the president's condition. The next few days are, apparently, going to tell the story."

"I see."

"And the president has a living will, in which he requests a do-not-resuscitate order be issued, in the event of something like this, so he won't be put on a respirator."

"I see."

"I think you should go ahead with your campaign announcement, just as you had planned. I hope being vice president will give you a big leg up on the nomination."

"Thank you, sir. I appreciate your statement on television. That will make it much easier for me to proceed."

"Then go to it, boy!"

"I will."

"Good-bye until later. I'll let you know if there's a change in the president's condition."

"Thank you, sir. I hope Sue continues to improve."

"She's coming home tomorrow."

"Give her my love."

"I will. Good-bye."

"Good-bye, Mr. President." Will hung up.

"Which president was that?" Sam Meriwether asked.

"The new one," Will said.

"And what did he have to say that needed scrambling?"

"I can't go into it," Will replied. "He did say that we should proceed with the campaign announcement as planned."

"Great! And because of what he said on television, nobody can fault you for jumping in."

"Along with a number of others," Will said. "Now we all have a lot of telephoning to do, so let's get started."

Everyone left to return to his or her own office.

Will took a handwritten list from a desk drawer and began dialing. He called Tom Black first.

"Yeah?" Tom said into the phone.

"It's Will. Saturday at noon, on the Capitol steps, I'm announcing for the presidency."

"Hot damn!" Tom yelled.

"We're busing a bunch of folks up from Georgia for background and to staff a Washington campaign office."

"Great! I'll have a camera crew there to film the announcement. We can use it in commercials. Let's you and I get together tomorrow and go over your actual words, so I can lift some sound bites."

"Let's do it Saturday morning," Will said. "Come to the house for breakfast at seven."

"I'll be there."

"By the way, Sam Meriwether is campaign manager."

"Good choice; I can work with him."

"Keep this as close to the vest as possible. Word is bound to leak, as I start calling people, but I don't want Saturday to be an anticlimax."

"Right."

Will said good-bye and hung up. The phone rang, and Kate was on the line.

"I don't want to talk right now," Will said. "I'll bring you up-to-date at home tonight, okay?"

"Okay," she said, and hung up.

He thought about who his next call should be to, and he dialed the number.

"Yes?"

"Mason Rutledge?"

"Yes."

"Mr. Rutledge, this is Will Lee; how are you?"

"I'm very well, Senator," Rutledge replied. "I hope you are, too." The voice was slow and patrician.

"I am, thank you. I'm calling you because I've decided to run for president this year."

"That's good news," Rutledge said. "I think you'll make a fine candidate."

Will noted that he had not said "fine president." "Thank you, sir. I've called to ask for your help."

"Well, I'm not a rich man, Senator, but I suppose I could manage something."

"I'm sorry, I didn't intend to ask you for a contribution to my campaign—at least, not a financial one."

"What sort of contribution would you like me to make?"

"One I believe would not take you away from Harvard Law or your duties there. I want my campaign to be on a firm legal and ethical footing from day one. I want someone to consult on campaign financing issues and to offer advice on ethical matters. I'd be very pleased if you would serve that function in my campaign."

"Well, that's very flattering, Senator," Rutledge said, "but I can't honestly say that I've already decided to vote for you. I'd like to see who else is running."

"It's not necessary that you vote for me, Mr. Rutledge," Will said. "I think you'd be making a fine contribution to the political process, in general, if you could help keep just one major campaign on track. I don't want to see the excesses of the past races this year, and I'm sure you don't, either. Your work at the Justice Department and your personal reputation make you an ideal person to make this contribution."

"Would you expect to use my name?"

"Yes. I would release your name, along with a list of other people who are assisting my campaign, and a description of your function."

"Well, I suppose that would be all right. The purpose is a noble one, and I wouldn't appear to be taking a partisan political stand."

"I'm not sure that's the case," Will said. "The mere mention of your name in conjunction with my campaign will cause many people to infer that you're supporting me. You would be free, of course, to clarify your position to your colleagues at Harvard Law and to the press. You need never make a statement supporting me, not even if you decide to. I'm quite content to have you as an outside, objective advisor to my campaign."

"I appreciate your candor, Senator," Rutledge said. "On that basis, I accept. I would be grateful if you would write to me, setting out what you expect my contribution to be, and I will respond in writing. Down the road a piece, it might be good to have such a communication on the record."

"I will do so immediately," Will said, "and I'm delighted that you'll serve in this capacity. I'm announcing at noon on Saturday, on the Capitol steps. Everyone so far associated with my campaign will be there, and we'd be very pleased if you would join us. When I introduce you, I'll stress your objective status."

"I'd like very much to meet your people," Rutledge said, "and I'd like to be there."

"Good. I'll have my office arrange airline tickets, and if you'd like to stay overnight, my wife and I would be very happy to have you as our guest in Georgetown."

"Thank you. Can I let you know?"

"Of course. My office will be in touch about the tickets today." Will gave him his private office number. "I hope you'll feel free to call me if you have any questions for me or any member of my staff."

"Thank you," Rutledge replied. "I look forward to receiving your letter, and I'll see you on Saturday."

Will said good-bye and hung up. Immediately, he dictated a letter to Rutledge. Now he had a campaign manager, a political consultant, and a Holy Man. It was a start.

17

Will and Kate sat before a blazing fire in his Georgetown study. He had poured her a scotch and himself a bourbon. "A lot happened today," he said.

"I expect so. Tell me about it."

"Biggest news first: Joe Adams called me right after his TV address and told me that, if the president should die, he will appoint me as vice president."

Kate began choking on her scotch. Will got up and clapped her on the back a couple of times. "I'm sorry," she said.

"I took it pretty much the same way, but others were in the room, and I couldn't let on."

"Is the president going to die?"

"The prognosis is poor," Will said.

"You know, I was never his biggest fan, but he did a good job, and he was nice to his wife."

"I hope when I go, someone will speak as well of me." Will laughed.

"The statement applies to you in full, except that I'm your biggest fan."

"Kate, sometimes I wonder about that."

"If I'm your fan? You can't be serious."

"It's just that you never seem to get very excited about anything that happens to me. Sometimes I'm not even sure that you approve of my line of work."

Kate put down her drink, got up, and sat on his lap. She kissed him thoroughly. "I'm sorry if I seem that way," she said. "Just for the record, quite apart from loving you dearly and completely, I want to see you go all the way this year. If I sometimes seem reticent, it's because I'm selfishly thinking what this is going to mean to *me*."

"I know that you're accustomed to our life the way it is, my love, but try and look at this optimistically. If I win, our lives are going to be more exciting than we could ever have dreamed, and if I lose, we'll be back to normal by Thanksgiving."

"Don't kid yourself, pal," she said, kissing him again. "Once you make that announcement on Saturday, nothing is *ever* going to be the same again. It may be better, it may be worse, but it won't be the same."

"You have a point."

"I just hope that, no matter how hard the wind blows, I can hang on to my job."

"I'll do everything I can to see that you do," he replied.

She kissed him again, then went back to her

chair and her scotch. "Oh, Jesus," she said suddenly.

"What's wrong?"

"If you're vice president, we'll have to move into the vice-presidential residence, won't we?"

"You know, I hadn't given that a thought."

"I believe you are acquainted with how much I hate moving."

"I believe I am. Maybe, since this would only be for the year, we could stay here."

"I'd love it if we could," she said.

"If somebody makes us move, then I suppose we could just pack our clothes and leave everything else here as it is for our return."

"I'll believe that when I see it," she said.

The telephone rang, and Will picked it up. "Hello?"

"Senator, it's Tim. I'm in a car about a few blocks from you with Leo Berg, who's agreed to run our advance operation."

"That's great news, Tim; tell him I'm very pleased."

"You'll get to tell him yourself; we'll be there in five minutes."

"What for?"

"I'll explain when we get there. We'll try not to interfere with your dinner." Tim hung up.

"We're about to have visitors—Tim Coleman and a man named Leo Berg, who used to run the White House Secret Service detail. I don't know what they want."

The doorbell rang, and Will got up.

"Tim lied; they weren't a few blocks away, they were outside." He let the two men in.

"Senator," Berg said, "thank you for the opportunity; I'm looking forward to it."

"I'm glad to have you aboard, Leo. Now what can I do for you two?"

"Senator, Tim tells me that there was an attempt on your life some years ago by a right-wing militia group."

Will glanced at Tim sharply.

"I'm sorry, Senator, but I felt Leo should know about this."

Will turned back to Berg. "That's correct. It was a group calling themselves The Elect, and it was run by a retired general named Willingham. Both Willingham and the assassin died in the attempt."

"Because of that, Senator," Berg said, "I want to ask for Secret Service support earlier than it would ordinarily be granted in a campaign."

"Do you really think that's necessary?"

"Sir, these militia groups are in touch with each other; if you've annoyed one of them, you've probably annoyed more."

"I don't know, Leo," Will said. "I don't want to ask for anything that other candidates won't be getting."

"They can make their own requests," Berg replied.

Kate piped up. "Listen to the man, Will," she said firmly.

Will sighed. "All right, I'm listening."

"I'd like to do a sort of preliminary survey for the Service," Berg said. "Then I'll contact them tomorrow to arrange for your protection from Saturday, and if you'll allow me to do this now, I think I can save you some intrusion by a lot of agents."

"Come into the study," Will said. "Can I get you a drink?"

"Scotch," Tim replied.

"Nothing for me," Berg said.

Will introduced Berg to Kate, and they all sat down.

"Now," Berg said, "let me familiarize you with what's going to happen from the point of view of the Secret Service, and Mrs. Lee, I'm glad you're here to hear this, because it's going to affect you, too."

"I'm all ears," Kate said.

"The Service will likely assign you a detail of sixteen men, Senator," Berg said. "A dozen of them will work in four-man teams on eight-hour shifts, and they'll be with you wherever you go. The other four will float, depending on the circumstances. Mrs. Lee, there'll be six assigned to you, and two will remain with you at all times."

"I don't think that will be entirely necessary, Mr. Berg," Kate said, "since I work at the CIA, and that is a very secure environment. They can escort me to and from work, though."

"Good point," Berg said, taking notes. "Is there a downstairs bedroom in the house?" Berg asked.

"Yes," Kate replied. "There's a maid's room at the rear. We don't have any live-in help, so it's empty."

"Good. There'll be two men in the house at all times, and that will allow them to take turns sleeping at night."

"Do they have to be in the house?" Kate asked plaintively.

"I'm afraid so. Don't worry, they're trained to be as unobtrusive and discreet as possible. Senator, they'll be in your office, as well, and in the corridor outside. And anywhere either of you goes, you'll be driven in a Service automobile, probably a Lincoln Town Car."

"How nice," Kate said dryly.

"Who lives in the big house across the street?" Berg asked. "It's dark."

"The ambassador to Saudi Arabia," Will said. "They're not there much."

"Good; maybe the Service can arrange to use it as an outpost. They'll go through the State Department for that. What's out back?"

"A garden, and beyond that another garden and another house," Will said. "The owner does something at Justice, I believe."

"Good. They'll want to know about that. Your neighbors on either side?"

"The *Times* of London rents the one on that side for their bureau chief," Will said. "The other one is owned by a lawyer with Ropes & Gray."

"Neither of those should be a problem," Berg said.

"Leo," Will said, "I want you to stress to the Service that life on this street should not be disrupted in any way."

"You're dreaming, Senator," Berg replied. "The

first time something controversial happens in the campaign, you'll have two dozen press out there, howling for a statement, and there'll be sightseers, too."

"Rather than have that happen, ask them to block off the street and allow only residents through," Will said. "I mean it, Leo, I'm not going to let this disrupt my neighbors' lives. Tell the Service I'll be intractable on this point."

"I'll see what I can do," Berg said, making a note. "You have a security system in the house, of course?"

"Yes."

"I'll want to see the central box and then check every window and door. There's every likelihood that it'll have to be beefed up."

"All right."

"The Service will want their own phone lines in the house, too. I notice you have a garage downstairs."

"Yes, the house is unusual in that respect."

"Two cars?"

"Yes."

"The Service will like that. What brand of garage-door opener?"

"I haven't a clue," Will said.

"I'll check it out, and we'll order some extra remote controls."

"As you wish."

"How many cars do you have here?"

"Two: a Suburban and a Lincoln Continental."

"Is there someplace you can store them?"

"What?"

"The Service will want their sedans in the garage. Don't worry, you won't be needing a car between now and the election."

"I suppose I could park the Suburban in my parking space in the Senate garage."

"And I could park the Lincoln in the Agency garage," Kate said.

"Perfect. Now, could I look around the house?"

"Sure."

Tim stood up. "You go ahead and have dinner," he said. "I'll show Leo around."

"Thank you, Tim," Will said.

He and Kate went into the kitchen, and Kate took some steaks out of the fridge. "So, it begins," she said, and there was a little sadness in her voice.

18

Will worked on a combination of Senate and campaign business through the morning; then, just before lunch, his pollster, Moss Mallet, arrived and was shown into Will's office.

"It was tight, but I have the results of your poll," Moss said.

"Tell me about it."

"There's good news, and there's bad news."

"Shoot."

"The good news is that nearly a third of likely Democratic voters have heard of you."

Will winced. "What's the bad news?"

"The bad news is that less than a third of likely Democratic voters have heard of you." Moss handed him a sheet of paper.

Will looked at the paper. "Jesus, nine years in the Senate, and I register with only thirty-two percent of Democrats?"

Moss handed him another sheet of paper. "Relax, it's not as bad as it sounds. Only forty-six percent know who George Kiel is, and he's the minority leader in the Senate."

"So much for an informed electorate."

"Listen, Will, this could be a lot worse. This is the first national polling we've done, you know, and I've seen guys you'd think were well-known who hardly raised a blip."

"That's comforting."

"Okay, here's something that *is* comforting," Moss said, handing him another sheet of paper. "Of those likely Democratic voters who know both you and Kiel, forty-one percent would vote for Kiel, in a head-to-head race, and forty-six would vote for you."

"What about the other thirteen percent?"

"A plague on both your houses, more or less."

Will sighed.

"Can't you see what this means?"

"Tell me."

"It means of those who know you both, you get a more favorable rating than Kiel."

"Should that make me deliriously happy?"

"I can promise you, it'll depress the shit out of Kiel."

"Well, that's something, I guess."

"Look, Will, if we can extend these numbers, it means that, as people get to know you, they'll like you better than Kiel. What more can you ask?"

"I guess you're right," Will said.

"I promise you, Tom Black is going to love these numbers."

"I'll feel better if he does," Will said. "Anything else?"

"That's it for now. Later, we'll do polling on issues, running mates, the works, but for right now that tells you where you have to go."

"And where is that?"

"On TV, my friend, and the more often, the better. I'd recommend doing an immediate campaign designed to raise public awareness of you."

"We don't have the money yet."

"Then get all the free time you can grab. Just remember, hardly anybody outside of Georgia knew who Jimmy Carter was when he announced. You're a lot better off than he was."

Kitty stuck her head in the door. "There's a report on CNN that George Kiel will announce on Monday," she said.

"That's good news," Will replied. "We'll beat him by forty-eight hours."

"Not really, not unless we start spreading the word now. This means people are already hearing Kiel's name, and not yours. I've had a bunch of calls from press asking what you're going to do, and I've been coy. I think it's time to telegraph your entry into the race."

"Okay, do it; tell them I'll have an announcement to make tomorrow, and you'll get back to them on time and place. Start angling for the Sunday-morning TV shows, too."

Moss stood up. "I've got to run, Will. I'm going to put together a polling proposal for the next month and send it to Tim. Let me know what you want to do."

Will stood up and shook his hand. "Thanks, Moss; I'll be in touch."

Late in the afternoon Tom Black came to Will's office, and the two of them compared notes on the announcement speech.

"Yours is too long," Will said. "I'd like to make it easy for the networks to run the whole thing on the news."

"Not going to happen," Tom replied. "If you give them a minute, they'll run seven seconds; if you give them five minutes, they might run half a minute. Our job is to break the announcement into segments, any one of which they can pick up at different times, and to have one paragraph loaded with the gist." He tapped Will's sheet of paper. "I like this: 'It's time to make a new center that we can all gravitate to.' Make that New Center, in caps, and we can craft something that will be a theme for the whole campaign."

"Start crafting," Will said. "I've got to make some begging calls to scrape up some money. Moss wants us to run a national TV campaign to increase awareness that I'm alive and running." He handed Tom the poll results.

"Not bad," Tom said, "but national TV spots are not going to happen anytime soon. We're going to have to put the money into specific states to win primaries, and let the media make you famous for it."

"You've got a point, but we're going to need the money, anyway, so I'd better get started."

"You do that."

Will started with a list of a hundred men and women who'd given substantial sums to the party in the past during his elections. Eighty-one of them were Georgians. At the top of the list was one Lurton Pitts, fried chicken king. Using a private line that he paid for himself, Will dialed the number. In a moment, he was put through.

"Will, how are you?" Pitts boomed.

"I'm real good, Lurton; how's the chicken business?"

"Not bad."

"That's good, because I'm about to hit you up for some money."

"I knew there must be a reason for that sinking feeling in my stomach. What's going on? You're not running this year."

"Yes, I am."

There was a brief silence. "Oh, Jesus," Pitts said. "You're going to go for it."

"That's right; I wanted you to be the first to know."

"Well, I'll be damned. I knew you'd do it eventually, but I guess with Joe Adams out, the time is now."

"I couldn't have put it better myself."

"How much you want?"

"Just a thousand."

"I can handle that."

"Plus a thousand from everybody you know and all their friends and relatives and all *their* friends and relatives."

"How about PACs?"

"Nope." Will had never taken any money from a PAC.

"How about soft money?"

"Not until after the convention. I'll have to take it as long as everybody else does."

"Damn, Will, I think my pulse just went up about twenty points."

"Mine's been that way all day."

"Where do I send it?"

Will found the number of his new post office box and gave it to Pitts.

"Will, you remember that first time, when I got those fellows together to talk to you about your Senate run?"

"I'll never forget it."

"I want to do that again."

"You bet. Sam Meriwether's going to be my campaign manager; he'll be in touch."

"Go get 'em, Will!" Pitts cried, then hung up.

That was why he'd called Pitts first; he needed to hear that kind of enthusiasm. He went on telephoning, and by dusk, he had raised a good seventy thousand dollars, and it would turn into a lot more when the people he'd called had had a chance to call their friends.

Tom Black handed Will a new sheet of paper. "Try this on."

Will read it. "It's good. Take it to Kitty and Tim, and see what they can do to help it."

Will watched him go, then went back to his telephoning. It kept him from thinking about how nervous he was becoming as his announcement approached.

19

Will stood on the Capitol steps in the still, cold winter air, in bright sunshine, surrounded by a busload of Georgians and a horde of television cameras.

"Good morning," he said. "During the past few days, we've seen American history take a sudden turn. The sudden and tragic illness of our president and the withdrawal of the vice president from the presidential race have cast the 2000 election in a whole new light, and a whole new slate of candidates is now stepping forward. I'm pleased to be among the first of them.

"I'm here to announce my candidacy for president of the United States."

The little crowd went as wild as a little crowd could.

Will waited until the cheering began to subside, then continued. "And I'm here to tell you why I'm running." He paused for a moment, then took a deep breath. This would be the sound bite that would be on every news program that evening. "I'm running because I see my country torn apart by partisan wrangling; I'm running because I see the political parties jockeying for petty advantage, instead of doing what we were sent to this building to do." He gestured over his shoulder at the Capitol. "I'm running because I want to lead this country toward a New Center, a New Center where every voice can be heard—Democratic and Republican. A New Center where conciliation and consensus can overcome ideology of any stripe and take us on toward new heights in the new millennium to come. We are a diverse country, but one idea has always driven us: We are all in this together!" Will paused for more cheering, smiling broadly, knowing that it was at this point that the TV news shows would move on to something else.

"I run as a Democrat," he said. "Make no mistake about that. I run on the ideals that have helped our party help this country to be great: individual liberty, without undue interference from government; good public education for all; a safety net for the elderly and the disadvantaged; sensible, cost-effective programs to help our weakest citizens become strong and self-sufficient; a strong and lean national defense; and above all, the guaranteed equality of *all* our people." More cheering.

"But I will tell you this: We can only have what we can pay for. We have lived beyond our means, and we can no longer do that. As I speak, the federal budget is balanced, and the administration I lead will keep it that way." More cheering.

"As I go out into this country I'm going to address all the issues that are vital to us; I'll praise good ideas and condemn bad ones—and the people who put them forward. But I'll do so in a constructive way that will build consensus. I invite every one of you to come along on this journey.

"I hold out my hand to every American—not just every Democrat, but every Republican and every independent in this land. I tell you that, together, we can do anything; that, from a New Center, we can take this country *anywhere we want to go!*" Will stepped back from the microphones, waving both hands and smiling. While the applause raged, he shook the hands of those around him, then stepped forward to the microphones again.

"I want to introduce you to some of the people who will be making this journey with me. First among equals is my wife, Kate." He held out his hand; she took it and joined him for a moment. "You're going to be seeing a lot more of me than you will of Kate, because she has important work to do here in Washington, and I'm not going to take her away from it. Wouldn't be good for the country." He introduced Sam Meriwether, Tim Coleman, and Kitty Conroy. "Finally, I want to introduce you to someone who hasn't decided yet whether to vote for me. I'm determined that this campaign will follow the letter and the spirit of the laws governing campaigns, and that the actions we take will be not just legal, but ethical. With that in mind I've asked former federal appeals court judge Mason Rutledge to be an objective arbiter of all our actions. Judge Rutledge has had a long and highly distinguished career at the bar, in the Justice Department, and in the courts. He has been, since his retirement from the bench, a professor of constitutional law and legal ethics at Harvard Law School. He will remain there during the campaign, but he will be on call when we need him to help us make the right decisions. And if he feels we haven't, he'll be free to call a press conference and tell you why. Judge Rutledge?" He beckoned the tall, handsome man forward.

Rutledge faced the cameras for only a moment. "I'm here," he said, "because I was impressed with Senator Lee's insistence on running a clean campaign, and I'm happy to help him do it. I expect I'll decide sometime before the first Tuesday in November whether I'll vote for him." He stepped back.

Will came back to the microphones. "Now we're going to invite you all to join us on a brief tour of our new national headquarters. There are buses here for those of you who need a ride, and the rest can follow. We won't keep you long. And the next time I see all you folks watching on TV, I'll be asking you for money." Loud laughter.

Preceded by two Secret Service agents, Will boarded a bus with his campaign workers and chatted with them while they were driven to the downtown office building that housed the headquarters.

Will, Kate, Sam, Tom, Kitty, and Judge Rutledge sat in the Lee kitchen and ate hamburgers while they watched the evening news and Will's performance before the cameras. They made the top, or near the top, of every newscast.

"It went beautifully, Will," Tom Black said. "I can cut at least three good commercials out of the footage we got."

"I was very impressed," said Judge Rutledge, who was staying the night. "It was a good announcement, not too long."

"I hope I can make 'not too long' the hallmark of my campaign," Will said.

Kate spoke up. "And I'm grateful, sir, for having been publicly let off the hook so early in the campaign."

"I promised, and I meant it," Will said. "Tom, what's next?"

"Buy some long underwear," Tom said. "We're going to New Hampshire."

20

Zeke Tennant woke habitually at dawn, and Sundays were no exception. He left the bed gently, so as not to wake his sleeping wife, Bonnie. He got out of his flannel pajamas and into long underwear, jeans, a flannel lumberjack shirt, and heavy socks and boots, then tiptoed out of the room.

Zeke's sixteen-year-old son, Danny, was leaning against the inside of the front door, peering out of a narrow slat at the world outside. "Morning, Daddy," he said.

"Morning, Danny. What kind of night did we have?"

"I thought I heard a noise, but I couldn't spot anything with the night goggles. Heard a helicopter, though; I'm sure of that. Must have been two, three miles off, to the west."

"Yeah, they come around with their heat-detection systems, trying to catch one of us out of the house at night."

"We had a couple of inches of snow, but it's stopped."

"You keep watch, and I'll get you some breakfast, then you can go to bed."

"Okay, Daddy."

Zeke threw some homemade sausage in the pan and got some eggs from the gas-operated refrigerator, then sliced some of Bonnie's bread. A few minutes later, he set two plates on the table by the front window, and they sat down to eat.

"That mirror plastic stuff on the outside of the windows was an ace idea," Danny said. "Nobody can see in."

"Yeah, there was a time when we wouldn't dare sit down in front of the window like this." The window was made of steel, and the panes of armored glass. As the sun came up, the scenery outside took on a gray cast from the mirrored material. They could see down the mountain road, some five miles, to the highway. Zeke had chosen the site to provide an early warning.

"You going to church?" Danny asked.

"You know we can't do that right now. I'm going over to Harv Shelton's place for a little meeting, though. You'll be okay here; the younger kids can keep a lookout, and I don't think they're going to try anything in broad daylight. And if they do, they'll have to deal with the land mines. You feed the dogs, then let them in."

"Daddy," Danny said hesitantly, "is anybody for sure looking for you right now?"

"You never can tell," Zeke said. "I've got a

failure-to-appear warrant out on me in Georgia; they can always use that for an excuse."

"But that's ten years old, isn't it?" the boy asked.

"All they need is an excuse to come up here legal, and if they want to, they'll do it."

"How long you reckon we could hold out against them?" Danny asked.

Zeke looked at him sharply. "As long as we have to, boy; you remember that."

"Yessir," Danny said.

Zeke finished his breakfast and took a turn around the house. There were three bedrooms and two baths, a little office for himself, a kitchen, and a large family room. He and his family and co-militiamen had built the log cabin themselves, and not from a kit. It had taken them two years, but they had done it. They were completely self-sufficient. The well had been drilled first, then the house built over it, so nobody could poison them; the cellar was stocked with dried and canned food, a year's worth. There were two huge propane tanks sunk into the earth—enough for two, maybe three years—and, if worse came to worst, there was the escape tunnel that ran two hundred yards under the woods, connecting with an old mine. On top of the house, reached by a ladder from the family room, was an eight-foot turret. Like the rest of the house, it had been built of two layers of logs and was lined with sandbags. The roof was six inches of poured concrete on top of logs, lined with cedar shingles and, on the southern exposures, an array of solar panels that kept a large bank of batteries in the cellar charged and ready. The whole exterior house had been repeatedly sprayed with a fire retardant. The place had been built so that no small arms could ever penetrate; it would take heavy military weapons to breach the walls, and the feds couldn't do that, for fear the media would find out. And if they did anyway, he had two M60 machine guns, with mounts in the turret.

Zeke got into a shoulder holster and jammed in his 9mm automatic, with two extra clips. He put a smaller automatic in his coat pocket, then strapped another to his ankle. He put on the sheepskin coat Bonnie had made for him and walked into the connecting utility building. He took the three-wheeler—not enough snow for the Sno-Cat, and too much for the pickup. He popped the steel garage door, started the engine, and drove out. The door closed automatically behind him. The two German shepherds on the front porch lifted their heads and watched him go. Keeping a sharp eye out, he roared down a well-beaten trail, scattering powder snow in his wake, and plunged into the woods. He drove for nearly two miles along the trail, then stopped at a heavy fence topped with razor wire and whistled loudly. A moment later, he heard another whistle, and a section of the fence swung open. He gunned the engine and continued toward the cabin ahead of him.

The garage door was open; he parked inside and pressed the button to close it. He walked into the house, hung his coat on a hook in the mudroom, and went into the living room. Half a dozen men greeted him.

"Hey, Zeke," Harv said. "You had breakfast?"

"Oh, yeah," he said.

"We just finished some eggs Benedict and champagne," Harv said. "Too bad you're late."

Everybody laughed.

Zeke lowered himself into a chair by the fireplace. "I could use a second cup," he said.

"Mary!" Harv shouted. "Get Zeke some black coffee, will you?"

"Coming," a female voice said from the kitchen. A plump, pretty woman in her late thirties brought in the coffee. "Morning, Zeke," she said.

"Morning, Mary, and thanks."

"Mary," Harv said, "if you'll excuse us, now, we've got some business to discuss."

"Bye, gentlemen," Mary said, closing the door behind her.

"Well," Zeke said, "what did it come to?"

Harv grinned. "A little over a million eight," he said. "I guess you want yours now."

"I reckon I do," Zeke said. "I reckon everybody does. Did you have to launder it?"

Harv shook his head. "Nah, it was all fresh out of three or four banks, a good mix of denominations, old and new bills. I put away some bundles of sequential serial numbers, nearly half a million."

"Why didn't you fence it?"

"Too soon. Everybody in the Northwest has heard that an armored car got hit. The feds are everywhere. We'll keep it a year or two, then sell it to somebody who can get it out of the country."

"Makes sense," Zeke said.

Harv went to the woodbox beside the fireplace and removed six bundles, tossing one to each man. "A quarter of a million each," he said. "I took my organizational fee and some expenses off the top."

"Fair enough," Zeke said, examining the bundle. The money was tightly packed and shrink-wrapped, then wrapped in brown paper.

"Don't go splashing out that stuff," Harv said. "The feds will be sniffing around, and we don't want some citizen reporting that he took a lot of cash in payment for something. Let it cool off for a while."

The other men nodded.

Harv glanced at his watch and picked up a remote control. The satellite TV came on. They were on mountain time, and the Sunday morning political shows were coming on. "Take a look at this guy," Harv said. "Any of you know him?"

"I know him," Zeke said.

"That's right, you're from Georgia. What do you think about him?"

"I think he's everything that's wrong with this country, all wrapped up in one man."

"Maybe we should turn our attention to him; it's been a while."

"You better believe it," Zeke growled. "Some friends of mine tried to take him out nine years ago, when he was first running for the Senate, but it all blew up in their faces."

"Was this Willingham and The Elect?" Harv asked.

"Yeah; he and another guy bought it, and the rest scattered, including me. That guy has been too hot to touch since then."

"What do you think about now?"

"I think if he got elected president, things would get worse for us. Christ knows I don't have any use for Republicans, but I'll be goddamned if I want another Democrat running things, especially this one."

"Well, we're refinanced now," Harv said. "You want to take this on?"

"It would be my privilege," Zeke said. "I'll take ten thousand from each of you for expenses."

The others nodded and began breaking open their packets of bills.

Zeke watched the image on the screen. "He's got it coming," he said.

21

It was Will's third Sunday-morning television program. He sat behind a desk and stared into the hot eyes of Barnabas Pauling, a right-wing political commentator known inside the Beltway as the Prince of Fucking Darkness, or Pod, for short.

"Senator Lee," Pod was saying, "your past is riddled with incidents of your placing expensive social programs ahead of fiscal responsibility . . ."

"Name three," Will said.

"Let's take welfare reform," Pod said.

"I voted *for* welfare reform," Will said.

"You also voted for a number of amendments designed to destroy welfare reform, before you finally gave in and cast your vote."

"There were gaping holes in the welfare-reform bill and there were a lot of children in those holes. I and some other sensible people tried to make the blow fall less harshly on them."

"Whatever," Pod said. "Now, your love for these *liberal* programs . . ."

"What programs are those?" Will asked.

"You know very well which programs I mean," Pod replied hotly.

Do you mean bills designed to improve public education? To fortify the Head Start program? To subsidize school lunches for kids whose parents can't afford them? Those are programs that the vast majority of Americans think are very important to the kind of country we live in." Will was glad it was color television, because Pod was turning red, now.

Sir," Pod said, his voice rising, "this country cannot afford a lot of new social programs."

"They're hardly new," Will replied. "Our people have been relying on them for a long time."

Pod turned to the moderator, who was suppressing a smile. "Ben, it's clear I'm not going to get any straight answers out of Senator Lee."

"Come on, Barney," Will said, "ask me some straight questions."

All right, Senator," Pod spat, "where do you stand on the balanced-budget amendment?"

"I'm all for a balanced budget and against the amendment. I think we ought to have the guts to balance the budget without mangling the Constitution."

"I thought so. How about gun control?"

"I've hunted all my life, and I don't want to make it more difficult for legitimate sportsmen to own hunting rifles and shotguns, but guns ought to be licensed so we know who owns them."

"So they can be confiscated by the government?"

"I don't know of any law that allows the

government to go around confiscating lawfully owned weapons, do you?"

"That's what people of your political stripe want, isn't it?"

"Nonsense. What I want is to keep as many guns as possible out of the hands of criminals and crazy people."

"The criminals are going to get handguns, anyway," Pod said.

"Not if we stop them."

With that, the moderator called on another commentator for questions, and Will greeted them with a smile.

Will walked quickly toward the car, with Tim Coleman hurrying to keep up. "Senator, I don't think you ought to get nose-to-nose with guys like Pauling this early in the campaign."

"It's a dirty job, but somebody's got to do it," Will said. "Besides, Moss is telling us that I need name recognition out there in the country. I wouldn't mind being remembered by the voters as the guy who didn't take any shit from the Prince of Fucking Darkness."

"Maybe you're right," Tim said. "I hope so."

"Moss is doing another poll tomorrow, to see if the announcement and the Sunday-morning shows have had any effect."

"I wouldn't count on too much."

"I'll take whatever I can get. Until we can qualify for public campaign financing we're going to be chronically short of money. I had to pay all the rent on the new headquarters in advance, and that wasn't much fun." They got into a car driven by a volunteer. A man Will didn't know was sitting in the front passenger seat.

"Morning," Will said, sticking out his hand. "We haven't met; I'm Will Lee."

"Agent Williams," the man said. "Secret Service. We had trouble catching up with you this morning, Senator."

"I didn't mean to be evasive, but we've been moving fast."

"There's another agent behind us in the car. With your permission, I'd like one of our people to do the driving from now on. This young lady wouldn't give up the wheel."

"Kathy," Will said, laughing, "next stop, let the man drive."

"I want to see his license," the girl said. Everybody laughed, including the agent.

"It's just that we're trained in evasive-action techniques," the agent said.

"I could have used you in the television studio a minute ago," Will said.

They drove to the new headquarters, and Will mingled with the Georgia volunteers, accepting a slice of pizza along the way. There were two television crews in the building, and he was giving running interviews.

"We hear Kiel is announcing tomorrow," a reporter said to Will.

"Be nice to have somebody to argue with besides Barnabas Pauling," Will said.

"Looks like you had the morning shows all to yourself," the reporter said.

"I'm sure Mr. Kiel will be all over them next week."

"Nevertheless, you got the jump."

"I'm going to need all the jumps I can get."

Will sat at the kitchen table with Kate, eating pasta and shrimp and watching a videotape of his performance on the Sunday shows.

"You stopped Pod in his tracks," Kate said.

"That's no real victory," Will replied. "The hard-core right wing will see it as Pod's win, not mine."

"The rest of the country would have enjoyed it, though."

"I hope so."

"What's on for tomorrow?"

"Didn't I tell you? First trip to New Hampshire. The primary is only seven weeks away."

"You didn't tell me."

"I'm sorry, Sweets; it's going to be like that for a while."

"I suppose so. You better take your long underwear."

"I don't have any long underwear. Anyway, Tim says they're having their mildest winter in years."

Kate put her hand on his cheek. "Just don't freeze your ass off. It's mine, remember?"

22

Will stood at the factory gate, freezing his ass off in eight inches of fresh snow, his chest racked with coughing and his nose streaming, and wondered why he had ever wanted to do this. His shoes were soaking wet, his overcoat was not heavy enough for a New Hampshire winter, and his new long underwear clung damply to his body, making him colder instead of warmer. All he could think of was bourbon and a roaring fire. It was five o'clock and already dark. This was his eighth appearance of the day, and he still had two to go. Two Secret Service agents lurked a few feet away; Will had demanded that they back off.

The whistle blew, and, a moment later, men and women began streaming out of the plywood plant, gathering their winter clothes about them. Will saw they were all wearing snow boots. Why hadn't somebody thought of that? "Hi," he said, taking off a thin glove and thrusting a bare hand at an approaching man. "I'm Will Lee, and I'm running for president."

The man stopped but didn't take the offered hand. "You a Republican or a Democrat?"

"I'm a Democrat," Will replied, smiling.

"Then go fuck yourself," the man said, and continued on his way.

Will's instinct was to aim a kick at the man's ass, but a woman was standing in front of him, shaking his hand. "Hey," she said. "I heard you say something at the football game last night. I liked it, and I might vote for you."

"I really appreciate that," Will said, wiping his nose with a sodden handkerchief. He was probably going to give half the town his cold.

"I like that stuff about the middle," she said.

"The New Center," Will corrected. He was anxious to stop some of the other people who were moving past him. "Good luck to you."

"And to you," she said, then went on her way.

Will got a couple of dozen people to acknowledge his presence before the crowd was gone, and he was left standing in the snow. A campaign volunteer, a college student from south Georgia, handed out the last of her leaflets and came over to him. "Senator, you look awful," she said.

"I feel awful," he replied. "I hope the van is running; I'm freezing, too."

"I'll get it started," she said cheerfully, and ran ahead.

Will trudged through the wet snow, feeling like a character out of *Dr. Zhivago*. An agent opened the door for him, then got into the backseat. The van was cold soaked, and the girl was having trouble getting it started. Finally, it came to life, and a rush of icy air came out of the vents. "Don't switch this thing off again, until we return it to the rental company," Will said.

The girl, whose name he could not remember, ran her gloved hand over the icy inside of the windshield, where their breath had frozen, and cleared a tiny portion of the glass. She drove, seeing nothing that could not be seen through the six-by-six-inch spot.

"We're going to end up in a snowdrift, and they won't find us until spring," Will said. "How do people live in weather like this?"

"It ain't Georgia, is it?" the girl said. "Freeze your buns off." As she turned a corner, the van began to move sideways. "Oh, shit," she said under her breath as she spun the wheel into the skid. She was too late; the van slid, broadside, into a large SUV idling at the curb.

"I'll take care of this," the agent said, opening the rear door.

"No, I'll do it," Will said. "You stay out of it." He waited while the girl inched the van forward so that he could get the door open. Thank God there was no TV crew, he thought.

A large man was climbing out of the vehicle, while a woman waited in the front seat.

"It was our fault entirely," Will said, preempting the man's coming outburst. "My driver has never driven in snow before, and I want to make this right. What do you think the damage is?"

The man stopped in his tracks and turned to

look at his damaged car. "I reckon a good fifteen hundred bucks," he said.

Will dug a checkbook and a pen out of his pocket. "Let's make it two thousand; bodywork is expensive these days."

"Fifteen hundred will do it," the man said wearily. "Make it out to Harry Hoskins."

Will wrote the check and handed it to the man. "I'm really very sorry," he said. "I know what an inconvenience this is going to be for you, and I wish there were something more I could do." He stuck out a hand. "I'm Will Lee, and I'm running for president. I hope this won't cost me your vote."

The man laughed. "Senator, you're the fifth candidate I've met today; there's two in the supermarket over there. Good luck to you." He got into his car and drove away.

Will climbed back into the van, which was now a few degrees warmer than the outside air. "Let's go."

The girl was practically in tears. "I'm so sorry, Senator; I don't know what happened."

"It wasn't your fault, Mary Ann," he said, suddenly remembering her name. "Make a note to rent cars with snow tires from now on."

"Yessir," she said.

Will sighed and fell fast asleep.

He was jolted awake as the van struck the curb.

"We're here," Mary Ann said. "It's the Kiwanis Club meeting, in the basement of the town hall, right there." She pointed. "I'll leave the engine running."

Will struggled out of the van. There was a man waiting at the front door of the hall to take him inside. Will peeled off his light topcoat and stamped the snow off his feet, leaving a puddle behind him. He was shown to the head table, shaking hands all the way, and a bowl of hot soup was put in front of him. He got that down gratefully, then started on the fried chicken, which wasn't bad. By the time he was ready to speak he was warm, if damp, and very sleepy. His missed his first cue, then hopped up and went to the microphone. He opened his mouth to speak, but nothing came out.

A man stood up and tapped the microphone, which was on.

Will tried again, and this time he managed a squeaking noise. He had no voice whatever. He grabbed a notebook from his pocket, scribbled something on it, and handed it to the man at his left. The man read it, stood up, and leaned into the microphone.

"It says, 'My name is Will Lee, and I'm running for president, and I've just lost my voice.'" The crowd roared with laughter.

As Will was making his way out of the hall, mutely shaking hands, he found his way blocked by a large man.

"What size shoe do you wear?" the man asked.

Puzzled, Will tried to speak, then got out his pad and wrote down 10D.

The man looked at the pad, nodded, and stepped away. Will was back in the van before he realized that the man who wanted to know his shoe size was the same man whose car his van had struck earlier.

It was after ten o'clock before Will got back to the depressing motel the campaign had booked him into. Kitty Conroy was waiting for him. "How'd it go?" she asked.

Will tried to speak and couldn't.

"Oh, my God!" Kitty said, helping him off with his coat. "You've got laryngitis?"

Will nodded wearily and headed for the bed.

Kitty stopped him. "Oh, no you don't," she said. "Not in those clothes." She began stripping them off him, aided by Mary Ann. The Secret Service agent stood by the door, watching morosely.

"We'll get you home first thing tomorrow," Kitty said. "You're no good to yourself, if you can't talk."

Will shook his head. "Not yet," he mouthed.

"All right, we'll see if you can talk tomorrow, then we'll decide. There's only one more day to go, anyway."

The door to the room opened, and another Secret Service agent walked in, carrying a large parcel. "This was just delivered," he said. "I've already checked it out."

Puzzled, Will opened the box and found a thick winter parka with a fur collar, a pair of snow boots, and a hunter's woolen cap with earflaps.

There was a note in an envelope, and Will opened it. The letterhead said, "Harry's Menswear."

"Dear Senator Lee," it read. "We don't like to have our candidates die on us in New Hampshire, so please accept the enclosed with my compliments. You'll not only live, but you'll fit right in."

It was signed "Harry Hoskins, the fellow whose car you bumped into earlier this evening."

Will fell into bed, already asleep. The next morning, still unable to speak, he wore his new winter clothes to the airport.

23

The anchorman gazed into the camera, rustled the useless papers in his hand, and read from the TelePrompTer to the national television audience of the primary-night special.

"The polls will be closing shortly in New Hampshire, and when they do, we'll tell you what our exit polls are showing. The weather was unexpectedly good today, and the turnout has been heavy. While there are half a dozen names on the ballot, three are expected to take the lion's share of the vote. Senate Minority Leader George Kiel is expected to win outright, with something more than fifty percent of the vote. Then Senator Mark Haynes, the firebrand liberal from Nebraska, and Senator Will Lee, the moderate from Georgia, appear to be running about neck and neck for second place and are expected to take in the region of eighteen percent each. That could change in Senator Haynes's favor, because Senator Lee had to fly back to Washington with a galloping case of the flu four days ago, so he couldn't be around for the home stretch. Let's go to Lisa Helford in Manchester for an update."

A young woman in fashionable ski clothes appeared on screen. "Thanks, Bob," she said. Immediately the screen was filled with shots of people lining up at the polls, and she continued, voice-over. "The unexpectedly heavy turnout was certainly due to the blue skies and warmer temperatures in New Hampshire, after weeks of weather that would be considered really filthy by anyone not from New Hampshire. The candidates braved it as best they could, and one, Senator Will Lee of Georgia, fell by the wayside, done in by the New Hampshire winter. An amateur cameraman caught him at a Kiwanis Club meeting five days ago, at the moment when his health failed him." The shaky screen and tinny sound of a home video camera showed Will approaching the dais, trying to speak, then scribbling something on a notepad. When the club's president read what Will had written, the room erupted in laughter.

"We caught a glimpse of Senator Lee at the local airport the following morning as he beat his retreat, and he seemed a lot better prepared for the weather, after a sympathetic Kiwanian who owns a men's store got him kitted out." An image of Will in his brand-new winter clothes filled the screen as he trudged across a snowy ramp to his airplane, turned and waved, only his eyes visible between his parka's fur collar and his cap, the earflaps of which were tied under his chin.

When the camera returned to the reporter, she

was laughing. "That's it from New Hampshire, Bob," she said. "Back to you."

Bob Blakely, the anchorman, was laughing, too, when he came back on. "Thanks, Lisa. Now let's go to our commentator, Bill Varner, who has been talking to New Hampshire voters for days. Bill, was that the height of fashion in New Hampshire last week?"

The camera panned to a desk where Varner sat. "Bob, that's the way you have to look up there if you want to survive the primary. Actually, Will Lee's early departure from campaigning may have hurt him badly. His campaign tried to make up for it by buying extra television time, but the pros I've talked to said it wasn't enough, that New Hampshire folks are used to seeing their candidates up close, and that television just doesn't do it. Also, everybody in the state saw that television report from the Kiwanis Club meeting and had a good laugh about it, and folks up here tend to look askance at candidates who can't get through a few weeks of winter without folding. What I'm predicting now is that Will Lee is going to lose at least five or six points out of this, and most of those votes are going to go to George Kiel, who will fatten his majority in the state. This could actually have the effect of derailing the Lee campaign, since the New Hampshire primary has been, for so long, a harbinger of things to come at the convention later in the year. So, if Mark Haynes does a little better than expected, we might very well see Will Lee withdrawing from the race—after he gets his voice back."

The camera went back to the anchorman. "If that happens, Bill, what's the overall effect on the race going to be?"

"Well, Bob, unless some dark horse appears from nowhere and turns Democratic voters on, George Kiel is going to be the out-and-out front-runner for the nomination. Kiel is a more conservative Democrat than Will Lee, though hardly a right-winger, and Hayes is so liberal that nobody gives him much of a chance for the nomination. The most he could hope for is a shot at vice president when he gets to the convention."

"So you think Will Lee could really be out?"

"Could happen, Bob, and it would be a pity, because I think a lot of Democrats around the country would find him an attractive candidate when they get to know him. He has an excellent reputation in the Senate, among both Democrats and Republicans. He's often compared to both Sam Nunn and Ted Kennedy, which is unusual. He's compared to Nunn because of his deep knowledge of defense issues, though he's much more skeptical of Pentagon requests than Nunn was, and he's compared to Kennedy, not for his politics, but for his hard legislative work and outstanding staff."

"What about his wife's job at the CIA?" the anchorman asked.

"I haven't heard anybody but Republicans complain about that. Katharine Rule Lee is a career CIA officer, and she's risen to a high level, being in charge of all the Agency's Intelligence analysts. She was something of a heroine a dozen years ago, when she was instrumental in the arrest of Ed Rawls, who is said to be the most damaging mole in the history of the Agency, except perhaps for Aldrich Ames. She's a very bright lady, by all accounts, but she intends to hold on to her Agency job come hell or high water, and she's not going to be seen on the campaign trail, except at the Democratic convention."

"Bob, on the off chance that Will Lee should be elected, is there some sort of inherent conflict in having a president whose wife is in an important CIA job?"

"I expect the Republicans would say so, Bob, but nothing like this has ever happened before. No first lady has ever been a government employee, either before or after an election."

"Would Will Lee be likely to consider appointing his wife as Director of Central Intelligence, if he were elected?"

"I don't think so, although Kate Lee is said to be an eventual contender for that job, should some future president appoint a career CIA officer instead of an outsider."

"Well, it's all very interesting, Bill, and the polls are closing in New Hampshire in just a minute, so after the break, we'll come back with our exit polling and see if Will Lee is going to be able to manage to stay in this race."

The cameras went to commercial.

Will, Kate, and a dozen of Will's staff sat around a large-screen television set at campaign headquarters. Will could talk again, now, though he had been advised not to, unless absolutely necessary.

"This doesn't look good," Tim Coleman said. "We sure could have used those four days."

Will nodded.

"I wish we had some poll results of our own," Tim said.

"We're about to get some," Will whispered.

Bob Blakely came back on camera, sitting at a V-shaped desk with three other people, among them Bill Varner. "Our director is telling us that we're going to have these exit-poll results flashed on our big screen behind us, and none of us has seen them yet, so this will be hot off the wire." He turned toward the screen behind him. "Here they come. Bill, you want to take us through this?"

"Sure, Bob, I . . ." Varner stopped talking. "Wait a minute, here, are you guys in the control booth running a game on us?" He pressed a finger to his earpiece. "This is really what's come in?" He listened again. "All right, here we go. Now, remember, these numbers are from exit polls, and we won't have the real numbers until midnight, but what we've got here is a major near upset. Our exit polls are showing Senator George Kiel not with more than fifty percent of the vote, as predicted, but with only forty-one percent. Next—and this is stunning, I don't know what happened—is Senator Will Lee of Georgia with *thirty-six percent*, and after him, Senator Mark Haynes with only eight percent of the vote."

"You think there might be something wrong with our exit polling, Bill?" the anchorman asked.

Varner had his finger to his earpiece again. "I'm hearing from New Hampshire that our people are standing behind these numbers, that they're real."

"And what is this going to mean, Bill?"

"It means that Will Lee is solidly in this race—he's still behind, but if these numbers hold, then something has happened in New Hampshire that we never expected. If he can bring in numbers like this while in bed with the flu for the last four days of the campaign, then he may really have something going for him."

Back at campaign headquarters, Will was being hugged by Kate and pummeled on the back by Tim Coleman and Kitty Conroy.

"Let's wait for the real results," he managed to whisper.

24

It was midnight, and ninety-eight percent of the ballots in New Hampshire had been counted, confirming the network's exit polls. Bob Blakely and Bill Varner still sat at their desk.

"Bill," Blakely said, "this has certainly been a big night for Will Lee. To what do you attribute this big surprise?"

"Bob, we've put together some footage taken earlier today, when the polls were still open, and we asked people who voted for Lee why they did. Let's listen."

A woman carrying a small child appeared on camera. "I met him a couple of times early in the campaign," she said, "and I just liked him. And when I saw that thing from the Kiwanis Club, I just laughed until I cried. I really felt for him."

An elderly man came on camera. "I heard that his car ran into another fellow's car right before that Kiwanis meeting, and Mr. Lee wrote him a check on the spot. That impressed me."

A young woman's face appeared. "Well, he's

charming, isn't he? He gives an honest answer to a question, and he looks you in the eye. He doesn't talk like a politician, even when he can't talk."

Another woman: "Listen, I've had the flu myself, and I know how bad it can be. But he kept going until he couldn't go anymore, and I admire that."

The camera went back to the studio. "Well, Bob, I don't know, I guess the folks in New Hampshire just liked the man."

"Bob, we haven't been able to get George Kiel to join us, but we've got Jim Thomas, Kiel's campaign manager, so let's go over to Kiel campaign headquarters." A bespectacled man appeared on the screen. "Jim, what happened up there today?"

"Well, Bob, we won the damn primary, that's what happened!"

"But you didn't get a clear majority, as you had been predicting you would. Why not?"

"Listen, it was *you* guys who predicted that, not us. We're just glad to have the victory."

"Do you think you would have won if Will Lee had had those last four days to campaign?"

"Sure, I do; I think we would have beat him even worse."

"Thanks, Jim." The camera went back to the studio, and Bob Blakely turned to the camera. "Well, we've got just one more stop to make before we're done. Even though George Kiel got the most votes, the big winner in New Hampshire seems to be Will Lee." Will appeared on the big screen from his campaign headquarters, smiling. "Senator, your staff has told us that you can't say much, because of your delicate voice, so give us just some idea of how you feel tonight, and we'll let you go."

Will's eyebrows shot up. "Well, Bob," he croaked, "I think I can win this nomination if I can just get sick enough."

Republican Senator Frederick Wallace of South Carolina picked up the remote control and switched off the television, still laughing.

His companion, Jeb Stuart Calhoun, the junior senator from South Carolina, took a swig of his bourbon. "Well, Freddie, what do you think of that?"

Wallace puffed on his cigar. "I think Will Lee kicked George Kiel's ass, that's what I think."

"And what do you think that means for us?"

"I think it means we ought to be worried."

"Jesus, Freddie, why? You think we have anything to fear from Will Lee?"

"Jeb, didn't you listen to what those New Hampshire voters had to say?"

"Sure, I did, and it didn't make any sense to me."

"Well, I guess that's why you're not president. Those people *liked* Will Lee, which shouldn't have come as such a surprise to me, since I like him myself. Think about it; how many *likable* presidential candidates have we had since Jack Kennedy died?"

"Ronald Reagan was likable."

"Right, right, who else?"

"Bill Clinton, although I personally hated the son of a bitch."

"Anybody else?"

Calhoun screwed up his aging brow. "Not that I can think of."

"And what else do Ronald Reagan and Bill Clinton have in common?"

"I can't think of a thing."

"They both were elected to two terms, you horse's ass!"

"Oh, yeah."

"Now tell me, Jeb, who would you rather run against? George Kiel, or that nice-looking, charming fellow who just kicked George's ass?"

"I see your point. But just because he did well in New Hampshire doesn't mean that'll translate to getting the nomination."

"Jeb, the folks in New Hampshire are the most hard-bitten, skeptical, cantankerous voters in this country. Just about every one of them has met two or three presidents and a whole lot of candidates. If Will Lee can charm them, he can charm anybody."

Calhoun drank some more bourbon. "Well, what are we going to do about it? Is the man clean?"

"Nobody's clean, Jeb, you above all people ought to know that."

Calhoun reddened. "Then there must be something we can get on him."

"I've known him since he came to work for Ben Carr," Wallace said, "and he's as clean as they come." He puffed on his cigar, then smiled a small smile. "That's not to say he's clean, though."

"You know something I don't, Freddie?"

"Jeb, I know a *hell* of a lot you don't, and don't you ever forget it."

"Come on, Freddie, what have you got on him?"

"There's a woman in Will Lee's past," Wallace said. "A very beautiful woman, in fact. Very telegenic."

"Tell me about it."

Wallace got up and poured himself another bourbon, then settled again in the wing chair before the fireplace. "It goes back a good ten years," he said, "back when Will was first running for Ben Carr's seat. He got himself roped into defending a young fellow down in Will's home country. The fellow was charged with raping and murdering a colored woman."

"You mean Lee got involved with a *colored* woman? I *like* it!"

"Jeb, the colored woman was the murder victim. Now shut up and listen."

"Sorry, go on."

"Will's client had this very beautiful girlfriend. She sat there in court every day and knocked everybody's eyes out. I guess she knocked Will's eyes out, too, because he ended up screwing her."

Calhoun leaned forward. "Let me get this straight: This woman was the girlfriend of Lee's client, and he screwed her?"

"Not only was she the client's girlfriend, but

she was the principal defense witness; she was the client's alibi."

"Lee screwed a *witness* in the trial? His *own* witness?"

"Well, it was a little more complicated than that. Will was still single at the time, although he'd been seeing Kate Rule for a while. But they had busted up at that particular moment, and the client's girlfriend had dumped her boyfriend, too, so, technically, Will and this girl were free, white, and twenty-one. And the girl had already completed her testimony in the trial."

"What about the boyfriend? Did he get off?"

"Nope. He was convicted of first-degree murder and rape and sentenced to die."

"And did he?"

"Not yet, but soon." Wallace permitted himself a small grin. "Unless he gets himself a first-class appeals lawyer."

"Has he got any grounds for appeal?"

How about his lawyer was screwing his girlfriend and allowed him to get convicted so the two of them could go on screwing each other?"

"You said this was ten years ago, and he's about to die. That means he's already exhausted the appeals process. Didn't this come up before?"

"It did, but it was mishandled by a stupid lawyer. What that boy needs is a better lawyer."

"You going to get him one?"

"Oh, I don't think I want to do anything as direct as that," Wallace purred.

"How you going to handle it?"

"I'm going to let you handle it, Jeb."

"Now, wait a minute, Freddie—"

"Relax. You've had some dealings with that little group of conservative lawyers—what are they called?"

"The J. Edgar Hoover Institute?"

"That's it."

"Freddie, those boys are *for* the death penalty."

"Well, sure they are, Jeb, like all right-thinking people. But they don't want to see it misapplied, do they? Make 'em look good to take an unpopular case, especially one that reflected poorly on a rising Democrat candidate for president."

Calhoun rubbed his chin. "Well, it might at that. I'll give them a call tomorrow."

"Jeb, you don't want to do that," Wallace scolded. "You want to talk to somebody who'll talk to somebody, then *he'll* talk to them."

"Right, right." Calhoun took a notepad from his pocket. "What's this murderer's name?"

"Larry Eugene Moody, if memory serves. He's in the Georgia state prison at Reidsville, on death row, of course."

"And the girl's name?"

"Charlene Joiner."

Calhoun stopped writing. "Isn't there a movie actress by that name? I saw something on television the other night."

Freddie Wallace smiled broadly. "You bet your ass there is."

The phone rang, and Wallace picked it up. "Who is it?"

"Freddie, it's Eft Efton; how are you?"

"Just a minute." He covered the phone. "You get on it, Jeb; I've got to take this call." He watched until Calhoun was out of the room, then returned to the phone. "I guess we got a little surprise tonight, boy."

"I guess so," Efton said. "I'm not worried, though. I'd love to run against a closet liberal like Will Lee."

Wallace sighed deeply. "You just don't get it, do you, boy?"

"Huh?"

"The man you want to run against is George Kiel."

"But he's the conservative."

"Eft, that liberal tag ain't gonna stick to Will Lee; he's got some credentials on national defense and a good record on the budget. And that ain't all; folks just naturally like him, and that can't be said of you. I mean, the hard core is gonna be with you all the way, but you're gonna have to attract the independents and a lot of Democrats if you want to get elected."

"Come on, Freddie, I've been toning down the rhetoric, or at least confining it to preaching to the converted."

"Eft, face it; you lack charm, and Will doesn't. Trust me, you want to run against Kiel."

"Well, I guess I'm not going to have much to say about who the Democrats pick, am I?"

"Maybe not, but *I* am," Wallace replied.

"What do you mean?"

"I've got a few irons in the fire; I'm going to get George Kiel the Democratic nomination, and no-

body's even going to know how it happened."
Wallace hung up the phone without another word,
and began sipping his bourbon again. It bothered
him a little that he was going to make a shit like
Eft president, but he'd rather have a shit that he
could control in office than somebody more
independent-minded, like Will Lee, even if he
did like him.

"Will, my boy," he said into the fire, "you're
never gonna know what hit you."

25

Zeke Tennant got down from the pickup truck at the dark crossroad, then turned to his son. "You take care of things, now. I don't want to have to worry about anything, and you won't be hearing from me for a while."

"Don't you worry, Daddy; we'll all be fine, and we'll wait to hear from you."

"Might be weeks or months; don't you worry."

"I'd never worry about you, Daddy."

Zeke got his duffel out of the pickup, then handed the boy his wallet. "Keep this for me." He leaned over and let his son kiss him on his cheek, then closed the truck door and watched as the boy made a U-turn and drove away into the early-morning hours. That was a good boy, he thought; he'd die defending their homestead, if necessary. He looked east; there was the faint glow of dawn.

Half an hour later, with the sun peeking over the horizon, the bus stopped in response to the flashlight Zeke was waving, and he got on and bought a ticket from the driver. You didn't have to show a picture ID to buy a bus ticket; all you needed was the cash. Zeke stowed his duffel in the overhead rack, then settled into his seat and tried to get some sleep.

Fifteen hours later, Zeke disembarked at the Las Vegas bus terminal and found a cab. Ten minutes later he got out at a modest apartment complex and walked through the parking lot to the building nearest the street. He let himself into the ground-level apartment, kicked the accumulated junk mail out of the way, and looked around. It seemed to be as he had left it: a furnished two-bedroom unit, with one bedroom set up as an office. He took his duffel into the bedroom, unlocked the closet with his key, and pushed the hanging clothes aside to reveal a wall safe with an electronic keypad. He punched in the code, opened the safe, took out a wallet and a checkbook, and put them into his hip pocket. Then he opened the duffel, dug to the bottom, and began stacking bundles of bound U.S. currency into the safe, keeping a couple of bundles for immediate use.

Zeke took a shower, shaved off his beard, leaving only the moustache, then packed the clothes he wore into a garbage bag for disposal later. He got dressed in garments he had left in the apartment, then poured himself a bourbon and turned on the TV. He was now Harry Grant.

Eight months before, Zeke had taken the same

bus to Las Vegas, carrying only what he wore and his duffel, which concealed a hundred thousand dollars. His first stop had been at a barbershop, where he had gotten a haircut and shave, leaving his handlebar moustache. This was important. He had then rented this apartment, paying a year's rent in advance. He had bought some nice, middle-of-the-road businessman's clothes, then had taken himself to a casino, where he had bought five thousand dollars in chips from one window, then more from another. Carrying the chips in a tray, he had sat down at a blackjack table and started to play.

Zeke was a card counter, and a good one. Playing carefully, never winning too much, he had nearly doubled his stake before he attracted the attention of a pit boss, who watched from a discreet distance. Zeke was untroubled by this attention; he lost some, then won some more. When he tired of blackjack, he headed for the backroom poker games, buying still more chips along the way.

He played until the wee hours, and when he had accumulated a little over fifty thousand dollars in chips, both bought and won, he cashed in everything, asking for a casino check. He had just laundered some money.

The following morning, he had taken the casino check and opened a bank account. Even in Vegas, a bank looked at you askance if you came in with that much cash. Over the time he had spent in Vegas, he had made other deposits, always in cash and always under five thousand dollars, to avoid filling out any federal forms.

Now, back in Vegas, he had a healthy bank balance, plus what he had brought with him. He ordered in a pizza, had a six-pack of beer delivered, and spent the evening watching TV.

The following morning he began running errands. He already had a Nevada driver's license and a Visa card from his earlier visit; now he had some business cards printed—Harry Grant, computer consultant, hardware and software. He bought a decent computer and a telephone-answering machine and had them sent to the apartment, then he went car shopping. He liked cars, and he was going to enjoy this. He visited half a dozen dealerships, then he found a two-year-old Lexus ES300, the smallest model. It had less than twenty thousand miles on it and was still under warranty, not that it mattered. He bargained hard, then wrote the man a check and waited while he called the bank. He drove away, pleased with his purchase. The car was luxurious and comfortable, but it didn't look all that different from a Toyota, so it was fairly anonymous.

That night, he gambled, losing a little this time, then picked up a prostitute at the casino bar and took her back to the apartment. She called herself Cherry. She looked around carefully.

"You're not going to give me any problems, are you, Harry?" she asked.

She remembered the name; good. "Of course

not, baby; we're just going to have a drink and ball. Nothing weird about Harry Grant." She was compliant, even enthusiastic, and Zeke enjoyed himself.

When they were both spent, and she was getting dressed, Harry led her into the office. "I want you to do a little favor for me," he said.

"I thought I already did that," she replied.

"Don't worry, there's no work involved, and it's worth another twenty."

"What do I have to do?" She sighed.

"Just a minute," he said. He wrote some words on a sheet of paper and handed them to her. "I just want you to record an answering-machine message for me. You've got a very nice voice."

"Okay." Zeke pressed the button, and she read, "You've reached Harry Grant computer consultants," she breathed. "We're on the line with other customers, but if you'll leave a message, someone will get right back to you."

"Very good," Zeke said. "Now it sounds like I'm a company, instead of just one guy."

"Glad to help. You going to give me cab fare?"

He handed her a fifty. "Here, baby; you've been great."

"You want to do it again, I'm available," she said, handing him a card.

Zeke waved good-bye to her and went to bed. Before he left Vegas, Harry Grant was going to be a real guy, known to lots of people.

26

Will let himself into the Georgetown house. A Secret Service man stuck his head out of the bedroom under the stairs and waved hello. Will waved back and tiptoed up the stairs, carrying his luggage. Although he had become accustomed to the constant presence of the agents on the road, he had not yet gotten used to having them in the house, but then, he hadn't been at home much the past few months.

Light showed from under the bedroom door, and he opened it.

His wife looked up from her book. "Hello, sailor," she said. "Like to give a girl a good time?" She let a strap of her nightgown fall off a shoulder.

Will dropped his bags, shucked off his clothes, and climbed, naked, into bed with her, while she slipped the nightgown over her head. There was no talk, just immediate lovemaking. When they were finished, he lay with his head on her breast. "God, I've missed you," he said. "A politician can't get laid on the campaign trail anymore, you know. Bill Clinton screwed it up for all of us."

"Well, gee," she replied. "A politician's wife can do very well for herself, what with three shifts of Secret Service men in the house. Those boys are always randy."

He bit her on a nipple.

"So, how was it?"

"Could have been worse, I guess; at least, I didn't get sick."

"That's an improvement, but how will you ever win if you're well?"

"There is that, isn't there?"

"I get the impression from the papers that it's going okay, but not great."

"A reasonable assessment," he agreed. "George Kiel is turning out to be more of a handful than I'd imagined. He's well ahead in the delegate count, and we've got less than a month before the convention, in L.A., and he still won't debate me."

"You having any fun at all?"

"Weirdly enough, yes. I like it when I can get in a room with fifty people and really answer their questions. Trouble is, the staff keeps pointing out that if I only talk to fifty people at a time, I can't get elected to anything."

"So, my darling, how would you feel about being vice president?"

Will sat up and stuffed a couple of pillows between his back and the headboard. "I really, really don't want to do that," he said. "I'd rather be slugging it out in the Senate than representing George Kiel at funerals."

"It might not be all bad," she said. "Joe Adams has done it well."

"Doing it well is not the point," Will replied. "The point is, that as VP, one has absolutely no power of any kind, and George is not the sort of guy who's going to share it. I'd get about the same treatment that Harry Truman got from FDR."

"You forget that Joe Adams is president of the United States, at the moment."

"I don't want to sit around waiting for George to kick off. What's the news on the president?"

"He wakes up from time to time, but doesn't seem able to communicate. I got that from Sue Adams."

"I'd rather not be VP, even under those circumstances."

"So, you're telling me that if Kiel nails down the nomination and then summons you to a hotel suite in L.A. and tells you that he can't win without you and, for the good of the party, you have to be VP, you're going to tell him to get stuffed? Lyndon Johnson didn't want to be vice president, either."

"I hope I'll have the guts to tell him to get stuffed," Will said, "but in a situation like that, you never know, do you?"

"No, you don't."

"So, how would you feel about being the *second* lady?"

"About the same as being *first* lady, I guess. I would do everything I could to ignore it, and as second lady it might even be easier to keep my job, or maybe even get promoted."

"If I stayed in the Senate, it would be even easier."

"Don't think I haven't thought about that," she said. "By the way, you do remember that we have dinner at the White House tomorrow evening?"

"I remember, and have the awful feeling that George Kiel is going to be there, too."

"And I'll have to make nice with his wife."

"Oh, yes. Won't that be fun?"

"She could win a Mamie Eisenhower look-alike contest," Kate said. "Even to the clothes."

"I love you when you're catty," he said, kissing her ear.

"I talked to Sue Adams again today," Kate said.

"And how is she? More important, how is Joe?"

"She said everything was fine. I'm not sure why I didn't believe her."

Will sat up straight. "Do you think Joe is worse?"

"I don't know. She was chipper enough, but there was something under the surface that I couldn't read. Still, they wouldn't be giving this dinner party if he wasn't all right, would they?"

Will relaxed. "You're right, they wouldn't. You know, I've hardly given Joe a thought for the past few months."

"Don't feel guilty; he's had his hands so full that he probably hasn't thought a lot about you, either. God forbid we should read about some incident in the papers, or start hearing rumors that he isn't quite right."

"I suppose I should give some thought to what I'll do if I do hear those rumors."

"What can you do?"

"I can press him to resign, I suppose. I'm not really comfortable with the knowledge that he's ill."

"But then Eft Efton would become the acting president, wouldn't he?"

"I suppose the country could stand even that for a few months, although it would give him a big leg up in the general election. I think he's going to get the Republican nomination."

"I hope he does," Kate said. "Wouldn't you enjoy running against him?"

"It would get dirty."

"On his part only, I hope."

"I hope, too."

"If it gets really bad, would you fight fire with fire?"

"You mean start digging into his personal life? Not a chance. I'll leave that to Larry Flynt and the tabloids."

"Eft won't leave it to them; he'll go all out to get anything he can on you."

"What is there to get?" Will asked.

"You can't think of anything?"

"I don't think I've ever done anything in my life that I can't defend, if I have to. There are some votes that I cast for political advantage that I'm not proud of, but I don't think that's the kind of thing Eft could use against me. He's had too many of those in his own career."

"I have to tell you," Kate said, "I have a sense

of foreboding about this. After the Clinton mess, everybody's fair game."

"Well, game, maybe, but not fair game. And the current atmosphere may cost the Republicans a lot of seats in the House."

"How about the Senate?"

"I think it's unlikely that we can get majorities in both houses."

"So, if you're president, you'll likely have a Republican-controlled Senate?"

"Probably, so I don't want to piss them off too much during the campaign. I've worked hard to build relationships with a lot of Republican senators, and I don't want to squander that in a dog-fight with Eft Efton."

They snuggled into bed, and she put her head on his shoulder, pressing her body against his. "How much time together do you think we'll get if you're president?"

"A lot more than now," he said, "but maybe less than we had before. I'll do the best I can; you know that."

"I guess I know that," she said.

"There's always Camp David and the bedroom on Air Force One."

She laughed. "I wonder if I could make love on an airplane full of staff, press, and Secret Service agents."

"We already know that the presence of agents doesn't slow you down," he said, kissing her.

"It didn't, did it?" She giggled.

"Not in the least."

"Want to do it again?"

"Will you settle for first thing in the morning? I'm pretty bushed."

"If I have to," she said.

"Maybe we can do it in the bathroom at the White House tomorrow night."

"Promises, promises," she said.

27

Terry Cogan drove through the flat south Georgia countryside toward Reidsville. Cogan was a small-time Atlanta lawyer, in his late thirties, who supplemented his DUI cases and ambulance chasing with occasional investigative work, and he was pleased to have this job, even if he wasn't sure who he was working for. He'd gotten a call from another lawyer in a big Atlanta firm, a friend of his father's, who'd sometimes sent cases his way, and the man had been tight-lipped about who was instructing him. Maybe it was better if he didn't know.

He made his way to the state prison, parked his car, and identified himself at the front gate, his way having been smoothed by a call from a state legislator of his father's acquaintance. Fifteen minutes later he was shown into a sparsely furnished room, and five minutes after that, a guard brought a man into the room and left the two of them alone.

"Hey," the man said. "I'm Larry Moody."

"Terry Cogan," the lawyer replied, offering his hand. Cogan had done his homework on Larry Eugene Moody, who had bulked up in the prison gym. The young man was thirty-five, and his blond hair was thinning and creeping up his scalp; otherwise, he looked much the same as in the pictures at his trial.

"Did Charlene send you?" Moody asked.

"Charlene Joiner? No. I'm an attorney, and I represent some people who are interested in your case, people who are opposed to the death penalty."

They sat down. "I'll tell you anything I can that'll help," Moody said. "I'm scheduled for October 30, and I'm getting worried."

"I can understand that," Cogan said.

"If I can just get a new trial, I know I'll be acquitted. That nigger girl who testified against me at my trial is dead, you know; she got killed in a car wreck last New Year's Eve."

Cogan had not the slightest doubt that Moody was guilty of the rape and murder of which he had been convicted. He knew that the girl Moody was referring to was a last-minute witness who'd testified that Moody had raped her when they were in high school. "I think you could be right," he said. "I've read the trial transcript, and I think that, without her testimony, you'd have been acquitted."

"Damn right I would have."

"It's a shame your lawyer wasn't smart enough to keep her off the stand."

"Will Lee? He's running for president now, did you hear?"

"I heard. I'm sorry you weren't better represented."

"Well, he did good, really," Moody said, looking at the ground. "I didn't tell him nothing about the nigger girl, so he sort of got blindsided at the last minute, when one of my old high-school teachers was on the stand and mentioned her. The prosecutor was all over that right away, and there wasn't really nothing Mr. Lee could have done."

"So you don't blame Will Lee for your conviction?" Cogan asked, making some notes on a legal pad. "I'd have thought you'd have been pretty pissed off at him."

"For what? He did the best he could, and that was damned good."

"Well, how about that business between Lee and Charlene?"

Moody laughed. "Listen, Charlene likes to fuck better than anybody I ever knew. I'd been in jail for a long time, so she was getting pretty horny, and when Charlene's horny, she can have just about any guy she wants. You ever seen her in the movies?"

"Many times."

"So you know how sexy she is."

"I sure do."

"Well, let me tell you something: Charlene on the silver screen ain't nothing compared to Charlene up close. Jesus, I get horny just thinking about it. When we were living together, I'd come home from work, and we'd do it, and we'd do it again at bedtime, and then again first thing in the morning, you know? We used to go to the drive-in movies, and we'd fuck in the back of my van, just for a change. So I know what Mr. Lee was up against when she showed up at his place that afternoon."

"Do you know what happened that day?"

"Oh, Charlene told me all about it after the trial. She liked talking about it."

"What, exactly, did she tell you?"

"She said she went out to the Lee farm, over by Delano, and she went back to this little house behind the big house, where Mr. Lee lived. It was on a little lake. Anyway, when she got there she saw him diving in the lake, and he was nekkid, so she got nekkid, too, and jumped in with him. So they fucked in the water, and then again inside the house, and then she did this little thing she used to do."

"What was that? What did she used to do?"

"She ate some ice cream, and then she gave him a blow job."

Cogan blinked at the thought.

"Let me tell you, Charlene knew her way around a cock. I mean, there's some guys here in prison who are pretty good at it for five bucks or some cigarettes, but Charlene was the absolute queen of the blow job, and I ought to know. If she gave me one, she gave me a hundred. And that thing with the ice cream, well . . ."

"I can only imagine," Cogan said, trying not to think about it. "Tell me, Larry, do you remember whether this little scene between Charlene and

Will Lee took place before or after she testified at your trial?"

"Oh, it was afterward, I think. Charlene and I had a little spat when she wouldn't fuck me in jail, and she wasn't talking to me at the time. And she had already testified by then."

"I see. Well, look, Larry, here's the thing."

"What?"

"Just about the only grounds you'd have for appeal would be that your lawyer was incompetent."

"Oh, I don't think he was incompetent; Charlene said he was real good at it."

"Larry, I'm talking about his being incompetent in the way he represented you at your trial."

"You mean, if I said he did a bad job, I might get a new trial?"

"Possibly," Cogan said, not looking at Moody. "Now, think back, Larry: Isn't it just possible that you did tell him about this witness, this black girl who said you raped her in high school?" Cogan didn't wait for Moody to respond, but plowed ahead. "And that maybe he could have done something to exclude her testimony, and because he didn't, you got convicted? I mean, if I had been representing you, I think I would have anticipated that and gotten her evidence excluded as irrelevant, or called other witnesses to refute her testimony." He watched Larry Moody closely for his response, and he thought he saw a little light go on in the eyes.

"Well," Moody said, his eyes narrowing, "now that you mention it, I think I might have told him I'd been falsely accused of raping that nigger girl. Nothing ever came of it, you know. There wasn't nothing to back up her story, just her word against mine. Even my old teacher said on the stand that she never believed I raped the girl."

"Well, it would help if you could remember exactly when you told him that and what the circumstances were," Cogan said. "Your story has got to be credible, you know; you've got to be believable. Think back and see if you can remember exactly when you told Will Lee about this black girl's accusation."

Moody massaged his forehead for a moment. "I got it!" he said. "It was the first time I met with him, in the Greenville jail. I'd just been arrested the day before, and the judge appointed Mr. Lee to defend me. He came to see me, and he asked me all sorts of questions about my background and where I was when that girl got murdered, and all that, and then he asked me if there was anything I wanted to tell him, anything he should know. And that was when I told him."

"What, exactly, did you tell him that day?"

"I told him I'd been falsely accused in high school by this nigger girl—of course, I didn't say 'nigger,' because Mr. Lee was a real liberal, you know."

"So, he did know before the trial about this incident, and he didn't take any steps to protect you from the testimony of this potential witness?"

"Yeah, that's it. I remember, now; I told him about all this that first time I met him."

Cogan was writing as fast as he could, now.

"Tell me, Larry, how often are you and Charlene in touch these days?"

"We write letters now and then, although I'm not much of a letter writer. She always writes me back, though, and once in a while I call her out in California, when I can catch'er at home. She's been trying to get me a good lawyer for an appeal, and Mr. Lee wouldn't do it."

"Charlene asked Will Lee to file an appeal for you?"

"Yeah, she did."

"And he wouldn't?"

"No, he wouldn't, the son of a bitch," Moody said, looking angry.

"But Charlene and Will Lee are in touch with each other?"

"Yeah, she said she talked to him on the phone."

"Do you know if Charlene and Lee have met recently? I mean, have they gotten together? Maybe had sex? Think carefully, now."

Moody's eyes narrowed again. "Well, I couldn't prove it, and Charlene didn't exactly say that, but I kind of got the impression, you know? You want me to ask Charlene the next time I talk to her? She'll tell me if she's been fucking him, I know she will."

"I don't think it's a good idea if you ask her straight out, Larry. I mean, if she flat-out denied it, then it would be hard to prove. Sometimes it's better if you don't know all the actual facts of a thing, you know?"

"If you say so, Mr. Cogan."

Cogan tossed his legal pad into his briefcase and stood up. "Well, Larry, it's been good to meet you."

Moody pumped his hand. "Do you think you can get me a new trial, Mr. Cogan?"

"I can't promise that, Larry, but I will look into it. I think it's just possible that the people I represent might find it to be a good thing for you to have a new trial. I'll be in touch."

Cogan drove back toward Atlanta, excited. He had been repelled by Moody and his blatant racism, but he might get more work out of this case than he had expected, so he could stand that. He resisted the temptation to use his car phone. He'd ask for a face-to-face meeting when he got back to Atlanta.

28

Will and Kate were delivered to the White House by a Secret Service car and escorted by an usher to the Blue Room for cocktails. There was a larger crowd than Will had expected, and a number of them were people he had not expected. George Kiel was there, as he had predicted, but so were Howard Efton, the Speaker of the House, looking uncomfortable in a tuxedo, and Robert Mallon, the governor of Arizona, who was Efton's chief opponent for the Republican nomination and, Will thought, the eventual vice-presidential candidate for the Republicans, on a slate with Efton.

"Well, I'll be," Kate murmured, looking around.

Susan Adams approached and kissed them both. "We're so glad to see you," she said. "This is the first time we've entertained at the White House since the first lady insisted on exchanging quarters with us."

"Any news on the president's condition?" Will asked.

"He's as before, and the first lady thought that, since Joe is now running the country, we should be living in the White House. Certainly, neither of us would have ever suggested it; it was presented to us as a fait accompli."

"I think the first lady was right," Will said. "This is where you and Joe belong."

"Joe's on the other side of the room, spreading joy," Sue said. "I know he wants a private word with you before the evening's over."

"Of course," Will replied. "Any time Joe likes."

The Speaker of the House materialized at Will's elbow. "Evening, Will," he said, with a warmth that caught Will off guard. "Katharine, you look lovely tonight."

"Thank you, Mr. Speaker," Kate said. Nobody had called her Katharine since high school.

"How are you, Eft?" Will asked.

"I'm better than expected, at this stage of the campaign," Efton replied softly, as if he didn't want to be overheard.

"You think you'll have a majority of delegates before the convention?" Will asked.

"Could be," Efton replied. "Then it looks like it'll be George Kiel and me in the general election. And you, of course; you'll be on the ticket, won't you?"

"Only if I'm at the top of it," Will said, surprising himself. He took Efton's comment as it had been intended, as a barb.

"That's the boy," Efton said, punching Will's shoulder. "Never say die!"

"Sometimes the voters say it for you, Eft," Will replied. "Excuse me, I want to talk to George." He steered Kate in the direction of his opponent for the Democratic nomination.

Kiel greeted him, smiling broadly. "Well, Will," he said, "I thought you'd be on the road."

"Funny, George, I thought you would be, too."

"Well, I guess I can afford a night off to have dinner with our acting president, but frankly," he said, smiling, "I'm surprised you can. My people tell me we're going to take the nomination on the first ballot by a hundred and fifty votes."

Will managed a broad smile. "You go right on thinking that, George." Will's best projection was that he was sixty votes behind, but he wasn't going to tell Kiel that. "I love an overconfident opponent."

Kiel managed a chuckle, then turned serious. "Will, you and I need to sit down and talk about some things. How about tomorrow morning at nine, in my hideaway office on the Hill?"

Will had no intention of sitting down with Kiel until he was forced to. "I'm afraid I'm off at the crack of dawn tomorrow, George," he said. "Maybe at the convention?"

"Well," Kiel said, "I suppose our relative positions will be better defined by that time."

"I guess they will," Will agreed.

An usher came into the room, rang a gong, and announced dinner. The crowd moved into a room that had been set with four tables of eight, as a string quartet from the Marine Band played in a corner. Will and Efton were at the same table, as were George Kiel and Mallon. Will wondered if there were some subliminal message in that. Was Joe Adams trying to tell the crowd something? He looked across the room to where Joe sat, chatting earnestly with a beautiful woman to his right. Joe looked tanned and fit, Will thought.

The guests worked their way through three courses of dinner, chatting noisily. Will was grateful that he and Efton were on opposite sides of the table; he was never comfortable in the Speaker's company, disliking both the man and his politics. Still, he had always been scrupulously polite to the man, except in campaign speeches. Will looked around the room, noting the composition of the guest list. There were prominent members of the Senate and the House from both parties, and Will could spot no members of the press, with the exception of the long-retired Walter Cronkite, who, with his wife, sat at the Adamses' table. They were on coffee when Joe Adams stood up and addressed the group.

"Good evening to you all," he said. "This is the first time that Sue and I have entertained in the White House since the first lady so kindly asked us to move in, and we are very pleased to have you all as our first guests.

"What you have in common, of course, is that, after the coming election, you will all play important roles in the running of the country. Almost certainly, the eventual nominees of the two parties are here, and by extension, the next president of the United States. So what Sue and I have here is not just a very special group of guests, but a very distinguished captive audience." There was a low chuckle from the crowd.

"You all know that I have declared my intention of withholding my endorsement of any candidate before the convention, and I believe my party can select a slate without my help, even at that time. Of course, after the conventions, I have to say that I'm leaning toward supporting the Democratic candidate." Loud laughter.

"Although I don't expect to take much part in active campaigning."

"Hear, hear!" Eft Efton shouted, and the crowd laughed again.

"I didn't say I was going to be neutral, Eft," Adams said with a smile. More laughter.

"I asked you all here tonight," he continued, "not to once again convey my hands-off position during the campaign, but to talk about your *hands-on* position. I hardly have to tell you that, in recent years, our political process has taken on a harsh, even bitter partisanship that has not served either the process or the country well. We have spent far too much time and energy fighting for political advantage instead of working to make this a better country. I want us all to stop it, and the current campaign is the time and place.

"Because of the position in which fate has placed me, perhaps I'm in a better position than most politicians to call for this change. During my months as acting president, I have bent over backward to govern in a bipartisan fashion, and some of you have responded to that effort, while others have been, shall we say, less enthusiastic." Nobody laughed.

"We're beginning the new millennium in extraordinarily good shape—a healthy economy, a lack of major military conflict and even political conflict, low unemployment, lower crime rates, and high optimism among our fellow countrymen. The last century has often been called the American Century. Well, let's have another American Century. Let's consolidate the gains that our fathers and grandfathers and we ourselves have fought so hard to earn, and let's go on to make this a better, safer, more peaceful country, while maintaining our leadership role as the world's only superpower.

"But I'm falling into clichés here, and I don't want to do that. I want to ask every one of you to go into this election as Americans, first, and party politicians second; I want an end to personal attacks and false moralizing; I want the next president to reach out to both parties and their constituencies; I want each of you here to dedicate himself to a new bipartisanship in this country. I believe there is more at stake right now in this country than at any time since the end of World War II, and if we can't face the next century working together, we have a great deal to lose.

"I know that there are those among you who think that you are all right and everyone else is all wrong. I know this is true because at times I have had those same feelings myself. Doing this job has shown me that I was wrong."

Then something happened that frightened Will. Joe Adams stood, his head down, staring at the table in front of him, saying nothing. For a moment, he thought Adams was near tears, then he realized that he had simply forgotten what he was going to say, or perhaps even where he was and who he was talking to. Sue Adams reached out and took her husband's hand, and still he did not continue. Somebody had to do something.

Will got to his feet, applauding; so did Eft Efton, and in a moment, the crowd was standing, cheering. Sue Adams led her husband from the room. At the door, he paused, waved to the crowd, then disappeared.

The applause died, and Will's eyes found Kate's across the table. He could see the fear in them.

29

Before dawn, Will kissed a still-sleeping Kate good-bye, went downstairs, gave his bags to a Secret Service agent, and got into the car. Tim Coleman and Kitty Conroy were waiting for him, sipping coffee.

"So, how was the Adamses' first White House party?" Kitty asked.

"Just great," Will lied. He had lain awake last night wondering if Joe Adams's slip was temporary or indicative of a slide into permanent senility.

"You don't sound as if it was great," Kitty said.

"Sorry, I'm still half-asleep."

"Well," Tim said, "this ought to wake you up: I had a call yesterday from Lou Regenstein."

"The movie mogul?"

"That's right; he's the chairman of Centurion Studios."

"I don't think I've ever met him."

"You've met Vance Calder, haven't you?"

"Yes, at a dinner party in New York a couple of years ago."

"Well, Calder is, apparently, a big fan of yours."

"First I've heard about that," Will said.

"You must have impressed him at the dinner party."

"We did talk a lot; I found him very bright. For a Brit, he seemed pretty well informed about American politics."

"He was born there, but he's been an American citizen for more than twenty years. And, in addition to being Centurion's biggest star, he's a major stockholder in the studio."

"I think I knew that; I'm not sure how."

"Anyway, both Calder and Centurion want to get behind you in a big way."

"How big?"

"Calder and the costar of his next film want to host a fund-raiser for you in L.A. right before the convention. He's promised to get a thousand people to his house, at a thousand dollars a head."

"He can get a thousand people into his *house?*"

"He's got twelve acres in Bel Air, and he'll do it on the lawn. It never rains in sunny California."

"A million bucks in individual contributions? Wow."

"And a lot of them will contribute to the party, too. There's more: Centurion is going to give a million to the party after you're nominated."

"That would make them the single biggest contributor, wouldn't it?"

"By a long shot."

"Tell them I accept."

"I already have. I hope you don't mind, but I thought it was better not to hesitate."

"You did the right thing, Tim," Will said. "This is a great way to start the last leg of the campaign for the nomination." He looked at Tim and Kitty. "So why do you two look so glum?"

"I guess you haven't seen the *Washington Post* this morning," Kitty said, handing it to him and pointing at a story below the fold:

FORMER CLIENT ACCUSES SEN. WILL LEE OF INCOMPETENCE IN APPEAL OF MURDER CONVICTION

"What the hell is this?" Will said, reading the piece.

"Larry Eugene Moody is appealing his murder conviction," Tim said. "His grounds are that he was incompetently represented by you in his original trial."

Will was having trouble reading the story in the moving car. "Go on," he said. "Just how was I incompetent?"

"He says—or his new lawyer says—that you failed to depose a key witness against him, and that you offered no other witnesses to counter her testimony."

"This would be the African-American girl who said he raped her in high school?"

"That's the one."

"It's true that her testimony probably got him

convicted. I thought I had it won until another witness blurted out the story about the alleged rape. Does the lawyer say how I was supposed to know she'd be called?"

"Moody says that he told you about the accusation in his first meeting with you, and that you did nothing to prepare for the witness."

"That's a bald-faced lie!" Will said. "Larry was convicted because he withheld that information from me. If I'd known about the incident with the girl, I would have known how to avoid opening the door on her testimony."

"Was there anyone else at that first meeting between you and Moody?"

"No, we were alone."

"Too bad; it'll be your word against *his*."

"All right," Kitty said, "let's run down what we've got here, and figure out how to deal with it. This story is, of course, immaterial to anything in the election. I think it's a sideshow staged by the Republicans; they're just hoping that enough mud will stick to hurt you. What we've got to do is to issue a statement this morning denying the charge of incompetence and stating the basic facts in the case."

"All right, I buy that," Will said. "You can type it up on the airplane and release it to the traveling press on the way west."

"After I hand that out, I think you ought to go forward in the plane and just chat with them informally about the murder case. You have nothing to hide, it's just Moody's desperate attempt to avoid being put to death, et cetera."

"All right. I can do that, but I have to avoid saying that Larry was guilty, though, God knows, he was. It wouldn't be ethical for a lawyer who represented someone in a murder trial to talk about his client's guilt while his case is under appeal."

"You might point that out to the press."

"I certainly will."

Tim spoke up. "I think it's interesting that, if Republicans are involved in this, they're out to get you even before the convention. That indicates to me that they'd rather run against George Kiel than you."

"A backhanded compliment, if I ever heard one," Will replied. Then something popped into his mind. "Wait a minute," he said. "You said that the fund-raiser in L.A. is going to be hosted by Vance Calder and his *costar*?"

"That's right," Tim said.

"And who is his costar?"

"Gosh, I forgot to ask," Tim replied.

"As soon as they're awake in L.A., call and find out."

"Okay; I'll call Regenstein back at nine their time."

Kitty was looking sharply at Will. "What is it?" she asked.

"I think I might know who the costar is," Will replied.

"Who?" Kitty and Tim asked simultaneously.

"It might very well be Charlene Joiner."

It took a moment for the penny to drop; then both their mouths dropped open. "Oh, shit," Kitty said.

"Charlene called me over the holidays and asked me to handle an appeal for Larry Moody. I refused."

"What else did she want?" Kitty asked.

"That was about it."

"*About* it? Come on, Will, what else?"

"That was it, really," Will said. He was not about to mention that Charlene had suggested they get together.

"This is not good," Tim said.

"Well, there are going to be a thousand people there. Maybe it'll be all right."

"You don't understand," Tim said.

"Understand what?"

"There's more to the news story about Moody's appeal." He picked up the *Post*, turned to an inside page, held it to the light, and read. "Moody's lawyer also charged that Will Lee had a sexual relationship with Moody's girlfriend during the trial, in which she was an important witness in establishing Moody's alibi. The girlfriend, Charlene Joiner, is now one of Hollywood's rising stars."

"Oh, Jesus," Will said.

"I agree," Kitty chimed in. "I thought we had killed that particular snake in your first senatorial campaign, but it's back."

"Maybe that's not a bad thing," Tim said.

"*What are you talking about?*" Kitty demanded.

"I wasn't all that active in that campaign," Tim said, "but as I recall, there was a school of thought that the, ah, incident with Charlene Joiner may have actually *helped* in the campaign."

"That was before Bill Clinton," Kitty said.

"Oh," Tim replied, "there is that."

"Yes," Will agreed, "there is that."

30

Senator Frederick Wallace strolled down a Capitol hallway toward his hideaway office, the best in the Senate. Seniority had its privileges. He nodded to many passersby, spoke to a few, and kept his trademark half smile fixed to his face. He let himself into the room and immediately stepped on something made of paper. He closed the door, held on to the doorknob for support, and reached down for the envelope on the floor. Freddie Wallace had a considerable gut, and he did not like bending over.

Wallace walked across the room to his big easy chair, tossed the envelope onto the coffee table beside it, opened a cabinet, and poured himself a shot of neat bourbon. It was not yet ten o'clock in the morning, but he always started the day with a shot of this very fine, private stock bourbon that a Kentucky friend supplied him with. It was something he had learned as a very young man from Harry Truman.

Truman had knocked his back, though, like medicine, and Wallace was far too appreciative of the skills of Kentucky distillers to rush the experience. He sipped at the bourbon, then picked up the envelope that someone had shoved under his door. It bore only his name, the Capitol room number, the zip code, and the admonition that the contents were personal and confidential. It bore an Atlanta postmark.

Wallace got a fat finger under the flap and tore open the envelope. Inside he found a single sheet of paper, no letterhead or return address. The page had been composed very neatly on what was obviously a manual typewriter, an uncommon instrument these days. He read:

Dear Freddie,

I hope you don't mind if I call you that. Although we've met only a few times, always in passing, I feel that I know you well. We have much in common: We are both old, wise in the ways of the world and, particularly, in the ways of politics, and we are both very crafty human beings, not to say sneaky.

We are also both in possession of some extremely sensitive knowledge regarding the recent health of an influential person. I trust I will not have to allude further to the person for you to know whom I mean; I would not like to do that in a written communication.

I know you well enough to feel certain that

you will, under what you deem the proper circumstances, use this information against another person who shares this knowledge with you and me. I don't want you to do this, Freddie, for my own reasons, so I am taking this opportunity to let you know that, should you allow your worst nature to come to the forefront, I am going to take it upon myself to make your golden years very difficult. I can do this, because I have documentary evidence of a part of your life that, if made known, could destroy your credibility in the Senate and make your marriage a perfect hell.

I am sure you know that I refer to the black woman with whom you have enjoyed a carnal relationship for more than twenty years, and who has borne you two sons. I am prepared, if necessary, to have her name and address released to the yellowest of the media, along with the names and university addresses of her children. They will all look fine on television.

If you can keep me happy, then I'm sure you can live out your tenure in the Senate and the remainder of your life, secure in the secrecy with which you have so carefully acted these many years. I should tell you, however, that although I would prefer not to muddy the clear waters of your life, it would not cause me the slightest regret to do so. In fact, if I should choose to confide in a certain magazine publisher, I might walk away with a million dollars, which, at my time of life, I could certainly use.

Trusting that you understand me clearly, I
remain

Yours most sincerely
Jonah

Senator Wallace knocked back the jigger of
bourbon, then spoke aloud a string of very bad
words. He had not lived this long and done this
well to be brought down by a common black-
mailer. He had to acknowledge to himself, however, that he, by his love of this dark woman, had
made himself highly blackmailable. He had
known, of course, that it would all come out
eventually, but he had planned to be comfortably
dead by that time, and the hell with the after-
math. He knew very well that his wife would immediately and noisily divorce him if she should
learn of his liaison, and, since their marriage, he
had depended upon her large fortune to keep him
in the style to which he had long ago become accustomed. He was not about to give that up, so he
had to move fast.

First, he dialed the private office number of the
syndicated conservative political columnist Hogan Parks.

"Yeah?"

"You know who this is?"

"Sure. How are you?"

"Mildly agitated," Wallace replied.

"About what?"

"Have you used the information I gave you?"

"I'm writing the column as we speak."

"Stop writing it."

"What's the matter, Freddie? Getting cold feet?"

"Goddammit, don't you use my name on the telephone!"

"Sorry about that; what's got into you?"

Wallace was not about to give an honest answer to that question. "It has come to my attention that I may have been misled."

"*What?* You would give me that kind of information when it might not be true?"

At the time, I believed it to be entirely true; now I'm not quite so sure."

"Even after his performance at dinner the other evening?"

"I may have misinterpreted that."

There was a moment's silence, then Parks spoke. "I think I'm inclined to write the column anyway."

"You can't do that," Wallace said.

"I think I might enjoy the fuss it will make," Parks said. "I don't have to use his name, or even identify his exact illness. Enough people in this town can connect the dots. And when it comes out that a certain other person had knowledge of the illness, it could change a very important outcome."

"Let me be very clear about this, Hogan," Wallace said. "If you run so much as a hint of this story before I say so, then by this time next week, you will no longer have a column. You will, in fact, have become the Matt Drudge of print journalism, with all the accolades that such a position enjoys. Do you understand me?"

"I believe I understand that you are threatening me," Parks replied coldly.

"Then you understand me very well," Wallace said. "You may consider what I have said a promise, as well as a threat. And I have the means with which to deliver on that promise. You know that, don't you?"

"You would do that to me?"

"Only if you insist on doing it to yourself."

"One mistake," Parks muttered, half to himself. "One mistake in a lifetime."

"That's all it takes, my friend," Wallace said, and hung up.

Wallace took a telephone book from a table drawer, looked up the private office number of a deputy director of the FBI, and dialed.

"Yes?"

"This is Freddie Wallace."

"Good morning, Senator; what can I do for you?"

"You can send an agent over to my hideaway office to collect a document. I want it analyzed immediately, in every possible way; I want to know who wrote it and where it came from."

"I'll have a man there in under half an hour."

"Thank you, and no official record is to be kept of this work, do you understand?"

"Completely, Senator."

Wallace hung up, took a razor blade from a drawer, and excised all references to his name and his black paramour, then dropped the remainder of the letter and its envelope into a larger envelope.

He flicked his cigar lighter, touched the flame to the excised paper, and watched it crumble in his ashtray. Then he stirred the ashes with a pencil until they were powder.

Near the end of the day, back in his hideaway office, Wallace received a phone call from his FBI contact.

"Senator," the man said, "I have carried out your instructions with regard to the document you sent me."

"And what have you found?"

"The letter was typed by an expert typist on an Olympia Reporter portable typewriter manufactured between 1956 and 1971. It is the sort of machine that was popular with journalists in the field, before the advent of laptop computers. Analysis of the signature, Jonah, indicates that it was signed by a male of sixty years of age or older, and the syntax and use of the language indicates a seventy percent probability that the writer was Caucasian and well educated. There were no fingerprints on either the letter or the envelope, except yours. No DNA residue was found on the envelope flap, so it was moistened without licking. There is, however, DNA residue on the stamp, indicating to us that the letter was stamped and mailed by a person different from the writer. It was mailed from a sub-post office on the west side of Atlanta, near a residential area popular with employees of the Atlanta Federal Penitentiary. Finally, the paper on which the letter was written meets the specifications and bears the watermark of stationery purchased in large quantities by the federal government for use by many branches, including the prison service.

"Our conclusions, therefore, are that the letter was written by an employee or a prisoner at the Atlanta Federal Penitentiary on a personal typewriter, and that the letter was entrusted for mailing to a guard or other employee, who removed it from the prison, bought a stamp, and mailed it."

"Excellent," Wallace said.

"If you like, we can extend our investigation to the prison, and I believe that, within a period of ten days to two weeks, we could identify the mailer and then learn from him the identity of the writer. However, I should tell you that, should we initiate such an investigation, this would involve the Atlanta office and would have to become an official matter. We deduce from the composition of the letter that it is extorsive in nature, and we noticed, of course, that a portion of the letter, probably including the extortion, has been excised. We would need your comments on the record about that."

"I don't believe any further investigation is warranted," Wallace said, "and I would like you to return to me immediately the original and any copies of the letter."

"Of course, Senator, and you may rely on our discretion. Is there anything else I can do for you?"

"Yes, would you get me a list of the names of all prisoners and employees at the Atlanta Federal Penitentiary. I'd like it delivered by hand to the address on the envelope by nine o'clock tomorrow morning."

"Of course, Senator."

Wallace said good-bye and hung up. He would see whom, among the inhabitants of that prison, he had met on a number of occasions, always in passing.

31

Zeke Tennant read the syndicated column in the Las Vegas newspaper with interest. He had been waiting for his pigeon to come west.

Senator Will Lee, in spite of being well behind front-runner George Kiel for the Democratic nomination, continues to drive his staff nuts by doing quixotic things like his appearance in Santa Fe, New Mexico, this weekend, at a fund-raiser in Santa Fe's main plaza for his friend, Congressman Roberto Chavez. Although it has been pointed out to him that New Mexico has only five electoral votes, and that his time could be better spent in more thickly populated states, he has insisted on going to the aid of Chavez, who is in a tight race against a right-wing Republican and whose support may be eroded by the presence of a Green Party candidate on the ballot. In past elections, the Green Party candidate has siphoned off Democratic votes, throwing elections to the Republicans.

Questioned on his campaign plane about this

trip, Senator Lee said, "Roberto Chavez is a top-notch congressman, and the nation can ill afford to lose him. He's also my friend, and it is personally important to me to see him reelected."

Santa Fe looked good to Zeke; he could drive there overnight and be there in plenty of time for the political rally. He thought Santa Fe and its Plaza might afford a good opportunity for a kill. He continued reading the column and was very interested in what it had to say.

In an hour-long chat with this reporter and others on his campaign plane, Senator Lee spoke at length about news reports concerning a case he handled as a lawyer some ten years ago, in his home state of Georgia. A prisoner on Georgia's death row, Larry Eugene Moody, has appealed his conviction for murder on the grounds that his legal representation was incompetent. Senator Lee, quite naturally, took umbrage at this description of his legal skills. He explained to me how he came to be assigned to defend Moody, at the request of a local judge, who later refused to release him from the case.

"The judge called another lawyer and me into his chambers and explained that, because of the illness of the county prosecutor and a shortage of lawyers, he was asking one of us to act as prosecutor and the other as the defendant's counsel. We agreed, reluctantly, and the judge flipped a coin to see who would do which job. Heads, I defended, tails the other lawyer did. It came up heads, and I found myself dragged into this case. Later I learned that the judge's coin had heads on both sides."

When we had stopped laughing, the senator told us of his hard work on the case and how he lost it in the end because his client had withheld information from him about a previous charge of rape that had not been prosecuted. When a defense witness inadvertently mentioned the earlier accusation, the prosecution was able to call the rape victim to the stand, and her testimony was pivotal in convicting Moody.

The senator from Georgia has also been accused of a liaison with an important defense witness, the defendant's girlfriend, who is now well-known as the actress Charlene Joiner. Lee explained that there had been only one encounter, on a weekend late in the trial, after Ms. Joiner had testified, and at a time when she had become estranged from Mr. Moody. They were both unattached adults. He pointed out that Ms. Joiner had confirmed these details in a press conference after the trial ended.

Senator Lee's staff have also been making this case all week, and their damage control seems to be working. The most recent polls have shown no drop in Lee's support; indeed, he is up a point or two in most polls, at the expense of George Kiel, and there have been reports of worry among Kiel's people. The Charlene Joiner connection seems to have had the effect of making Senator Lee more human, and the fact that she has become an important movie actress hasn't hurt. She is nothing like the pathetic Paula Jones; she is talented, accomplished, and quite beautiful, seemingly without the aid of surgeons. Whatever his appetites, Will Lee certainly has better taste in paramours than Bill Clinton.

Zeke put down the paper, got out a suitcase, and started packing. He went into the master-bedroom closet, removed a panel, and took out a Czech sniper's rifle, which broke down and went into an ordinary-looking briefcase. He hid the rifle's silencer under the spare tire, since only that was illegal, and headed out of Las Vegas.

Zeke drove at the speed limit. Even though he was fully prepared for a stop by the police or highway patrol, with his driver's license, credit cards, and other ID, he had no wish to invite attention. He had plenty of time; Will Lee's political rally wasn't for two more days. He looked out the window, enjoying the desert scenery. Zeke had been brought up in greener places, and the vistas of the Southwest were exotic to him. Half a mile ahead, a coyote ran across the road, carrying something in its mouth.

He got to Santa Fe at noon the following day and made his way to the Plaza, driving slowly around it, noting the Indian jewelry sellers displaying their wares on the sidewalk in front of the old Governor's Palace. There was only one hotel directly on the square, La Fonda, which stood at the southeast corner. He used his cell phone to reserve a room, then parked in the ground-floor garage and checked in. He took a long nap and woke late in the afternoon, with the sun low in the sky. His room gave a partial view of the Plaza, not good enough to shoot from, but then he had no intention of firing from a room he had rented. He would have to do some exploring.

He shaved, showered, dressed, and, reading from a brochure, took an elevator to a roof restaurant on the east side of the hotel. There was an outdoor bar, and he took a seat, looking around him. The rooftop terrace was on the wrong side of the building for shooting, but above him was more roof. He ordered a margarita and strolled around the restaurant, looking for access to a higher area. At the back side of the hotel was a trellis planted with some sort of climbing plant. It went up a good twelve feet to what seemed to be the roof. It should do nicely.

Zeke went back to the bar and concentrated on finding a woman to pick up. After all, he had another twenty-four hours, and he had to do *something* with his time.

32

Freddie Wallace let himself into his hideaway office and found another envelope waiting for him, this one of the plain brown variety. He took it to his usual comfortable chair, poured himself his morning shot of bourbon, and opened the envelope.

Sir:

Enclosed please find the lists you requested of employees and inmates at the Atlanta Federal Penitentiary. Some corrections have been made, which makes the lists accurate as of yesterday. Please be assured of our discretion in this matter, and please let me know if you require further assistance.

The note was typed and not signed, but Freddie knew whom it was from. He switched on a reading lamp and, sipping his bourbon, began reading the list of employees. Somewhat to his surprise, he knew two of them—the warden, who had once testified at a hearing before a committee on which Freddie sat, and the captain of the guard, a former constituent who had once sought his help in obtaining employment in the federal prison system. He thought carefully about both men, then discarded them both as potential authors of the letter he had received. The warden would have had no motivation to write it, and the captain of the guard was in his debt.

Next, he turned to the list of prisoners, which was considerably longer than the list of employees. Freddie had a prodigious memory, and he recognized a number of the names as belonging to people whose cases had made the newspapers when they were tried. Finally, he was left with three candidates for Jonah: the first, Emilio Costas, was a real-estate developer whose backing turned out to have been from the Cali Cartel of Colombian drug lords and who had made a substantial contribution to Freddie's last campaign for the Senate. The contribution had been returned when the man's backers became known. The second was a lawyer who had actually worked in Freddie's Senate office more than ten years before and who had been imprisoned for stealing from a government agency by whom he had subsequently been employed. The third was the notorious CIA mole and traitor Edward Rawls.

Freddie gave careful thought to each candidate. Certainly, Costas was capable of doing anything that might get him out of prison, but Freddie could not see how threatening a United States senator could aid in that effort. The lawyer, he had known a great deal better than in passing, but Jonah's description of their acquaintance could have been to simply throw Freddie off the scent. Still, he had helped the man, getting him transferred to Atlanta, to be near his family, and Freddie did not judge him aggressive enough to be the kind of threat in question, nor would he have had any reason to protect either the vice president or Will Lee.

Edward Rawls was another matter. He had, indeed, met Rawls in passing on a number of occasions—a dinner party at the home of a CIA official, when Rawls had testified before a Senate committee; at a White House diplomatic reception; and on at least two other such occasions that Freddie could recall. Freddie allowed his mind to range over the history and reputation of Edward Rawls, looking for nexuses. He found two, lodged in long-unused brain cells. Rawls had very likely known Joe Adams when Adams was in the Senate, serving on the Senate Select Committee on Intelligence. He would also have known Will Lee, who was counsel to the same committee at the time. Most important, he recalled that Katharine Rule Lee had been the instrument of Rawls's downfall in the CIA, but before that had occurred, he had been something of a mentor to Kate. They had known each other well. This was promising.

Now, Freddie thought about those relationships. What did Rawls have to gain from them?

Well, from Joe Adams, nothing. Adams was out of Rawls's reach, now, both politically and medically. Joe Adams might well not even remember who Rawls was. Will Lee, on the other hand, might be very useful indeed to Rawls. If Lee were elected president, a pardon of Rawls, his wife's old friend, would be within his gift. So, Freddie reasoned, Rawls had every reason to protect Will Lee.

Freddie made his decision, and it was not a hard one. He switched on his computer, typed a short letter, printed it, and sealed it in an envelope. On the envelope, he wrote the name "Jonah," then sealed it. Taking care not to leave a fingerprint on either letter or envelope, he dropped them into another, larger envelope. Consulting a large, computer-generated address book, he addressed the larger envelope to the captain of the guard at home, then he made a call to the Atlanta Federal Penitentiary.

When the man came on the line, Freddie, without mentioning his name, made sure the captain knew who was calling, then he made his request. The captain gladly granted the favor. Freddie hung up, feeling smug and safe once again.

Two days later, Ed Rawls was stopped by a guard as he left the dining hall after breakfast, on the way to his job in the prison library. The guard escorted him on rather a long walk, down a stairway two levels underground and down a hallway Rawls had thought disused. The guard stopped before a steel door, unlocked and opened it. It swung on rusty, noisy hinges.

"What's going on?" Rawls asked.

The guard took an envelope from his pocket. "Open it and read what's inside," he said.

Rawls took the envelope, opened it, and unfolded the single sheet of paper.

Jonah,

You have made a serious miscalculation, and you are now about to suffer for it. Further, should any word of what you claim to know ever become public knowledge by any means whatever during my lifetime, I will see that you spend the rest of your life in prison, without hope of parole or pardon, and every day of it in the place you are about to enter. Don't ever come to my attention again.

The Whale

Rawls looked at the guard. "What the hell?" he said.

"See you in a week, Ed," the guard said. He took the letter back, spun Rawls around, pushed him through the door, slammed it behind him, and locked it.

Ed Rawls had just time to see that he had been thrown into a concrete room barely large enough to lie down in, and furnished only with a single water tap in a corner over a hole in the floor. Then the door was shut, and he stood in the dark, wondering how this could have happened.

33

Zeke checked out of his room at La Fonda around four in the afternoon. He allowed a bellman to carry his luggage to his car, then tipped the man, who went back into the hotel. Zeke waited a minute, then walked out of the parking lot and down the street toward the Plaza.

Signs posted in shop windows gave the time of the rally as six o'clock, giving him plenty of time to size up the job. Near the center of the park in the Plaza, workmen were completing a wooden platform, which rose about four feet from the ground. Zeke walked around behind the platform and looked back toward La Fonda. Good; a perfect line of sight to the northwest corner of the hotel's roof. He walked back to the hotel.

In the garage, he removed the briefcase from the trunk of the car, then dug out the silencer from under the spare tire and placed it in the briefcase with the rifle. He walked back into the hotel and turned left toward the elevator that went to the roof. He pressed the button for the top floor and rode up alone. He stepped out into the rooftop bar, which was deserted, since it didn't open until six, then went directly to the trellis. He looped the briefcase's strap over his shoulder and began climbing. Shortly, he was on the roof. He walked around the perimeter of the building, examining each side for escape routes. The way he had come would be best, of course, but after six, he might be seen by someone in the rooftop restaurant. On the south side, however, was a cast-iron drainpipe running straight to the ground, ending behind an adobe wall. He remembered that the garage had a window on that side of the building.

Satisfied, he walked to the northwest corner of the building and, staying low, peered over the parapet. Perfect. He had a full view of the wooden platform in the center of the Plaza park. Zeke glanced at his watch, then sat down, leaned against the parapet, took a paperback novel from his pocket, and began to read.

Will was awakened at five o'clock by Kitty Conroy, in his suite at the Eldorado Hotel. They had landed in Santa Fe earlier in the afternoon, and after half a dozen brief meetings with local Democratic supporters and a couple of media interviews, he had had time for a nap. He was groggy, though, and he attributed the way he felt to altitude sickness. After all, Santa Fe was seven thousand feet above sea level, and that took some getting used to.

Will showered, freshened his shave, and got into a freshly pressed pair of jeans and some borrowed cowboy boots. He agreed to a suede jacket, but declined the offer of the wide-brimmed hat. Photographs in odd hats came back to haunt you.

"We're going to walk up to the Plaza," Kitty said. "It's only a couple of blocks from the hotel, and you can shake a lot of hands on the way."

Will's right hand had toughened up a lot over the past few months; you had to get in shape for campaigning. Together with Kitty, he started for the elevator, accompanied by two Secret Service agents.

A mariachi band was playing in the Plaza, and Zeke put away his book and peered over the parapet. There was a thickening of the crowd at the northwest corner of the Plaza park; Will Lee was walking toward the platform, shaking hands.

Zeke quickly assembled the rifle, screwing the silencer onto the end of the barrel. Then he took the fat telescopic sight from the case and, peering through it, looked down at the Plaza. He could see Lee clearly and up close. Except for some glare from the setting sun to the west, it was an excellent setup. He'd wait until Lee mounted the platform and faced the crowd to speak; then he'd go for a head shot. Then he saw something he hadn't expected.

There was a box of security around Will Lee, and at each corner was a man in a suit. What Zeke had not expected was that each of the four men wore an identical metal button in the lapel of his suit. What the hell was the Secret Service doing here? Lee hadn't even been nominated yet. As he thought about this, he concentrated his gaze on the lead agent, and he saw the man suddenly squint, as some sort of light swept across his face. Then the man looked up and directly at Zeke, alarm on his face. He pointed at the northwest corner of La Fonda.

Zeke realized that the setting sun had been reflected into the man's eyes by his telescopic sight. The man continued to look at Zeke, and he raised a fist to his lips, and said something into a microphone hidden in his cupped hand.

Christ! Zeke started breaking down the rifle and packing it into the briefcase. He'd never have climbed onto this rooftop if he'd known the Secret Service was in town. He was lucky there wasn't an agent in his lap right now. They would have checked the rooftops earlier that day.

Keeping low, Zeke jogged toward the rear of the building. The trellis was too risky; there'd be cops coming up that elevator to the roof restaurant, looking for him. As he reached the rear parapet, he heard a commotion from the direction of the restaurant. Quickly, he slung the carrying strap of the briefcase over his shoulder, swung a leg over the parapet, grabbed the drainpipe with both hands, and, clamping the instep of each foot to the pipe, slid rapidly down the side of the building, four stories to the ground.

He ran to the window that let light into the garage, which was hinged at the top. He swung it open and looked inside. Nobody in sight. He wriggled through the window, dropped to the garage floor, and ran to his car, slinging the briefcase into the trunk. He got the Lexus started, then drove slowly out of the garage. The attendant was out of his cubicle, standing in the street, looking toward the Plaza. The sound of sirens came from that direction. The man didn't even see Zeke turn right toward the cathedral, then right again. Consulting a map, he came to Alameda, then turned onto Old Santa Fe Trail. As he did so, a police car passed him, going in the opposite direction toward the Plaza and the hotel, its lights flashing, its siren wailing.

Zeke drove slowly west, leaving the downtown area. He passed apartment complexes and a golf course, then began following signs to the interstate. Another two minutes and he'd be out of town.

He'd been stupid. He should have noticed that, with the sun setting, his scope would reflect. And he hadn't known the Secret Service was on the job. That was going to make his work more difficult.

But, he thought, not impossible. He drove down the interstate to Albuquerque and took I-40 west, toward Los Angeles.

34

Ed Rawls was released from solitary confinement one week to the minute from the day he had been put in. For seven days he had not shaved, bathed, slept in a bed, or eaten anything but unsalted dried beans and stale bread. He stank; his scalp itched uncontrollably, as did his armpits and his crotch; judging by the looseness of his trousers, he estimated he had lost ten pounds. He was incensed.

He was allowed to shower, shave, change clothes, and eat, then he was taken to the captain of the guard.

"Morning, Rawls," the captain said.

"Good morning, Captain."

"You enjoy your little vacation?"

"No, sir, I did not. Perhaps you can tell me why I received such treatment."

"You angered a powerful man," the captain said. "I don't know exactly how, but the letter you read must have explained it."

"It was something about Jonah and the whale,"

Rawls said, looking baffled. "It didn't make the slightest bit of sense to me."

"Come on, Rawls; he isn't the kind of man to act unless he knew what he was doing."

"Who are we talking about, Captain?" Rawls asked.

"You know as well as I do."

"I'm afraid I don't. I can only think that this fellow has gotten me mixed up with somebody else. Have I ever given you or anybody else in this pen the slightest trouble?"

"No, you haven't, and you're not going to start now."

"I have no intention of making waves, Captain, but neither do I want to be punished for something I haven't done. Can you tell me what it was I was supposed to have done?"

"You didn't do it to me, Rawls, so I don't know."

"Come on, Captain, who is this whale guy?"

"That'll be all, Rawls; keep your nose clean, and you won't have to go back in there."

Dismissed, Rawls left the captain's office and was returned by a guard to his job at the library.

A coworker named Ames saw him coming. "Hey, Ed, where you been? Rumor is you did some time in the hole."

"The rumor is right," Rawls said, "but did it say anything about why?"

"Pissed somebody off, I guess," Ames said. "By the way, my parole came through."

"Good for you, Charlie; when do you get out?"

"Tomorrow morning, thank Christ."

Rawls beckoned Ames behind a bookcase. "Charlie, what are you going to do when you get out?"

"Jesus, I don't know," Ames said. "My daughter says I can come live with her, until I find a job."

"How old are you?"

"Fifty-five."

Rawls nodded. "Where does your daughter live?"

"Chattanooga, Tennessee."

"You got any friends anywhere else in the country?"

"I been writing to a guy I went to college with; he lives in New York."

"Charlie, you want to make some easy money on the outside?"

"How would I do that, Ed? I don't want to bust my parole."

"You know what a third-party mail drop is, Ames?"

"Nope."

"That's when somebody mails something to you, and you forward it to somebody else. The person who mails it is the first party, you're the second party, and the guy you mail it to is the third party."

"You want me to mail you stuff, Ed?"

"No, Charlie, just the reverse. I've got some money on the outside; I'll make it worth your while." Rawls was fully prepared to go back into solitary, but he didn't think he'd have to.

A week later, Freddie Wallace let himself into his hideaway office, picked up a couple of pieces of mail from the floor, and answered the phone. "Yes?"

"You know who this is?" Hogan Parks said.

"I believe I do," Wallace replied. "You have my thanks for restraining yourself on that other matter."

"Always glad to be of help," Parks said. "Funny thing is, something nearly as juicy arrived on my desk this morning."

"And what's that, my friend?"

"Seems a prominent member of the United States Senate was once a card-carrying member of the Ku Klux Klan."

Wallace kept control of himself. "Is that a fact?" he managed to say.

Apparently so," Parks replied. "Somebody sent me a copy of a list of members of a South Carolina chapter, and his name is right there. Looks authentic, and a letter accompanying it says that the FBI can confirm it, because they had an undercover agent in the same group."

"Well, I'd be mighty careful about spreading that kind of dirt," Freddie said, forcing himself to sound confident.

"I thought I'd ask you right out if you can confirm this report," Parks said.

"Well, now," Freddie breathed into the phone, "seems like we've got something of a standoff here. Because if you print that, then a paper or two might learn about a certain journalist who got himself arrested for propositioning a vice cop in a Georgetown gay bar a few years back."

"I guess we have got a standoff," Parks admitted. "But what makes you think I'm the only one who's received this report? What if it went to a wire service or, worse, a tabloid?"

"Right now, I'm dealing with you, and not anybody else," Freddie said.

"Okay, I'm quiet; if you read about it in the papers, it didn't come from me. Will you accept my word on that?"

"Of course I would, my friend," Freddie said. "I've never had any reason to doubt your word."

"Somebody's out to get you, pal," Parks said, then hung up.

Freddie hung up, too, and he was sweating. Then he looked at the mail in his lap. There was a plain brown envelope addressed simply to the room he sat in. He ripped it open.

Dear Freddie,

I thought you'd like to know in advance that a copy of the enclosed Klan membership roll has gone to three political columnists. I'm going to let you guess who they are. Suffice it to say they all have a national readership.

I've done this because I heard about what you did to that poor Rawls fellow, apparently thinking he was me. It's no skin off my nose, of course, but it did give me a hint of how vindictive you can be, so I thought a little shot across your bow was in order. If the columnists call you for a comment, or if you can figure out who they are, then you have a chance of stopping the story.

I'm aware of some other things about you that would make good reading, in addition to the one mentioned in my earlier letter. If you make any other attempt to locate me, or if the information about the previously mentioned person's health leaks, or even if you mess with Rawls again, I'm going to become the Johnny Appleseed of yellow journalism.

Don't mess with me, Freddie. You're out of your league.

Love and kisses,
Jonah

Quickly, Freddie examined the envelope. It was postmarked New York City. The letter seemed to have been set in type, so it had probably come from a computer printer, impossible to trace. Freddie held the paper up to the light and found a watermark; it read: State of New York, and the seal was there, too.

"Jesus God," Freddie said aloud to himself. "Who *is* this son of a bitch?"

35

Will stood and looked at his campaign airplane. It was an elderly Boeing 737, leased from a creditor of a failed regional airline, and adapted, slightly, for his purposes. It contained a desk and a sofa where he could sometimes catch an hour's sleep, plus a lot of first-class-sized seats for staff and press. It was seedy, smelly, and, at the moment, broken. "How long?" he asked the pilot.

"At least four hours," the pilot said. "They're driving a part up from Albuquerque. Could be six hours."

Will turned to Kitty. "Make the necessary adjustments in the schedule, but before you do, rent me a car."

"A car?"

"And don't mention it to the Secret Service."

"Senator . . ."

"Just do it, Kitty, please."

Will drove north, with no particular destination in mind. He just wanted to get away from the business of campaigning for a while, and this was the first real opportunity he had had in months. He enjoyed driving himself again and not having to talk or listen. He was not a happy candidate.

He came to a fork in the road and took the one toward Los Alamos, because he had never been there. All he knew about the place was that the first atom bomb had been built there, and that there was a huge laboratory where weapons were still designed.

Will had known that running for president was going to be hard, but he had never realized *how* hard. On the plus side, he had a good organization, great volunteers, a knowledge of the issues, and well-thought-out positions on everything. On the minus side, fund-raising was lagging, and even with federal matching funds, he was coming up short on television money.

Then there was George Kiel. Will had underestimated the planning that Kiel had been doing for this campaign, apparently for years. The man had an unmatchable network of people in what seemed like every party organization in the country, and he was taking a lot of campaign money that Will wouldn't touch. The result was an avalanche of very good, if conventional, television advertising that was hurting Will in many states, and the fact that Will was behind in delegate votes for the coming convention.

But what bothered Will more than anything was his belief that Kiel could not beat Eft Efton in the general election. He could see this scenario playing out: Kiel is nominated, and party big-wigs, terrified that he might lose to Efton, bring unbearable pressure on Will to accept the vice-presidential slot on the ticket.

Will did not want to be vice president, not even with the promise that, after two terms, he could be the party's nominee for president. Still, he didn't know if he could stand up to the pressure when the demand came.

The road was rising, winding through spectacular mountain and canyon scenery. Will rolled down his window, and cooler air than he had expected rushed into the car. Finally, he pulled over to a roadside parking place and got out of the car. He was high above the Rio Grande, and the landscape stretched to the south toward Santa Fe. He could make out adobe buildings in the town, even see where the airport should be. Western scenery always amazed him, and the clarity of the air made this spectacular.

He wanted to talk to Kate right now, but she was in her office at the CIA, and when he talked to her there, he could never know if their conversation was being recorded. He wanted her to tell him not to take the VP nomination, that she would leave him if he did, that she would hate him for backing down to the party. He wanted her to scream at him, to put some iron back into his backbone.

He breathed deeply of the thin mountain air, but he didn't seem to be able to get enough oxygen. He tried to imagine being vice president, and he couldn't. There was one man who could help him. He took his cell phone from a pocket, dialed the White House number, and asked for Vice President Adams.

A secretary answered the call, recognized his voice, and put him on hold. A moment later Susan Adams came on the line.

"Will? How are you?"

"I'm all right, Sue, if a little tired. Can Joe find a moment to speak to me?"

"He's in an important national security meeting right now, Will, and his schedule is really tough today. Is there anything I can help with?"

Adams wasn't going to talk to him. "I just wanted to talk to him about the vice presidency."

"The *vice* presidency? Are you considering that spot on the ticket?"

"Not really, but I know a moment might come when I might have to consider it, and I wanted Joe's take on whether I should do it."

"Will, I can tell you what Joe will say."

"Then please do."

"Joe has always hated being vice president, you know that."

"I knew he wasn't entirely happy with the job."

"He was unhappy right up until the moment he became acting president. From that moment on, he was glad he took the job."

"So if I take the vice presidential nomination, all I have to look forward to is the hope that George Kiel might clutch his chest and turn blue?"

"I don't think Joe would put it as strongly as that, but that's what it boils down to."

"That's pretty depressing," Will said.

"Will, you know that Joe wants you to have the top job. That hasn't changed."

"To tell you the truth, I was beginning to wonder."

"Joe just feels that he has to be seen remaining neutral in all his actions until the nomination is decided, no matter what his personal feelings."

"What about at the convention? Is he going to take a position before the voting?"

"He hasn't decided what to do about that," Sue said. "He's thought about it a lot, believe me."

"How is Joe feeling, Sue? I mean, really?"

"He's just fine about ninety-five percent of the time," she replied. "I'm not sure that any of us can expect more than that."

"I wish I were fine ninety-five percent of the time," Will said.

"I've never heard you like this, Will. What's going on?"

"I don't know, Sue; maybe I'm flagging."

"Don't do that, Will; it's too important. You don't want to leave the country to George Kiel or Eft Efton, do you?"

"It's not what I want, Sue; it's what the party and the electorate want."

"I think you can make them want you."

"I think I can beat Eft; I just don't know if I can take the nomination from George."

"You can do it, Will; I believe that, and so does Joe."

"Well, I'm glad *somebody* believes it."

"You've just got to work every minute, Will, and take every break. If you work hard, you'll get lucky."

"Thanks, Sue; I'll try to keep that in mind."

"We're looking forward to seeing you at the convention, Will. I think things will start to gel for you in Los Angeles."

"I hope you're right, Sue. Thanks for taking the time to talk to me."

"I'll tell Joe you called," she said, then hung up.

Will closed the little telephone and put it away. The mountain air still didn't have enough oxygen.

He got into the car and drove up to Los Alamos, which he thought looked like a seedy small town designed by a team of convicts. He drove down empty roads and occasionally passed guarded gates, through which roads led into woods.

He found himself in Bandolier National Forest, and the scenery took on an alpine look. There were amazingly few cars on the roads, and he liked the emptiness of the landscape.

He turned back toward Santa Fe and remembered that the scenery always looked different on the way back. He wondered if the depressing political scenery was ever going to change for him.

36

Zeke Tennant drove west across New Mexico and Arizona. He found Gallup depressing and Sedona nice. He stopped at the Grand Canyon and had lunch and a good look at a very big hole in the ground. He drove on south and west and watched the scenery dissolve into desert, guarded by huge cacti. He passed through towns with familiar names.

"Kingman, Barstow, San Bernardino," he sang, but he never caught sight of Route 66. He stayed overnight in a motel in San Bernadino, then, the next morning, bought a large map of Los Angeles and did some studying. It didn't take long to get his bearings.

The L.A. Coliseum was in a neighborhood he didn't care for, but after driving around for a while he found a neat block of houses, and one of them had a sign outside advertising a room for rent. The landlady, a slightly overripe but attractive woman of about forty, Mrs. Rivera, looked him over and, when he offered her a month's rent in advance, found him acceptable. Zeke left his suitcase in his room, then went for a drive. He was looking for construction sites and, in less than an hour, found two that seemed promising.

Next, he drove back to the Coliseum and drove slowly around it until he saw a sign that read L.A. COLISEUM EMPLOYMENT OFFICE. HIRING NOW. He parked in the nearby lot, combed his hair, and walked into the office and up to a counter. "May I have an employment application, please?"

The woman behind the counter gave him a form and a ballpoint pen and indicated a table where he could sit and complete the application.

Zeke used his Las Vegas address and identity, Harry Grant. Asked for his skills, he thought about it, then put down carpentry and electrical work. As an afterthought, he put down "installation and repair of computers and sound systems." He had done all of those jobs in other existences. He turned in the application and sat down to wait.

A few minutes later a man appeared behind the counter. "Harry Grant?" he asked.

"That's me," Zeke said, standing up.

The man looked him up and down and, apparently, liked what he saw. "Come with me," he said, raising the countertop to let Zeke through. He led the way to a windowless office down a hallway and offered Zeke a chair. "My name is Hiller," he said, looking at Zeke's application. "I see you live nearby. How long you been there?"

"Moved in today," Zeke said. "Just got into town."

"Where from?"

"Las Vegas; I've been there for the past eleven years."

"Doing what kind of work?"

"Well, I've done a little of everything at one time or another, but for the past four years I've had my own business, installing computers and home-entertainment systems."

"What happened to your business?"

"I did okay at it, but it's tough being self-employed. I got to the point where I was going to have to start hiring help, and I thought, well, I don't really want to do that; I'd rather just find something good and work for somebody else. I kind of got tired of Vegas, too."

Hiller nodded. "You haven't put down any references," he said.

"Like I said, I've been self-employed. I could give you the names of a couple of people I did installations for."

"Good. What are they?"

Zeke rattled off two names and phone numbers in Las Vegas, along with the name of his banker. He had prepared for this long ago.

"You mind if I call these people now?" Hiller asked.

"Go right ahead."

Hiller held out a plastic bottle. "While I'm at it, you may as well fill this for me. I assume you don't mind taking a drug test."

"No, sir, not at all." Zeke followed the directions to the men's room. On the way he passed a window that offered a view of the huge interior of the building. There was a lot of construction going on. He used the john, filled the plastic bottle, dawdled a bit, and returned to the office.

"Well, those folks thought well enough of you," Hiller said, taking the bottle from him and labeling it. "Do you have an electrician's license?"

Zeke did, but in Georgia, under his own name. "No, sir, but I could probably pass the test."

"What kind of carpentry work have you done?"

"Everything from framing to finish work. I did two years as a cabinetmaker's apprentice when I was eighteen, building kitchens, and I'm good at installations."

"Well, you're an interesting fellow, Harry," Hiller said. "I've got a need for some temporary people at the moment. You interested?"

"I'd prefer something permanent," Zeke replied, "but maybe what you've got might lead to that?"

"It might very well. Tell me, can you work from architectural drawings?"

"Yes, sir; that's what I did at the cabinet shop, and my boss let me work pretty much on my own."

"Good. Right now we're getting ready for the Democratic convention, and we're stretched pretty thin. With your range of skills, I could offer you twenty an hour to start, and after the convention, if you show me you can do the work, I might have something better for you."

"I think twenty might be all right to start," Zeke said, "but I think I can show you I'm worth more than that, if you'll give me the chance."

"Harry, when I run this drug test, what am I going to find?"

"Urine," Zeke replied. "I like a beer after work, but I've never been a drug user."

"Good. Let's say you're hired, pending the test results. It'll take me a day to run the test and get you processed. Have you got your own tools?"

"Yes, sir," Zeke lied.

"I'll call you tomorrow and let you know for sure, but I think you can expect to be back here the day after tomorrow at 8 A.M. sharp to start work." He rose and shook Zeke's hand.

Zeke left the office and got back into his car. He needed some tools, and he thought he knew where to get them. He drove around for a while until he began seeing a lot of bars and pawn-shops. At the second pawnshop he found what he was looking for. Some poor bastard, down on his luck, had pawned a first-rate set of carpenter's tools, and Zeke got the lot for two hundred dollars. At a surplus store he bought some cover-alls, work boots, and a hard hat.

He put his tools in the trunk of the car and began driving again, back to the construction sites he'd seen earlier. He circled a large excavation until he heard a siren and somebody yelling, "Fire in the hole!" A moment later, a satisfyingly large explosion went off.

"Oh, yeah!" Zeke muttered under his breath. He looked hard at the little shack on the edge of the excavation, festooned with signs warning of danger and high explosives. "Nothing like advertising," he said aloud, laughing.

When he got back to his rooming house later in the day, his landlady called to him as he passed her living room.

"Mr. Grant?"

"Yes, Mrs. Rivera."

She fumbled for a piece of paper in her pocket. "A Mr. Hiller called. He said to tell you everything is okay, and you can start work tomorrow, instead of the day after."

"Thank you, ma'am," he said.

"It's okay if I call you Harry?" she asked.

"Sure, it is," he said.

"My name is Rosa," she said. "Maybe you would like to have supper with me this evening? You like Mexican?"

"Sure do, Rosa." He grinned, looking her up and down. "I like Mexican real good. But, ah, where's Mr. Rivera?"

"In Mexico, I think, but who cares?"

"Not me," he said, giving her his best smile.

37

As his campaign airplane approached Los Angeles, Will picked up the telephone, the only item on the aircraft that he felt worked consistently well, and called Kate at home.

"Hello?" she said.

"Good evening; this is the next president of the United States."

"Oh, God, not another dirty phone call."

"Show a little respect, Missy, or when I'm president, I'll exile you to the Department of Agriculture."

"Could you breathe a little harder, please? I don't feel I'm getting the full effect."

"I promise you the full effect just as soon as you arrive in L.A."

"Oh, well, there's a problem; I can't come tomorrow."

"What?"

"A flap at the office. I can't go into it, but . . ."

"Kate, I need you here."

"Will, I'm sorry, but . . ."

"Kate, I haven't asked much of you during the campaign, but this is important. The delegates are arriving, and I want them to see you with me on television. Peter, too."

"So, you want to use my son for window dressing?"

"You bet I do, and you as well. And ANYWAY, I thought it might be a memorable experience for Peter to be at the Democratic convention and see his stepfather nominated for the presidency."

"Wait a minute, do you know something I don't?"

"Just take it for granted."

"Will, I'll just be a day late, that's all. You know I wouldn't be late if it weren't important."

"The fund-raiser is the day after tomorrow," Will said. "You can't miss that."

"Oh, is this the one where I get to shake the hand of Charlene Joiner and thank her for screwing you?"

"That's the one, and short of thanking her, you have to be nice. The press is primed for this event, and it must go well. Look on the bright side; you get to spend some time with Vance Calder, too. You met him in New York, remember?"

"I believe I may have a vague recollection of having met the biggest movie star in Hollywood and the handsomest man on earth, yes. I'll make you a deal; you spend all your time with Charlene, and I'll spend all my time with Vance."

"You want me to spend all my time with Charlene?"

"Well, no, but I figure you won't be able to,

anyway, whereas I can cling to Vance like a mussel, and everybody will think it's charming."

"We've got the biggest suite at the Bel Air Hotel, so we can put Peter down a hall somewhere, so he won't hear his mother's pitiful cries."

"That's good geography. Can we put Charlene in Mexico?"

"Probably not; she is, after all, our hostess."

"I hear there's a market for her services in Tijuana."

Will felt a need to change the subject. "The Secret Service will meet you at LAX, and you'll get VIP treatment all the way."

"You mean I won't have to wait for my luggage and a rent-a-car?"

"You'll go straight from the airplane into a limo, and from there, straight into my bed."

"Will the Secret Service help with that, too?"

"We won't need any help."

"How many events do I have to go to while I'm there?"

"One thousand and sixty, at last count."

"That's what I thought."

"Some of them might actually be fun," Will said. "The rest, you'll have to pretend."

"And I'm so good at pretending."

"You'll manage; it won't be any duller than a CIA old boys' reunion."

"It wouldn't be any duller than that if you were running for head of the Los Angeles sewer department."

"Speaking of the old boys, do they ever mention the campaign and your place in it?"

"At first they did, in sly sorts of ways. I think they finally got over it."

"They're not worried what life would be like if the first lady were working at the Agency?"

If they are, they're too clever to let me know it. Come to think of it, maybe I should start dropping hints that they'd better be nice to me."

"Wait until I have the nomination, then let 'em have it."

"Where, exactly, are you now?"

Will looked out the window. "We're flying over the eastern suburbs of Los Angeles, which go on forever and ever."

"Are you landing at LAX?"

No, at Santa Monica. The airplane can just about get in there, and Kitty thinks it'll be easier to manage the press there than at LAX."

"What do you mean, 'the airplane can just about get in there'? How long is the runway?"

"Shorter than LAX's, I think, but long enough."

"Will you be on TV when you land?"

"If I'm not, I'm firing Kitty."

"Then I can watch. Oh, boy! Will you try and say something new and different?"

"I try to do that every day, but it doesn't always work. I have to settle for what's new and different to the particular audience."

"Send me a signal," she said. "If you love me, scratch your crotch."

Will burst out laughing. "On national television?"

Never mind. Charlene would probably think it was a signal to her."

"I'll see you the day after tomorrow," Will said, still laughing.

"Count on it, my love."

"I love you."

"You better."

38

As the 737 landed, Will looked across a taxiway into a boiling crowd at the Supermarine terminal. "Oh, look," he said to Kitty Conway, as they raced past, engines in full reverse, "a spontaneous demonstration."

"Yeah," Kitty replied, "and it only took three weeks to put together."

A Secret Service agent sitting across the aisle from Will briefed him as they taxied back toward Supermarine. "This is the biggest crowd we've managed yet, and I want you to know the setup," he said. He took a sheet of paper from his pocket and displayed a diagram of the area. "We had Supermarine pull all aircraft off their ramp to make room for the crowd. A podium and sound system have been set up, where the airplane will stop, and this area to your left will be press only, except for cameramen, who will be scattered all over the place. If you feel a sudden urge to plunge into the crowd, remember this: The first rows of people, three or four deep, are our buffer zone.

All the people there are campaign workers or invited guests; we've run the name, date of birth, and social security number of every one of them through our computers to make sure that none of them has a criminal record or has ever made a threat on a president or a politician.

"Behind them is the general public, and if you push that far into the crowd, it will be almost impossible for us to protect you. That's how we lost George Wallace; he pushed past the buffer zone, Arthur Bremmer was waiting for him with a handgun, and Wallace spent the rest of his life in a wheelchair."

"I see," Will said. "The crowd seems pretty happy; I don't think we'll have to worry about an Arthur Bremmer."

"Senator," the agent said, "with all due respect, that's the stupidest thing I've ever heard you say. Remember how happy the crowd was in Santa Fe?"

"Yes, that was a good rally."

"Well, there was a man on a rooftop, probably with a rifle and a telescopic sight. We rushed the roof, but he got away from us."

"Why didn't you mention this before?"

"We didn't want the press to get hold of it, and we thought it was just as well that you didn't know." He reached into a small duffel on the seat next to him and took out a vest that matched Will's suit. "We'd like you to wear this," he said. "It has a lining made of Kevlar, and it will stop small-arms fire."

"This is Southern California; it's a little warm

for a vest, isn't it?" Will looked at Kitty. "What do you think?"

"I think I would not like to be alive," she said, "if I let you leave this airplane without it, and you got shot. Please wear it for me."

Will slipped out of his suit jacket and into the vest, which was surprisingly light. "It fits," he said. "How did you get it to match my suit?"

"We got the outer fabric from your tailor," the agent said, "and the vest was made from his pattern by our man. We've got three more."

"Looks like I've got a new tailor," Will said. "I didn't know the Secret Service provided that service."

"If you're nominated," the agent said, "you're going to have a new wardrobe of protective garments—an overcoat, a trench coat, some other things. The colder the weather, the more we can protect you."

The airplane came to a halt, and everybody stood up.

"Funny," Kitty said, "I feel as though the campaign is starting right now; as if nothing we've done so far matters; just everything from here on in. Do you feel that way, Senator?"

"I think I do. It's very strange." The door to the airplane opened, and the noise filled the cabin. Somewhere a band was playing "Happy Days Are Here Again." "Let's go," Will said.

He stepped out onto the gangway, and the roar of the crowd struck him like a breaking wave. Clips of old newsreels flashed through his mind— Eisenhower, Kennedy, Reagan, stepping out of airplanes, hands in the air, waving, smiling. He felt like Woody Allen's character Zelig, superimposed on some old black-and-white footage. His knees were weak as he walked down the steps. Then, as he mounted the platform, the roar became even louder, and suddenly, he felt as if an enormous rush of energy had passed from the crowd to him, and, for the first time, he was one with his audience.

The band stopped playing, and the audience slowly grew quiet. Will began to speak, and magically, what had become his standard stump speech grew into something else—rehearsed, yet improvised. He was modest, then amusing, then serious, then finally, inspiring. He knew he had never spoken so well, and when he ended and stepped back from the microphone and listened to the crowd cheer, he felt he had crossed into some fresh, new political territory.

The Secret Service agents herded him and a handful of staff down a funnel of screaming people toward a line of waiting vehicles. Will shook hands on either side of him, felt people grabbing at his clothes, heard them shouting at him. He looked into their faces and found himself wondering if one of them was his Arthur Bremmer, concealing a gun behind a smile, eager to become a footnote of history by ending his life.

Then he was in the back of a Secret Service limousine with Kitty and Tim, and they were moving faster and faster. To Will's surprise, they drove straight across the runway and out of the other side of the airport. "Isn't this dangerous?" he asked.

"We got the FAA to close the airport for a few minutes, until we were clear," Kitty said. "Senator, what happened back there? I've never heard you speak like that."

"I don't know," Will said. "I got this incredible rush. That was a very well-trained crowd, Kitty."

Kitty shook her head. "Only a couple of hundred of them were ours. The rest just showed up. Something is happening here, I swear it is. I've never experienced anything like it before."

"Neither have I," Will said, his heart still pounding. "Don't let it stop."

39

The motorcade turned into the back drive of the Bel Air Hotel and pulled into a parking lot behind a two-story building. Will was led down a tunnel and through a ground-floor door into the handsomest hotel suite he had ever seen. It looked, he thought, like the home of a very rich and very tasteful Hollywood producer. He heard voices, and the first person he saw was Charlene Joiner.

She was standing facing the door, next to Vance Calder and a short, well-tailored man Will had never met.

"Will!" Charlene cried, and rushed forward, kissing him on the cheek.

"Charlene," he said, "it's good to see you." It had been ten years since he had seen her, and she had then been in her early twenties. A decade had made her even more beautiful, and the perfect hair and Armani suit helped. He felt an involuntary stirring in his crotch.

"I believe you've met Vance Calder?" Charlene asked.

Will shook the movie star's hand. "Of course. It's good to see you again, Vance."

"And this is Lou Regenstein," Charlene said, pointing Will at the shorter man, "the chairman of Centurion Studios."

"Mr. Regenstein, I'm very happy to meet you."

"Please, Senator, it's Lou."

Lou it is. I want to thank all three of you for the magnificent effort you're making for my campaign. I believe it is the most generous act I've ever heard of, and I'll never forget it. Won't you all sit down?"

Everyone sat on facing sofas before a fireplace, while Will took off his jacket and removed the vest, which, along with Charlene, was making him warm. "Forgive me, but I don't think I need to be bulletproof for this occasion," he said, slipping back into his jacket.

Everybody laughed.

"I want you to know," Calder said, "that the fund-raiser is fully subscribed, a thousand people at a thousand dollars a head." He handed Will a check for a million dollars, made out to his campaign.

Will accepted the check and looked at it. "Outside of a couple of defense expenditures, that's the biggest check I've ever seen," he said. "However did you round up so many people?"

It was easy," Charlene said. "We simply announced the party would be limited to a thousand, so we had an immediate demand for tickets."

"Hollywood loves anything exclusive," Regenstein said. "We hear rumors that tickets are being scalped as we speak."

Will laughed. "Maybe we should scalp a few ourselves."

Everybody laughed.

"How is Arrington, Vance?"

"She's very well, and so is our son, Peter."

"We have a boy named Peter, too; he's arriving the day after tomorrow with his mother. He's at Choate."

Charlene jumped in. "If you're on your own, will you come to dinner tomorrow at my house in Malibu? I'm having a few people in."

Yeah sure, Will thought. "I'm so sorry, Charlene," he said, "but you have no idea the schedule I'm keeping while I'm here. Your fund-raiser counts as recreational time."

"Maybe next trip. I'd love to meet Kate," Charlene said with patent insincerity.

Regenstein stood up. "Well, Senator, we'd better be going; I'm sure you've got a lot to do."

Will stood, too, shaking the man's hand. "Thank you again, Lou, for all your help on this fund-raiser, and I haven't thanked you properly for Centurion's incredibly generous gift to the party."

Everyone laughed.

"Will," Charlene said, "can I have just a moment of private time with you?"

"Of course," Will said, looking around the room for rescue. Kitty, Tim, and two Secret Service agents were with them, and Kitty was whispering to an agent.

Will shook Vance Calder's hand again. "I'll see you at the party; Kate and I are both looking forward to it."

"Arrington is looking forward to seeing you again," Calder said.

Everyone filed out of the room, except the Secret Service agent to whom Kitty had been whispering.

"Could we be alone for a moment, Will?" Charlene asked.

"I'm sorry, Charlene, but the Secret Service insists on being with me at all times."

The agent nodded vigorously. "It's policy, ma'am."

Charlene looked annoyed, but she returned to her seat on the couch. Will sat on the sofa opposite.

"It's good to see you doing so well out here, Charlene," Will said. "Starring with Vance Calder—that's something."

"Oh, Vance is a dear," she said. "I've been fucking him ever since we started work on our movie. He's over at my trailer every day at lunchtime."

Will was speechless. He glanced at the Secret Service agent, whose eyebrows had shot skyward.

"Don't look so shocked," Charlene said. "It's a tradition at Centurion. Vance has always fucked his leading ladies."

"What did you want to talk to me about, Charlene?" he asked. He hoped it was not about fucking Vance Calder.

"It's about Larry Moody's appeal," Charlene said.

"Yes, I heard about that," Will replied dryly.

"The people from the J. Edgar Hoover Institute called me and asked if I would ask you to file a brief as part of the appeal."

Will was startled at the mention of the right-wing group. "What sort of brief?" he asked, baffled.

"Well, as you know, the basis of their appeal is that Larry had legal counsel that was . . . inadequate."

"I believe 'incompetent' was the word they used."

"Yes, well, they're hoping that you'll file a brief confirming that your representation of Larry at his trial was less than your best. I mean, you had the senatorial campaign going, and Senator Carr was ill, and . . ."

"Are they *insane?*" Will demanded. "Do they really think for a moment that I would state to an appeals court that I am an incompetent attorney?"

"Now, Will, it's just a matter of form, and it's to save Larry's life, that's all."

"It's not a matter of form, Charlene. No self-respecting attorney would ever do such a thing. I'm sorry that your friend faces the electric chair, but he put himself there, first by raping and murdering a young woman, second by insisting on his innocence, instead of allowing me to plead to a lesser charge, in return for a reduction in sentence, and third, by lying to me from day one."

"I know all that, Will, but I'm very fond of

Larry; he helped me at a difficult time in my life, and I'm still grateful to him."

"That speaks well of you, Charlene, that you would stand by your friend, but I'm afraid I can't be of any help to you in this matter. You must understand that it's absolutely impossible for me to do anything for Larry now."

Charlene sighed deeply. "Well, if that's your last word."

"It is, I'm afraid." Will stood up to encourage her to do so.

Charlene stood and came toward him, her arms out.

Will grabbed her by the shoulders and held her at a distance while he pecked her on the cheek. "It's good to see you," he said, steering her toward the door, "and I want to tell you again how grateful I am for your help with the fund-raiser. It was an incredibly generous thing to do." They had reached the door, and the agent held it open.

"See you at the party," Charlene said, and before Will could back away, she leaned forward and kissed him on the ear, using her tongue.

"Good night, Charlene," Will said, trying to keep his voice steady and noting the expression on the face of Kitty Conroy, who was waiting to come in.

As Charlene passed out of the room, Kitty stepped in. "Can I get you a Q-tip?" she asked as the door closed.

"Thanks for keeping an agent here," Will said.

"What did she want?"

"She wanted me to file a brief in Larry Moody's appeal, admitting that I gave him incompetent representation."

"Oh, is *that* all?" Kitty hooted. "And I thought she wanted your body."

"Maybe she did," Will said defensively. He dug the check out of his pocket. "I guess she thought the price was right."

Kitty looked at the check. "Jesus Christ, I never thought I'd see such a thing in my whole life."

"Just get it into the hotel safe, and don't take any detours to Las Vegas on the way."

"Don't you worry," Kitty said, reaching for the door, "and I'll ask the Secret Service to post extra guards to keep Charlene out."

40

Zeke presented himself for work as requested, and Hiller, who had hired him, walked him down to the floor of the Coliseum, where a large platform was under construction at one end of the space. Hiller called another man over.

"Hank, this is Harry Grant, who's just coming to work for us. I think you might find him useful. Harry, this is Hank Greenbaum; Hank will be your foreman."

Zeke shook the man's hand. Ordinarily, Zeke would have refused to work with a Jew, but there was no point in creating a fuss about race right now.

"Good to meet you," Hank said. "I hear you have quite a range of skills to offer us."

"I'll help wherever I can," Zeke replied.

"Tell you what, climb up on that ladder there and tell me what you think of the framing plan of our platform."

Zeke climbed up and surveyed the work for a

couple of minutes, making mental notes. He came back down. "Who designed the framing?" he asked.

"A kid in our in-house design office."

"Not a structural engineer?"

"No, we thought he could handle it."

Zeke shook his head.

"You see a problem?" Hiller asked.

"How many people at a time are you likely to have standing on it?"

"Maybe as many as two hundred," Hiller replied.

"And what are you flooring it with?"

"Half-inch plywood, then carpeting," Hank replied.

Zeke shook his head again.

"You think it's dangerous?"

"I think that, under a lot of weight, it could be a little rickety."

"Let's go take a closer look," Hank said, "and you can tell me what you'd do to make it better."

The three men walked under the platform and through the framing.

Zeke looked around. "You see how he's got this series of boxes designed? I think we could make it a lot more rigid if we put cross-members in each box, and then I'd use three-quarter-inch plywood for the flooring. That ought to keep it rigid, and it would feel a lot more substantial underfoot, too."

"I agree," Hank said to Hiller, "but I'll have to have approval for the extra expenditure. It shouldn't be too bad; we can exchange the half-inch plywood for the three-quarter and get full credit. I might even be able to get them to throw in delivery."

"Do it," Hiller said, "and thank you, Harry; that was well spotted."

Zeke shrugged.

Zeke did the shoring up himself, and Hank Greenbaum watched him closely. By quitting time all the cross-members were in, and the framing was ready for the plywood flooring.

"Good job," Hank said. "You're going to be real useful around here. I like the way you use tools."

"Thanks," Zeke replied. "What you want me to do tomorrow?"

"Come on up to my office and take a look at some plans," Hank said.

Zeke followed Greenbaum up to a small room above the platform and watched as he unrolled some architect's plans. "This wasn't done by no kid," he said, looking at them.

"Nope, this was an expert job," Hank agreed. "These are the plans for the podium. It's pretty elaborate, as you can see, wide, with raised paneling. It has room for all the telephone and sound-system wiring and the TelePrompTer equipment, and, directly under the podium, there'll be a closet where all the junction boxes will be located. That way, if there's a problem during the convention, we can solve it without sending men out onto the platform."

Zeke nodded. "What's this?" he asked, pointing

to another kind of box at the center of the podium.

"The Secret Service is supplying that. It's basically a three-sided box made of quarter-inch steel plate. It's accommodated into the design, so that it won't show, but anybody standing at the microphone will be protected on three sides from gunfire."

"It doesn't have a floor," Zeke pointed out.

"You think it needs one?"

"Nah, only authorized people would be under the podium, anyway, and I'm sure the Secret Service will check it out for bombs more than once."

"You ever had any experience working with the Secret Service?" Hank asked.

"No, I'm just going by what I read in the papers about how they work. They'll be all over us like flies."

"I guess they will," Hank said. "They've already been around to case the place, and they've approved the plans for the platform and the podium. I understand you've done a lot of installation of cabinetwork."

"That's right, I have."

"Then I'd like you to take whoever you need and assemble and install the podium. It's due in tomorrow morning from the cabinetmakers. Then, when you're done, the painters will come in and finish it."

"What about the electrical work?" Zeke asked.

"That's being done by an outside contractor."

"I think it would be a good idea if, after I've got the thing installed, I worked with them on running the wiring and siting the junction boxes. I've done a lot of that."

"It's okay by me," Hank replied.

"Can I take these drawings home with me tonight and do some planning? Then I can go right to work on the installation as soon as the cabinetwork arrives tomorrow morning."

"Sure, go ahead, but for God's sake don't lose them. That's my only copy."

"Don't you worry," Zeke said.

That night after supper, Zeke spread the plans out on Rosa's dining-room table, set up a lamp, and began his work.

"What you doing, baby?" Rosa asked, coming from the kitchen, where she had been washing dishes.

"I'm planning something very important," he said, pointing at the plans. "Do you know that the man who might be the next president of the United States is going to be standing right there, making a speech? You can watch it on television in a few days."

"Oh, really?"

"Yeah, it's going to be pretty exciting," Zeke said.

41

Freddie Wallace answered the door himself at his Georgetown home. It was late, and his visitor looked both tired and worried. "Come in, my boy," Freddie said, in his most avuncular manner. "Come in, and have a drink."

"Thank you, Senator, I could use one," the man said. He was in his early forties, well dressed, and possessed of the sort of accent that spoke of generations of Ivy League ancestors.

Freddie led the man to his study. "Bourbon?" he asked. "I've got some awful good bourbon."

"Scotch, if you have it," the man replied.

"I've got some awful good scotch, too," Freddie said. "At least, that's what I'm told; I never drink the stuff myself." He poured a double of a single-malt whiskey, dropped in a couple of ice cubes, and offered it to his visitor.

The man accepted the glass gratefully and took a very large gulp of the whiskey.

"I suppose you're wondering why I asked you here at this time of night," Freddie said, waving the man to a chair before the fireplace and taking one himself.

"Yes," his guest replied.

"You and I have been helpful to each other in the past, John," Freddie said, to remind the man of past indiscretions.

The man said nothing.

"I have a feeling you know what I want from you," Freddie said, and he knew immediately that he had hit the mark.

"I can't imagine," the man said stiffly.

"Now, John, you and I both know that, sometimes, a man can be in a position to help his country in ways that are not obvious to the casual onlooker."

The man gazed forlornly into the fire.

"Just tell me what you want," he said.

"Tell me about Joe Adams."

The man winced. "What about him?"

"You see him as often as anybody, except maybe his wife."

"I suppose."

"It's come to my attention that Joe has not been himself of late."

"He seems fine to me."

"Really? That doesn't jibe with my information."

"What information is that?"

Freddie leaned forward in his chair, as much as his ample gut would allow. "Now, laddie, let's not play games. I don't want to make this any more difficult for you than I have to."

"I'm not playing games," the man said, "I just don't know what you're talking about."

"Your tenure in the White House is coming to an end, John," Freddie said. "When the new man, whoever he may be, takes over, you'll be out in the cold, unless you have some sort of inside track to George Kiel or Eft Efton."

"I don't," the man said.

"Well, if you want to continue to rise in this city, you're going to need the help of people of influence," Freddie said, "and, especially, protection from those who would, shall we say, make your life more difficult."

"How would anybody do that?" the man asked.

"Laddie, we've all done things in our lives that we're not proud of. All of us have committed small sins, while others . . ." He let the sentence trail off.

"I'm sure you've read my FBI file, Senator," the man said testily. "And if you have, then you know that I've led a blameless life."

"I'm sure that's true," Freddie said, without admitting to having read the file, which he had. "But blame can always be apportioned. Sometimes things get past even the FBI. Not everything is in their files."

"Senator, do me the courtesy of being direct with me," the man said. "Tell me what you want, and what you're threatening me with to get it."

"John, I have uttered no threat of any kind," Freddie said soothingly.

"Haven't you?"

"Certainly not. Let me pose a question to you."

"Go ahead."

"If you believed that a threat to the stability of the country existed in the behavior of a high, elected official, would you want to protect your country?"

"Of course I would, but I'm not aware of any such threat."

"Suppose this high, elected official were ill, and his illness posed a threat?"

"Senator, what are you talking about?"

Freddie was becoming exasperated with the man's intransigence. "I'm talking about Joe Adams," he said.

"Do you seriously think that the vice president is some sort of threat to the country?" the man asked.

"I think he could be, under the right circumstances."

"What circumstances, exactly?"

"Use your imagination, laddie. Think about the pressure cooker the man is living in."

"Joe Adams handles pressure as well or better than any man I've ever met," the man said.

"He wasn't under much pressure at that White House dinner," Freddie said, "and he stumbled badly there."

"He just became emotional," the man said. "He believed passionately in what he was saying to his audience."

Freddie was becoming annoyed now. "Son, do you take me for a fool?"

The man looked him squarely in the eye. "Frankly, Senator, I don't know what to take you for."

Freddie was growing red in the face, and he knew it. Why the hell was he having so much trouble confirming these rumors? This Jonah character had prevented him from getting them into the press, which might have caused them to be confirmed, and now, this supposedly weak man sitting before him was being stubborn. "Laddie, you're about to find out whether there's life in this town after being a White House staffer, and you're about to find out what I can do about it."

The man stood up. "Senator, it's late. Thanks for the drink; I'll be going now."

Freddie was on his feet. "You're playing with fire, boy."

"No, Senator, *you're* the one who's playing with fire. I'll tell you something: If I have to have enemies in this town, I'd just as soon you were among them. Good night." The man turned and walked straight out of the house.

Freddie stood there, shaking. He would not be spoken to that way. Who did this little twerp think he was? He threw his crystal glass into the fireplace.

Outside on the street, the man removed a slender dictating recorder from the breast pocket of his jacket, rewound it, and listened for a moment. Every word was plain.

42

Will stood before the California delegation, the largest and, from his point of view, most important of all. They had given him a standing ovation upon his introduction. "I've already talked myself blue in the face all over California," he said, "but I'd like to answer any questions you may have."

"Tell us where you stand on the Castle Point naval base," a man in the front row said.

Will took a deep breath. "That's a tough one, but I'll be frank: It's very likely that the base will be closed."

"You know how important that base is to California, don't you?" the man asked.

"I certainly do. Military bases are important to every state; they're big employers, and they pump a lot of money into the local economies."

"Then why do you support closing it?"

"I'm still waiting for the final report from the commission before I make that decision, but I have to tell you, it doesn't look good, and I'd like to tell you why."

"All right, go ahead."

"As important as military bases are to the states, they're even more important to the country as a whole. We don't have any weapons system that costs as much to build or maintain as a large military base costs us. Year after year, we try to close a few, so that we can make big savings on the defense budget, but year after year, congressmen and senators fight to keep them open, because it means votes to them.

"So the president set up a special commission to make recommendations on which facilities should be closed, and barring any really huge errors in their recommendations, I'm committed to accepting them. My home state of Georgia is likely to lose a big base, too, but if it makes sense for the country, I'll accept that.

"The good news is that there's never been a better time to reduce the number of bases. We're in the middle of a booming economy, and that means that the people who lose their jobs will find it easier to find new ones. California has the lowest unemployment rate it's had for thirty years, and those people will quickly be absorbed into new jobs. Remember, too, that if Castle Point is closed, it will very likely be put to private, commercial use, and that will create a lot of new jobs." He pointed to a woman in the third row.

"Tell us exactly where you stand on abortion."

"All right; like the country as a whole, I'm torn on this question. On a personal level, I'm opposed to abortion; I would not suggest to any woman I know that she have one. But in the end, it has to be the woman's choice, and I won't allow my personal feelings to intrude on that. I don't think that I or any other politician has the right to tell a woman what to do in those circumstances, and I won't support any law that infringes on her personal choice."

"Where do you stand on national health insurance?" a man shouted from the back of the room.

"I think that, eventually, we'll come up with some sort of workable program that will gain bipartisan support. The Clinton plan was shot down by a television campaign that told a lot of lies about how the plan would work—lies like you wouldn't get to choose your own doctor. Now, as a result of the failure to pass that plan in the Congress, the insurance companies have a death grip on how our doctors treat our illnesses, and I think that's wrong. I doubt that there's a person in this room who doesn't know someone who's been denied an operation or other treatment because of the intransigence of an insurance company. You hear a lot from the Republicans about not wanting to create another bureaucracy, but in fact, what we have now is an enormous *insurance* bureaucracy that is making decisions about our individual medical care. Every time they deny treatment, they make more money, and that's wrong."

"How do you feel about the Clinton impeachment business?"

"I think it was a sustained, right-wing-Republican, political tantrum from the Starr investigation, to the Judiciary Committee hearings, to the House impeachment vote, to the presentation of the house managers. President Clinton's sins were just that, and not impeachable offenses. The whole process was an outrage against the Constitution, and the Republican Party is going to have to bear the political consequences for what they did. It's my hope that a great many of the instigators of impeachment will be voted out of office in November."

That got a rousing round of applause. Will spent another half hour answering their questions, then moved on to other state delegations, where he answered, mostly, the same questions.

In the late afternoon Will returned to the Bel Air to find Kate and Peter waiting for him, Peter before the big-screen television in the suite's living room.

"You look a little tired," Kate said, kissing him.

"I've been tired since January," Will replied. "I hope that being president is a lot less work than running for the office."

"Don't count on it. Listen, there's something I have to talk to you about."

"Let's go into the bedroom. Peter, you okay here?"

"Sure, Will. Can I have a Coke?"

"There's a refrigerator in the bar; help yourself, and stay out of the booze."

"Yeah, yeah." The boy laughed and went into the kitchen.

Will went with Kate into the bedroom and closed the door. "Is something wrong?"

Kate took a pocket dictator from her purse. "Could be; listen to this; Sue Adams messengered it to me this morning. One of the voices is John Campbell, from Joe Adams's staff; I think you'll recognize the other one." They sat down on the bed, and Kate switched on the machine.

Will listened intently, and when the tape was finished, his mouth was open. "My God," he said. "How did Freddie find out about this?"

"It sounds to me as though he doesn't know for sure," Kate said. "But the old bastard is clearly willing to do whatever it takes to find out."

Kate did not mention the letter that she had received from Ed Rawls:

Kate,

Freddie W. knows about J.A., but I have him neutralized, for the moment. I'm not sure how long I can keep my foot on his neck, though. He figured out that it was me and had me thrown into the hole for a week, but I may have made him think it's somebody else. He could probably have me killed, if he wanted to.

Jonah

43

Zeke crept out of Rosa's bed and, leaving his clothes on a chair, tiptoed into his own room. He took a zippered canvas bag from under his bed and checked its contents: a pair of dark coveralls, a ski mask, a pair of driving gloves, a dozen feet of clothesline, a set of bolt cutters, and a fifteen-inch length of lead pipe, wrapped with two rolls of friction tape at one end.

He slipped into some jeans, a T-shirt, and a pair of canvas boat shoes that wouldn't leave a tread mark, then crept down the stairs and out of the house. It was a ten-minute drive to the construction site he had picked out, and when he arrived he drove around the block twice, looking for LAPD patrol cars and the night watchman. He saw no cars, but the watchman was walking the perimeter of the site. Zeke parked and watched until the man returned to his shack. Zeke got into his coveralls, rolled the ski mask so that it looked like a watch cap, slipped on the thin gloves, then grabbed the bag and headed for the fence. He cut his way through the chain links with the bolt cutters and slipped through. The watchman was still in his shack, probably dozing.

Zeke ran lightly over the rough ground to the shack. From inside he could hear the sounds of an old movie coming from a small TV set. He pulled down the ski mask, removed the lead pipe from his bag, stood behind the door, took a deep breath, and coughed loudly. A moment later, the TV went off and the door opened. Zeke waited for the man to take a step or two, then swung the pipe in a short arc toward the back of his neck. There was a faint thump, and the man fell in an uncoordinated heap. Zeke dragged him back into the shack and, with the length of clothesline, lightly hog-tied him, then stuffed the man's own handkerchief into his mouth. He turned the TV back on and turned up the volume.

Zeke left the shack and, standing in its shadow, waited three minutes, watching for traffic. There was little to be seen, and no patrol cars. He ran toward the explosives shed. He cut through the padlock with the bolt cutters and let himself inside. There were no windows, so he switched on the light; everything he wanted was there. He had to resist the temptation to take it all, but he settled for two pounds of plastic explosive, which was about the size of a brick, and some detonators.

He stuffed everything into the bag, checked for traffic again, and ran back to the opening he had cut in the fence, then to his car. He tossed the bag into the trunk, got in, and drove away. A few blocks down the street he stopped, shucked off the coveralls, and threw them, along with the shoes, the gloves, and the ski mask, into a Dumpster; then he drove home and crept up the stairs again.

He stowed the bag under his bed, then tiptoed back across the hall, used the toilet, flushed it, and got back into bed with Rosa. She rolled over and threw an arm over him. The woman slept like a stone; his alibi was tight.

The following morning, Zeke stood with Hank Greenbaum as the unassembled podium was brought to the platform on a forklift and lowered gently to the plywood floor.

"How long will you need to install the thing?" Hank asked.

"I'll have it together tonight and ready for painting," Zeke said, "but I may have to put in some overtime."

"That'll be fine," Hank replied. "How much help do you want?"

"Just one man."

"Rico!" Hank hollered to a man across the platform. "Get over here and help Harry put this thing together."

Rico walked over. "Sure thing," he said.

"Take your orders from Harry," Hank said, and walked away.

The two men began unloading sheets of custom-built paneling from the forklift. Shortly before noon, as the podium was beginning to take shape, two men in suits arrived.

"Secret Service," one man said, and they both flashed ID.

Zeke hadn't been ready for this, and his first impulse was to kick the man in the crotch and run like hell.

"We're just looking the platform over," the agent said to Zeke. "What are you two men doing here?"

"We're assembling and installing the podium," Zeke replied.

"Let me just make a note of your name," the agent said. Looking at the laminated ID badge hanging from Zeke's pocket, he jotted down some information, then did the same with Rico. "How do we get under the platform?" the agent asked Zeke.

"There's a door at the back, and one at the front," Zeke replied.

"What are we going to find down there?"

"Nothing, except a closet where all the telephone, electrical, and sound-system wiring is led in."

"Thanks, carry on," the agent said, and the two men walked away.

Zeke went back to work, breathing easier.

When the quitting whistle blew, Zeke turned to Rico. "I'll take it from here," he said. "There's not much more to do."

"Whatever you say," Rico replied. "See you tomorrow."

Zeke continued to work on the podium as the rest of the work crew made their way off the

Coliseum floor. Finally, he was alone. Using a power saw, he cut a section out of the floor under the podium, then hinged it, creating a trapdoor. He had planned this to give quick access to the wiring closet below. Nobody would think it was anything but a good idea.

He let himself down into the closet, switched on the light, and gazed at the wiring installation. Slowly, he identified each wire and where it led. Each wire was marked with a strip of masking tape, and its destination was written on the tape. He located the wire that would lead to the microphone, on the premise that, once the mike was installed and working, nobody would pay any further attention to it. The wire turned out to be red, which would help him identify it again later. He looked around the closet, which was nothing more than a six-foot-by-eight-foot framework of two-by-fours, clad in quarter-inch plywood. All that this room needed for his purposes, he decided, was a ceiling. He took some measurements, then went behind the platform where materials were stacked, found a piece of scrap plywood that was big enough, trimmed it with his power saw, and went back into the closet.

He cut a number of holes in it for the various bunches of wires to run through, then he reran all the wires and tacked the plywood to the framework. It was hardly noticeable, since it did not impede the work of the electricians, but now he had a gap of four inches between the new closet ceiling and the plywood that made up the floor of the platform. The gap would be there when he needed it, very near the new trapdoor.

He cleaned up after himself, gathered his tools, and went whistling home, content with his day's work.

44

Will pulled his black bow tie tight and examined it closely. He had once seen Vance Calder perform that task in a movie, and his result had been a lot better than Will's.

Kate came out of the dressing room, where she had been applying her makeup. "Better let me take a look at that," she said.

"Wow," Will breathed. "That is some dress!" It was black, short, and low-cut.

"I thought it would be good for the Hollywood glitterati to know that there are tits back East," Kate replied coolly.

"How does it come off?" Will asked.

"Later; now let me at that bow tie."

She did something to it, and when Will checked it in the mirror, it looked almost as good as Vance Calder's. There was a rap on the bedroom door. "Come in," Will said.

A Secret Service agent poked his head in.

"No bulletproof vests tonight," Will said adamantly.

"No problem, Senator," the agent replied. "We've already checked the name, date of birth, and social security number of every guest and every Calder employee, including the caterers. Everybody's clean. The car is ready when you are."

Will glanced at his watch: five-forty-five. They were to be there early for an early dinner with the Calders before the other guests arrived. "Are we ready, Kate?"

Kate smoothed the front of the dress. "We're ready. Where's Peter?"

The boy appeared from the kitchen, looking surprisingly mature in his dinner jacket.

"The starlets are going to be all over you," Kate said, straightening his tie.

"That's my dream in life," Peter replied, kissing his mother carefully on the cheek, so as not to muss her makeup.

"I understand the Calders have paired you up with someone for dinner," Will said.

"Oh, great!" Peter grunted. "I'll have to entertain somebody's granddaughter, I guess."

"Every woman is somebody's granddaughter," Kate said, steering him toward the door.

For the occasion, the Secret Service had come up with a limousine that Will thought looked very presidential. The three of them piled into the rear with one agent and made themselves comfortable.

Peter pointed to a complicated telephone console with many buttons. "I'll bet you could start World War III with that," he said.

"Probably," Will replied. "Anybody you're mad at? I'll order up a cruise missile."

"How about the biology department at Choate?" Peter said. "Biology was never my best subject."

It was only a short drive to the Calders' Bel Air residence. A uniformed guard stood at the gate, along with a Secret Service agent, and a crowd of press had already gathered outside the gate. A galaxy of strobes went off at their approach, and Will waved through the window. "Kitty has only allowed a couple of pool cameras onto the grounds," he said, "and a couple of print reporters."

"It's like a Hollywood opening," Peter said.

They drove up to the house, which was a low, sprawling Spanish-style residence with a tiled roof. Vance Calder and his wife, Arrington, were waiting at the front door. Next to them stood Lou Regenstein, and Charlene Joiner was on his arm, in an Academy Award–class dress, with cascades of newly styled blond hair spilling over her shoulders.

"Well, here we go," Kate said, eyeing Charlene.

"Don't bite," Will replied as they got out of the car.

There were handshakes and cheek pecks all around; then, as they went into the house, Will spotted what he thought must be the most beautiful creature he had ever seen. He recognized her immediately as the teenage star of a new television series that had gotten a ton of publicity lately.

"And here's Peter's date," Vance Calder said. "Peter, this is Astrid Bergson; Astrid, this is Peter Rule."

For just a moment, Peter had the expression of a felled ox, then he recovered himself and shook the girl's hand.

Vance leaned over, and whispered to Kate, "Don't worry, she's only sixteen, too, and very sweet."

They had entered a broad hallway that ran all the way through the house to the gardens beyond, and Vance steered them into the adjacent living room, where a butler was waiting with flutes of champagne on a silver tray.

Everyone chatted like old friends.

Peter and Astrid, Cokes in hand, stood near the fireplace. "I've seen your TV show," he said. "I think it's terrific."

"Thank you," the girl replied. "I hear you're at Choate."

"That's right. How can you manage both school and the show?"

"Oh, there's a law about that. I'm tutored every day, and my grades are very good. How are you enjoying L.A.?"

Well, mostly, I've limited myself to the pool at the Bel Air Hotel."

"You should see some of the city while you're here."

"I'd love to do that," he replied.

"How about I show you around some this weekend?"

"Fantastic!"

"I'm coming east in a couple of years," she said. "My deal with the show is that I can leave when college starts. I'm planning to go to the Yale Drama School."

"Yale sounds great," Peter said. "I think I'll go there, too." He gave her his best smile. "I was thinking of Harvard, but what the hell?"

She laughed a wonderful, tinkling laugh, through gorgeous teeth.

Peter sighed.

They sat at a round table, talking animatedly, while four courses of extremely pretty Californian cooking were served, with accompanying wines. Will silently thanked Arrington Calder for having had the presence of mind to seat Kate and Charlene on opposite sides of the table. It occurred to him, with a start, that Peter was probably the only male at the table who had not slept with Charlene Joiner.

45

By the time they were on dessert, the noise level in the hallway outside the dining room had risen to a dull roar. The paying guests were arriving and, if the volume of their laughter was any indication, were already beginning to get their thousand dollars' worth.

Arrington Calder set down her coffee cup. "I think it's time for us to go and mingle with our guests. Will, we've a microphone set up on the terrace; perhaps you'd say a few words to them first?"

"Of course," Will said.

Arrington took his arm and led him out of the dining room, through the hallway, and out onto a terrace, which was elevated over the broad rear lawn and gardens. Everybody followed. As they stepped onto the terrace, applause broke out.

Vance stepped up to the microphone. "Good evening, and thank you all for coming," he said. "I think it's time you all met the reason we're here.

Ladies and gentlemen, the next president of the
United States, Senator Will Lee!"

The crowd roared its approval as Will stepped
to the microphone. Finally the applause died.
"Good evening to you all. First of all, I want to
thank our hosts, Vance and Arrington Calder, for
being so kind as to allow us all to invade their
home this evening."

Much applause.

"Second, I want to thank them, as well as
Charlene Joiner and Lou Regenstein of Centurion Studios, for organizing this event, and for
extorting so much money from all of you. It's
important for you to know that, although there
is a limit of one thousand dollars per person that
can be contributed to a candidate, there is still
no limit on what an individual can contribute to
the Democratic Party, which can use the funds
in the general election. Lou Regenstein and his
board of directors have been so wildly generous
as to promise a million dollars to the party, and I
hope each of you will consider following their
example."

Much laughter and applause.

"I've promised Lou that I'll do everything in
my power to see that that money is spent on my
campaign, and not George Kiel's!"

More laughter and applause.

"Now I'd like to introduce you to my family:
This is my wife, Kate, and our son, Peter." He put
an arm around each of them and pulled them
forward as more applause broke out. "Kate is here
so that she could meet Vance Calder again, and

Peter is here so that he could meet Astrid Bergson."

Much laughter.

"This is one of Kate's few campaign appearances since I announced, last January. As you may have heard, the national security depends on her being at her desk in Langley, Virginia, nearly all the time, and there's a pretty good argument to be made that she is more important to her country there than on the campaign trail."

More laughter.

"This is Peter's first campaign appearance since he was twelve years old. He has been, of course, occupied with school, although it's going to be very hard to get him to go back, after having met Astrid."

More laughter.

"Tonight, I want to thank you for more than your financial contribution: I want to thank you for your personal contribution to the political life of your country. People from that far-reaching community we all think of as Hollywood have always taken an interest in national affairs, just as the nation has always taken an interest in them. So many of your faces are so well known to the American people that they have come to think of you as their neighbors out west, and they want to know where you stand when it's time to choose the nation's leaders. I am very proud and very grateful that so many of you are standing with me."

Much applause.

"The Democratic convention opens tomorrow,

and tonight, all across this city, there are other parties like this taking place, though perhaps not quite so well attended as this one. I don't want you to think of your colleagues who are supporting other candidates as your opponents. By this time next week, our party will have chosen its candidates, and we will all be working together to see that they are elected. There will be parties, too, for candidates of the Republican party, and though you may rightly think of them as opponents, after the first Tuesday in November, we are all—Democrats and Republicans—going to have to work together to make this country all that it can be.

It is at the center—not the left or the right—where the work gets done, and that New Center is where we are all going to have to meet each other and our obligations to our country. We are all in this together, and together we will take this country into the new millennium!"

Will stepped back from the microphone to huge applause. He pulled Kate and Peter forward, and they all waved at the crowd.

When the applause had finally died, Vance Calder came to the microphone again. "Now that you've gotten your money's worth, dinner is being served. We've felled a large number of oxen, and for those of you who are California vegetarians, we have denuded the San Joaquin Valley for your dining pleasure."

Will, Kate, and Peter walked down the steps and onto the huge lawn where the guests were gathered.

Peter whispered into Will's ear. "Now can I break off and talk to my date?"

"Sure," Will whispered back, "but don't do anything you wouldn't want to see on the front page of the *Los Angeles Times* tomorrow."

Peter fell back and took Astrid Bergson's hand.

Will did his level best to shake every hand at the party. He and Kate wandered through the crowd, talking with the guests, laughing at jokes, and thanking everyone. Outside of Washington or Georgia, Will had never been to a party where there were so many familiar faces, faces that he had watched hundreds of times at the movies and on television. He posed for pictures with most of them.

Then there was a tug at his elbow, and Charlene was there. Kate had fallen back into the crowd.

"We need to talk alone," Charlene said.

"Not even if you have a gun," Will said, sotto voce, through a smile. "Not here, not with everyone taking pictures. I hope you understand." He turned and grabbed an actor's outstretched hand, thrilled to be saved from a tabloid fate.

46

If Will had felt busy before, the tempo of his existence increased markedly with the beginning of the convention. The delegates gathered and caucused, the platform committee met and argued, while Will's representatives fought for his positions; deals were being made at every opportunity; and promises were made that would never be kept.

Will's parents arrived. Billy and Patricia Lee were housed in a suite adjoining Will's, and both began working the telephones, calling delegates in their hotel rooms and on their cell phones, extracting assurances where they could. On the evening of the first ballot, Billy called a meeting in Will's suite. He looked grim.

"All right, listen up," he said, and the two dozen people in the suite grew quiet. "We're not going to win the nomination tonight," he said, and there was a collective gasp. "I've counted and re-counted, and we just don't have the delegates.

The good news is, George Kiel doesn't have them either." The room burst into babble again.

Will stood up. "Everybody shut up and listen to Dad," he said.

Billy looked around, then continued. "I make it that Kiel is twelve to fourteen delegates short, and we're about thirty-five short. What we have to do this evening is to make sure we don't lose even a single delegate on the first ballot. If we can do that, then we'll have a better shot on the second ballot, I *think*. It's important that, after the first ballot, we pick up some delegates, even if it's only half a dozen. I want instructions to go out to our people on the floor to tell our delegates to hold fast, and not expect to walk away with this thing. If we can get through two ballots tonight without losing, and maybe pick up a few votes, then we'll have a real shot at winning tomorrow night. Now you've all got your lists of people to call. Will and I will be calling the delegation chairmen on the floor, shoring them up, and I want each of you to make sure that every one of our delegates with a personal phone gets at least one phone call on the floor. It'll make 'em feel good. Now go to it!"

Most of the campaign workers left for a meeting room in the hotel where a phone bank had been set up. Each of them had a list of names and numbers to contact.

"Will," Billy said, "what worries me most is California. They'll hold on the first ballot, because they'll have to, but on the second ballot, we're going to lose some people."

"Because of the Castle Point naval base?"

"That's right. I've heard from some friends that Kiel's people have been promising some of the California delegates that, if he's elected, he won't close the base."

"But he's already committed to following the commission's recommendation on Castle Point, just as I have."

"Right, and we have to hammer that home with every California delegate. When they call the roll, California is the fifth state to be called, and the first big state. If there are significant defections, it could start a snowball effect for Kiel. But if we can hold, it may give a lot of other delegates some backbone. So you and I are going to personally contact every California delegate we can."

"Let's get started," Will said. By tradition, he couldn't appear at the convention until after the balloting, so he began working the phones.

Zeke was under the convention platform with two Secret Service agents. It was the third set of agents he'd given the tour, and this pair was being very meticulous. He went through every under-platform installation, working from a detailed set of drawings, pointing out the wiring plans for lighting, sound system, TelePrompTers, and telephones.

The agents knew what they were doing, Zeke realized. These guys were technically oriented, and they understood everything pointed out to them.

"How many telephone lines?" an agent asked.

"Six to the podium," Zeke said. "Another six to the rest of the platform and the green rooms. It's a Lucent Partner Plus office system, with a max of twenty-four extensions, and they're all in use."

An agent popped the cover on the main phone panel and went through it, line by line and extension by extension.

"It's been checked and rechecked by the people who installed it," Zeke said. "It's working perfectly."

The agent nodded. "I just wanted to be sure there was nothing in the box but telephone wiring."

The man had given Zeke an idea. He'd planned to detonate with a timing device, but now he realized that these people might very well spot that. The telephone system offered a more elegant solution.

Above their heads, a roar went up from the crowd.

"Sounds like they've finished the balloting," an agent said.

Will sat with his father before the big-screen TV in the living room of his suite, a list of delegates before them. The last of the big states, Texas, was polling its delegation for the second ballot.

"If we can get past Texas without losing too many delegates, we can hold our own," Billy said. "But not much better than that."

The television commentators were having a

field day; they had not seen a race this close for many a convention.

The Texas vote was announced by the delegation chairman, to a roar from the whole convention.

"We're alive," Billy said, "but there are still fifty delegates from other, smaller states to go."

They held Utah and Vermont, then lost two Virginia delegates. Washington, West Virginia, and Wisconsin came in as expected.

"We have a net loss of one delegate," Billy said. "It's not much, but it scares the hell out of me."

Only Wyoming was left to vote, with only three delegates, all of whom had voted for Kiel on the first ballot. They were sitting together in the front row.

"Mr. Chairman," the delegation leader boomed into the microphone, "before announcing our vote, I request a poll of the delegation!"

The crowd erupted into wild laughter and applause.

"The delegation will be polled," the chairman said. "The clerk will call the roll."

"Mr. Weston," the clerk said.

"Mr. Chairman," Weston said, "I wish to cast my vote for the next president of the United States, Senator Will Lee of Georgia!"

"That's one," Will said. "I hadn't expected that."

"Your mother has been on the phone with Governor Tobias, talking cattle." Will's mother had been the cattle farmer in the family.

"Ms. Evans," the clerk called.

A woman stood up. "I cast my vote for Senator Will Lee!" she shrieked.

"Mr. Tobias," the clerk called.

The governor stood. "Mr. Chairman, Wyoming is unanimous for Senator Will Lee!"

"Well, I'll be damned," Will said.

"We've got a net gain of two," Billy cackled. "I wish it was six, but it'll have to do."

They went through the delegate count again, to be sure they had missed no votes, then Kate came across the room with a cordless phone, her hand over the receiver. "Will, George Kiel is on the phone," she said.

Will looked at his father.

"I guess you know what this is about," Billy said. "You'd better talk to him."

Will took the phone. "Hello, George," he said.

"Will, we have to talk."

"Go ahead."

"No, I want us to meet; I've got a bungalow at the Beverly Hills Hotel. Will you come over here?"

Will didn't like the idea of talking on Kiel's turf, and he hesitated.

"Will, we *have* to talk; there's something you don't know."

"All right, George, but it will have to be alone—nobody else at all. Agreed?"

"Agreed." Kiel gave him the bungalow number. "Your Secret Service people will know the back way in. Nobody will see you."

"I'll be there in twenty minutes," Will said, then hung up the phone. He looked around the room. "Now I have to decide whether I can stand being vice president," he said.

"You could do worse, Will," his father said.

"I know it," Will replied. "I knew it might come to this, but now I've got to decide before I get to the Beverly Hills Hotel."

"You've already heard what all of us think, Will," his father said. "Do whatever you feel is right, and we'll be with you."

"Kate?"

"Whatever you want is good enough for me," she replied.

Will stood up and got into his jacket. "I'll be back as soon as I can," he said.

47

The Secret Service car drove up Sunset Boulevard, past the Beverly Hills Hotel, then made a left and drove uphill for a couple of hundred yards. A guard at a nearly hidden gate looked at the agent driver's ID, then opened the gate. A moment later, the car glided to a stop before a cottage that was nearly buried in a jungle of California landscaping.

Will got out of the car, walked to the door, and rang the bell. George Kiel opened the door. "Wait here," Will said to the agent. He walked inside, and Kiel closed the door behind him.

Evening, Will," Kiel said, offering his hand. Kiel was a big man, six-two or -three, and heavy. He was dressed in a suit, and he took off his jacket and tossed it on a chair. "Can I get you a drink? I'm having one."

"Bourbon on the rocks," Will replied.

Kiel motioned to a chair before the fireplace, where a gas log was cheerfully pretending to burn. "Have a seat."

Will sat down; Kiel brought the drinks and sat down, too.

"You know, Howard Hughes used to live in this cottage."

"Oh?"

"Yes, and I expect a lot of starlets were sampled right here."

Will didn't respond to that.

"How's your week going?" Kiel asked.

"Actually, it's going pretty well, after the balloting this evening," Will replied.

Kiel chuckled. "Tobias did a one-eighty on me," he said. "How'd you do that?"

"I sicced my mother on him," Will replied, sipping lightly at his drink. He was going to need a clear head for this.

"I may as well warn you, Will, I'm going to pick up a substantial number of California votes tomorrow night."

"By promising to keep Castle Point open?"

Kiel shrugged.

"George, if you break your commitment to follow the commission's recommendations, why will those folks believe you won't break your new commitment to them?"

"Just think of it as politics, Will."

"It's bad politics, George."

Kiel ignored that. "Will, I want to compliment you on the way you've run your campaign. You've done it in a principled manner, and I admire that. In a way, I'm sorry to see you fall short."

"So far, you've fallen short yourself, George;

remember, we gained delegates on the second ballot."

"So you did," Kiel admitted. "All two of them."

"We expect to win on the fourth ballot," Will said. This was a bluff, and Will thought Kiel probably knew it, but he was surprised to see a flicker of doubt flash across the man's face.

Kiel took a deep breath. "It won't get to a fourth ballot; my people tell me we'll win on the first ballot tomorrow night."

Now it was Will's turn to wonder if Kiel was bluffing. Did he know something Will didn't? He'd said something like that on the phone. "If you do, George, I'll be the first to support you. I'll turn over what's left of my war chest, after our bills are paid, and I'll campaign for you actively. *If* you win the nomination."

"That's very generous, Will; it's what I'd expect from you."

Will decided to keep his mouth shut and let Kiel do the rest of the talking.

"Will," Kiel said finally, "I want you to run on the ticket with me in the second spot."

Will took a breath to speak, but Kiel held up a hand.

"Don't turn me down yet," he said. "You haven't heard everything I have to say."

Will nodded.

"I'll make you the most powerful vice president in history," Kiel said. "I'll put you in charge of all domestic policy, including economic policy. You know my interest in foreign affairs. There'll be a domestic policy advisor on staff, as usual, but he'll report to you."

Will was stunned; he hadn't expected this. "That's very . . ." He couldn't think of a word.

"Unprecedented," Kiel said.

"It certainly is."

"Well?"

Will's mind was thrashing through the gears; he needed time. "George, you said on the phone that there was something I didn't know. What is that?"

Kiel got up slowly and went to the chair where he had thrown his jacket. He reached into an inside pocket, withdrew a single sheet of paper, read it quickly, then put it back into the pocket. He fumbled through the jacket and came up with another piece of paper, then came back to his seat. "Will, if you'll run on the ticket with me and we're elected, I won't run for reelection after my first term. I'll give you my word on that."

Will was stunned anew. "George . . ."

"Listen, I don't want this to go any further, but my health isn't all it should be. I don't think I could manage eight years, maybe not even four."

"George," Will said, "I hope you're not promising to die in office."

Kiel burst out laughing, and Will laughed with him.

"Christ, I hope not."

"And what happens, three and a half years down the pike, when your doctor tells you you're fine, and it's okay to run again?"

Kiel looked at the paper in his hand, then gave it to Will. "Put that in your pocket," he said.

Will read the letter:

Dear Will,

Confirming our conversation of tonight, I want you to know that it is my firm intention, should I be elected president, not to run for a second term. Should you decide to be my running mate this year, and if we are elected, I will put you in charge of all domestic and economic policy, reporting directly to me, and near the end of my first term, I will announce my intention not to seek reelection and enthusiastically endorse you to succeed me as president.

I do this because of my high personal regard for you and your abilities, and I hope you will accept the vice-presidential slot on my ticket.

With warmest regards,

It was on Kiel's personal stationery, signed and dated.

Will was flabbergasted. Kiel's offer was certainly unprecedented, and to put this sort of political promise in writing was unheard of. "George, I'm very flattered to be asked to run with you."

"Then do it, Will. We'll make a great team."

"I need to talk with Kate about this," Will replied. "Can I sleep on it and give you an answer in the morning?" He handed the letter back to Kiel.

"Keep it," Kiel said. "Show it to Kate, and to your folks, too; I know you rely on their advice." He cleared his throat. "One thing: This offer is predicated on your withdrawal before the balloting tomorrow evening. If you decide to fight until the end, then we're in a different ball game. Understood?"

Will stood up. "Understood. I'll be in touch in the morning." He shook Kiel's hand and made his exit.

On the way back to the Bel Air, Will read and reread the letter. It seemed airtight. What an offer! Under these circumstances, being vice president was extremely attractive. He couldn't wait to show the letter to his family.

Nobody had gone to bed. Kate, his father and mother, Kitty Conroy, and Tim Coleman were all there.

"So what happened?" his mother asked.

"I think I can best explain that by reading a letter George gave me," Will replied. He read the letter aloud.

"That's unbelievable," Billy Lee said when Will had finished. "Not the deal he's offering you, but that he would put it in writing. I've never heard of a politician doing such a thing."

Will handed him the letter. "Signed, sealed, and delivered. What do you think I should do?"

"While you were gone I talked with Thad Morrison," he said. Morrison was the governor of

California. "He's been getting calls from his delegates about Castle Point."

"Oh?"

"Kiel has, apparently, promised them that, if they change their votes, and he's elected, he'll keep Castle Point open."

"He as much as admitted it to me tonight. What do you think it's going to cost us?"

"Thad thinks at least eight delegates, maybe one or two more, will change their vote on the first ballot tomorrow evening."

"And Kiel needs, what—fourteen votes to win the nomination?"

"That's right," Tim Coleman said, "and if eight or ten California delegates change their votes, it won't take much of a snowball effect to give him the nomination on that ballot."

"So, what we've got here is a carrot and a stick," Will said. He held up the letter. "Carrot."

"And the stick is the loss of the California delegates," Tim said.

Kate spoke up. "Why don't you fight it to the finish? What have you got to lose? Kiel will still want you for vice president."

Will shook his head. "George made it clear that the offer is good only if I drop out before the balloting."

"He's bluffing," Billy said.

"Of course he is," Patricia Lee said.

"Trouble is," Kitty said, "we can't be sure."

"That's what a bluff is all about," Billy replied.

"The California delegation is caucusing at noon

tomorrow," Tim said. "We've got until then to decide."

"I told George I'd give him an answer tomorrow morning."

"Morning ends at noon," Tim pointed out.

"Oh," Kate said, "Sue Adams called; she said that Joe wants to meet with you tomorrow at ten."

"Where?"

"He's at the Roosevelt, downtown."

"Okay, let's all sleep on this," Will said. "And I'd like to talk to Joe about it, too." He stood up. "Good night, everybody."

Kate fell asleep immediately; it took Will longer. His last thought before drifting off was that he would accept George Kiel's offer.

48

They all sat down to breakfast at eight o'clock. Will dismissed the room-service waiter and served everybody himself. "All right," he said as he sat down, "I want an opinion from each of you. Kitty, you first."

"Kiel has us boxed," she said. "It's a big stick, and a big carrot, too. Take it."

"Tim?"

"Looking at it in terms of the general election, I think you could beat Efton, but it would be very close. I think that with you and Kiel on the same ticket, the odds are better. Accept."

"Mother?"

"Screw George Kiel. Go for the nomination." She said it quietly but emphatically.

"Dad?"

"I'd like to see you president before I die," Billy said, "but I guess I've got another four years in me. It's a great offer; take it."

"Kate?"

"Everybody's right, it's a great offer," she said. "Sorry, Patricia, but it is the smart move. The downside is, we're in the goldfish bowl for twelve years, instead of eight, assuming all your dreams come true. It's got to be your decision, Will, but I'm with you either way."

Will squeezed her hand. "Thanks, love."

"I've got to call Thad Morrison first thing," Billy said. "What do you want me to tell him?"

"I want to hear from Joe Adams before I decide," Will said. "Tell him I'll call him before the caucus."

Will was admitted to the presidential suite at the old Roosevelt Hotel at 10 A.M. sharp. Joe and Sue Adams were reading the papers and having coffee. They both stood up to greet him.

"I'm glad to see you, Joe," Will said, accepting some coffee and an armchair. "How have you been?" He thought Adams looked well—rosy-cheeked, maybe a little heavier than when he had last seen him.

Adams shrugged. "At least as well as can be expected," he said, "maybe better."

Sue spoke up. "We're limiting Joe's activities this week as much as we can. He's agreed to introduce the nominee, whoever he is, on the last night."

Will nodded. "I've got to make a big decision this morning, Joe, and I'd like your advice."

"I think I can guess what the decision is," Adams said. "George has made you an offer?"

Will handed him Kiel's letter, and watched as the vice president read it.

Adams's eyebrows went up. "A better offer than I had expected," he said. "An excellent offer, in fact, and I think it's significant that he gave it to you in writing. It gives you a considerable weapon if he should change his mind about a second term after a taste of power. I think you could actually hold him to his promise. I suppose he'll withdraw the offer if you continue to run."

That's right," Will said. "The consensus among my people, except for my mother, is that I should accept. But I want your opinion, Joe."

"I think it's a great offer," Adams said, "but don't you think you've got a shot at the nomination? Why do you want to quit?"

"I don't want to, but it looks as though we're going to lose eight to ten of the California delegation. George has told them he'll keep the Castle Point base open, even if the commission recommends closing it."

Adams furrowed his brow. "I thought George was firm on accepting the commission's recommendation," he said.

"The California delegation is caucusing at noon."

"I can see how this might put George over the top," Sue Adams said.

"When do you have to give George an answer?" Adams asked.

"This morning. I'm about out of time."

Adams nodded. "Will, would you excuse me

for a few minutes? I'd like to make a couple of calls in the bedroom. Sue, will you keep Will entertained?"

"Of course," Sue replied, pouring Will another cup of coffee.

Adams left the room.

"How is he, really?" Will asked.

"He's doing all right," Sue said. "And while he's making those calls, there's something he's asked me to talk to you about."

"Sure, what's up?"

"The president is dying," Sue said. "The first lady is making a decision soon about whether to take him off the ventilator. If they do that, his doctors' best guess is that he can't last more than a few days, maybe a few hours."

"I'm sorry to hear it," Will said.

"The question then arises, what should Joe do about the vice presidency? I know Joe promised you that, if the president died, he would appoint you vice president, and he's willing to keep that promise."

"I see," Will said.

"The question is, do you still want it? There's a lot to consider."

"There certainly is," Will agreed.

First of all, there's the question of the nomination. If you go for it and don't get it, then as VP, you're just another lame duck, and you're out of the Senate. That doesn't make any sense. Then, if you accept George Kiel's offer, it would be very strange for him to be running for president with the vice president as his running mate. Finally, if you get the nomination and Joe appoints you, he thinks we're unlikely to get Senate confirmation. The Republicans are not going to want to give you a weapon of status to use against Efton. They might have accepted you six months ago, but not with so little time left before the election."

"So what you're saying is that, under any circumstances, Joe's appointing me would not be a good idea."

"That's about it," she said.

"But if Joe doesn't appoint somebody, then Efton is in line for the presidency, if anything should happen to Joe."

"Yes, but Joe has the option of appointing a more benign Democrat, somebody the Republicans wouldn't see as a threat."

"Does he have somebody in mind?"

"He's thinking of Jim Browner."

Browner was the senior Democratic senator, a man in his early eighties.

"Jim's not running for reelection, anyway. He's had five terms, and it would be an opportunity for him to render a final service to his country."

"I think that's a splendid idea," Will said.

Joe Adams returned to the living room and sat down. "Did you and Sue talk about the vice presidency?"

"Yes, Joe," Will replied, "and I agree it's best you don't appoint me. I think Jim Browner is a fine choice."

"Good," Adams said. "Now, you've asked for

my advice; here it is: I think you should turn
down George Kiel's offer and continue your campaign for the nomination."

Will was taken aback. "May I ask your reasons?"

"I can't tell you my reasons, Will, but that's my
advice, and I feel strongly about it." Adams looked
at his watch. "Good God, I've got another appointment in about one minute, and I have to
put on a tie." He stood up and held out his hand.
"It's good to see you, Will."

Will shook his hand and kissed Sue; then he
left the suite and returned to his car. He looked at
his watch: 10:30. "Let's go back to the Bel Air,"
he told the driver.

He sat at his suite's dining table again, the same
group around him, and told them about his meeting with Joe and Sue Adams.

"I have to admit, I'm astonished," Billy Lee said.
"I thought Joe would tell you to accept Kiel's offer."

"Frankly, so did I," Will said. "But he was strong
in his recommendation that I continue to go for
the nomination."

"I wonder who he telephoned when he left
you," Tim Coleman said.

"I wonder, too," Will said.

"So what's it going to be, Senator?" Kitty
asked.

Will got up and retrieved an envelope from
his briefcase. He took George Kiel's letter from
his pocket and wrote something on it, then he

put it into the envelope, sealed it, wrote "Personal and Confidential" on it, and handed it to Kitty. "Send somebody over to the Beverly Hills Hotel with this," he said. "Then get me Governor Morrison on the telephone."

"You're still in it, then?" his mother asked.

"I'm still in it."

49

Will waited for the governor of California to come on the line. It was ten minutes before noon, and the California delegation to the convention was about to meet in caucus.

"Hello, Will?" Governor Morrison said.

"Thad, how are you?"

"Rushed. We're about to meet."

"I wanted to talk to you personally before you caucus," Will said. "It's about the Castle Point naval base."

"I hope you've found a way to change your position, Will," Morrison said. "George Kiel has."

"I know; he told me."

"So, what's it going to be? I've got to go into that meeting and tell my delegates where you stand."

"I can't change my position, Thad. I've taken a public position on accepting the commission's findings, and I've done it for the right reasons. I want you to tell your people for me that it's my belief that we'll never get the defense budget under control if we're going to allow political interference of this kind, and I won't be a party to it."

"George doesn't seem to have a problem with it."

"Thad, let me put a couple of questions to you."

"Shoot, but be quick."

"First of all, are your delegates going to support a candidate who makes a political promise to accept the commission's findings, then reverses his position for self-serving reasons?"

"That's a legitimate question; I'll put it to the delegates."

"One more: If George is willing to reverse himself now to get your delegates' votes, what's to prevent him from reversing himself again after the election?"

Morrison was briefly silent. "I'll put that question to them, too," he said finally.

"That's all I've got to say, Thad. Do your delegates understand that the nomination may be riding on how they vote on this?"

"If they don't, I'll explain it to them."

"Will you call me back and let me know how they vote?"

"I can't do that, Will; this is a closed caucus, and the results are not to be revealed until the vote tonight."

"Thanks for listening, Thad."

"Good luck, Will." He hung up.

Will replaced the receiver and turned to the group in the living room of his suite. "Well, that's it; it's all I can do."

"What did Morrison say?" Kitty asked.

"Just that he'd put my views to the delegates."

Tim Coleman spoke up. "I've been doing the math," he said. "If we lose eight or ten votes from California, it doesn't have to cause a snowball, not if we do our work in the other delegations. If we can change a few votes our way, we can hold for at least another ballot."

"We can't go on coming in second," Will said. "I think that, after this ballot, we'll have trouble holding delegates from all over the country. If we lose this one, even by a few votes, we're done."

Patricia Lee spoke up. "Will, why don't we talk about who your choice for vice president is going to be when you win?"

Everybody burst out laughing.

"That's my ma," Will said.

Across town, Zeke went into an electronics shop and began buying. He bought a telephone voice-mail system that was compatible with the Lucent equipment being used for the convention podium, a number of other parts, and some Lucent labels.

Back in his room, he unscrewed the top of the voice-mail box and, using the wiring diagram that had come with the unit, traced the printed circuits for various functions. When he had all the functions traced, he soldered a thin wire to a circuit, then attached the other end to a flashlight bulb. Using the system's built-in recorder, he recorded a list of voice-mail options. Finally, he connected the voice-mail system to Rosa's phone line and, using his cell phone, called the number.

"Welcome to the podium of the Democratic convention," his own voice said. "Please choose from one of the following three options: If you wish to be connected to the podium, press one; if you wish to hang up, press two; and if you wish to set off an explosive charge that will blow the podium and anyone near it to eternity, press three."

Zeke laughed aloud at his own joke. He pressed three and watched as the flashlight bulb lit up. Bingo! Then he rerecorded the third option. Now it said, "If you wish to be placed on hold for the rest of your life, press three." That should keep anyone who was accidentally connected to the number from pressing three.

Chuckling to himself, he packed the equipment into a bag and left for the Coliseum.

"Senator," Kitty said, "can I ask the obvious question? I mean, I know the answer, but I'd like to hear it from you."

"Go ahead," Will said.

"If George Kiel can play this game, why can't you? Why can't you just call Thad Morrison back and tell him you'll keep the base open, then, after you're elected, close the fucking thing. Would you really rather be right than president? Because, to tell you the truth, I'd rather be wrong and be the president's press secretary."

"Come on, Kitty, you know better than that."

"All right, you wouldn't make the next edition

of *Profiles in Courage*, but you'd have a shot at running the country, you know?"

"Kitty, if somebody had told me six months ago that I'd find myself in this position, then maybe I wouldn't have taken so firm a stand on the commission's report; maybe I'd have found a way to weasel out of it or rationalize it, or something. But that's not the way it happened. As it turned out, I took that position, then I repeated it ad nauseam to get other senators to support it, then I told everybody who'd listen that I wouldn't change it. So I'm stuck with it, and that's that. So, if we're going to win this thing, we're going to have to find another way to do it. Let's get started."

Zeke waited for a lull in the afternoon's proceedings. Then, when the maintenance workers were on a coffee break, he went into the closet under the podium and installed his system, connecting it to the last of the six telephone lines coming into the podium. Only one of the numbers was given out; a caller dialed the first number, and if it was busy, the call rolled over to the second number, and so on, until all six lines were busy. When they were, a caller would get a busy signal. Only if the caller directly dialed the number for the sixth line would he reach Zeke's voice-mail system, and only the telephone company and Zeke had that number. Zeke had copied it from the installer's records.

He attached a Lucent label to the black box; he doubted if anyone would notice it, but if somebody took the lid off the box, the insides would look like nothing more than part of the phone system. He would attach the explosives later, after everyone was used to seeing the box there in the closet, and after the closet had been inspected numerous times.

Tim Coleman put down the phone in Will's suite. It was a little after five.

"What?" Will asked.

"That was an acquaintance of mine who was at the California delegation's caucus."

"You didn't tell me you knew anyone like that," Will said.

"I didn't want to mention it, in case the call never came."

"And what was the result of the caucus?"

"Fifteen delegates switched their votes to Kiel."

Will sagged. "Kiel was only fourteen votes short of the nomination."

Patricia Lee spoke up. "It's not over," she said. "We've still got a chance to gain votes from other delegations."

Tim shook his head. "I don't see how we can make up that many votes before tonight."

"Let's get to work," Will said.

50

Will and his inner circle of around two dozen people had a buffet supper in his suite as the convention opened and the balloting began. His campaign had put every possible person on the convention floor to canvass delegations, looking to change as many votes as possible.

"California!" the chairman called out.

The television screen was filled with the face of Governor Thad Morrison, who was deep in conversation on a cell phone.

"California!" the chairman called again.

Morrison held the phone against his chest and grabbed a microphone. "Mr. Chairman," he said, his voice booming around the Coliseum, "California wishes to delay its vote until the end of balloting."

Will grabbed Tim Coleman. "What's going on?" he asked.

"I don't know," Tim replied, shaking his head. "I've heard nothing from my source; as far as I know, we're still losing fifteen votes."

"Something is going on here," Will said. "I wish to God I knew what it was."

Tim had a chart and was marking the votes of the various delegations, while Kitty used a calculator to do a running total.

The balloting finished.

"We've got 222 votes, and Kiel has 256," Kitty said.

"Then we're done," Tim replied, his shoulders sagging.

"We haven't heard from California," Patricia Lee said.

"California!" the chairman called out.

"Here we go," Kate said.

"Mr. Chairman," Thad Morrison called out, "California votes thirty-nine for Will Lee . . ." Cheering broke out.

"That gives us 261," Kitty said, "and we need 270 to win the nomination. Kiel only needs fourteen votes."

"And," Morrison continued, "fifteen votes for George Kiel."

The Kiel supporters erupted. Pandemonium reigned in the hall. The chairman banged his gavel to no avail.

Will put his head back and closed his eyes. Why hadn't he taken George Kiel's offer? He could have been president in four years.

"Something's happening," Tim said, pointing at the big-screen TV. Thad Morrison was back at the microphone, shouting something.

"What's he doing?" Will asked.

"He's trying to get recognized," Tim said.

Gradually the chairman regained order. "The chair recognizes Governor Thad Morrison of the great state of California."

"Mr. Chairman," Morrison said, "I request a poll of the delegation."

"What's the point?" Kitty asked. "We've lost."

As the polling began, a phone rang and somebody answered it. "It's for you," a worker said, handing Will the phone.

"Not now," Will said, riveted to the TV.

"It's the vice president."

Will took the phone. "Hello?"

"Will," Joe Adams said, "I want to apologize to you."

"Joe, it's all right; it was my decision, not yours."

"You don't understand," Adams said.

"What do you mean?"

"I assume you're watching TV."

"Yes."

"They're polling the California delegation."

"Yes, I'm watching."

"I've been on the phone with Thad Morrison three times this evening; that's why California didn't vote at first."

"And what were the two of you talking about?"

"I've been trying to nail down some information all afternoon, and I finally confirmed what I had suspected."

"And what was that, Joe?"

"I found it suspicious that George Kiel would

reverse himself as he did about the Castle Point base. It would have been unlike him to do that."

"But he did."

"And for a reason."

Tim was tugging at Will's sleeve. "We've got two of our lost California delegates back," he was saying.

Will waved him away. "What's going on, Joe?"

"There was a leak from a staffer on the commission on base closings."

"What kind of a leak?"

"The commission is going to recommend that Castle Point remain open."

Will's jaw dropped. "I don't believe it."

"Believe it. George Kiel found out about it; that's why he promised Thad Morrison he'd keep the base open."

"And when did Thad Morrison find out about this?"

"I was telling him when California was called on to vote."

Tim was yelling. "We've got three more delegates back!"

"Tim tells me we've got five California delegates back, so far," Will said. "That means George can't win on this ballot."

"And more to come, I hope," Adams said. "I think the delegates from the Castle Point area wanted to make a point; they've voted as they promised their districts they would. Now, with this new information, they feel they can vote as they wish. Let's hope they wish you were the nominee."

"We've got twelve back!" Tim shouted. "We need two more to win."

A moment later it was over. The chairman spoke up. "The chair records fifty-four votes for Lee, none for Kiel! Senator Will Lee is nominated!" His last words were drowned out by the roar from the convention floor.

People were dancing around Will's suite, hugging and kissing. Hands clapped him on the back; women smeared him with lipstick; Kate, Peter, and Patricia Lee all embraced him.

So, Will," his mother said, "who's going to be your vice-presidential nominee?"

Someone came to Will with a phone. "It's George Kiel."

Will got everyone quiet, then picked up the phone.

"Congratulations, Will," Kiel said.

"Thank you, George. It was a tough fight; you ran a hell of a campaign."

"Will, I want to put everything I've got at your disposal. I've got about four million dollars in the kitty and a lease on an airplane that's a lot nicer than yours."

"Thank you, George, I'm very grateful to you."

There was a silence. Will decided to break it. "George, I'd be honored and very pleased if you would be my running mate."

"I'll give that very serious thought, Will. When can we talk more about it?"

"Let's have breakfast tomorrow morning at eight," Will said. "My place, this time?"

"Your place at eight," Kiel said, then hung up.

Will put the phone down.

Patricia Lee spoke up. "Did I just hear you offer George Kiel the job?"

"You did."

"But we didn't talk about this," Tim Coleman complained. "We should have discussed it."

"There was nothing to discuss," Will said. "George came within a hair of winning the nomination. It would be an insult to nearly half the delegates not to ask him. He's got as good an organization as we have; he's better plugged in with party officials all over the country than I am; he's an expert on foreign policy, and I'm not. And," he said, smiling, "he's got four million dollars and a very nice airplane to offer us."

"Well chosen!" Kitty shouted.

Somebody discovered a case of champagne, and corks began to pop.

Will's father sidled over. "You didn't say whether Kiel accepted," Billy Lee said to his son.

"We're having breakfast tomorrow morning," Will said.

"Be careful what you give him; he could be hard to handle."

"I'll keep that in mind," Will said.

Across town, Zeke and Rosa watched the insanity on the floor of the convention.

"Oh, I'm glad he won," Rosa said. "I like this Will Lee."

"I'm glad he won, too," Zeke replied, staring at the screen. "I can't wait to hear him give his acceptance speech on the podium tomorrow night."

51

Zeke waited in line with the other workers while the Secret Service ran each of them through the metal detectors. He wasn't worried until he saw the dogs. Two Labrador retrievers were coming down the line with their handlers, sniffing at everyone. Zeke shifted the box to his other hand to keep it as far away from them as possible. He'd never dealt with sniffer dogs, and he began looking around for the quickest way out of the building.

A dog passed him, sniffed at his clothes and his lunch box.

"Hold out the cardboard box," his handler said.

Zeke held out the box. His plan was to hit the man with his metal lunch box and run like hell. It wasn't much, but it was all he had. He had packaged the explosive into two zippered plastic bags, then scrubbed any explosives residue from his hands. After changing clothes he had sliced open a large chocolate cake he had bought, hollowed out the bottom, inserted the explosive, and re-placed the top. Now the dog was showing a great interest in his cardboard box.

"Set the box on the table and open it," the man said, and his hand was on his gun.

I have one more shot at this before running, Zeke thought. He set down the box and untied the string.

The agent opened the box and turned to his dog. "Rocky, we're not looking for chocolate cake here." He turned to Zeke. "This dog would do *anything* for chocolate. What's the cake for?"

"For the guys on my crew. It's their last day, and my girlfriend baked it for them."

"Okay," the man said, and turned to his next customer.

Sweating, but breathing easier, Zeke walked into the Coliseum with a pound of gelignite.

Will opened the door himself. George Kiel was standing there, dressed for golf. At the bottom of the path a passel of reporters stood, shouting questions at both of them.

"Come on in, George, and let's get away from the noise. You playing golf today?"

"At the Bel Air Country Club," Kiel said. "My clubs are in the car; you want to join us?"

"Wish I could, but it's a big day, and I've got a speech to write."

"You didn't already have it written, Will?" Kiel asked. "That shows a lack of confidence."

Will passed Kiel a tray of pastries. "It shows a

superstition about not anticipating too much. Have a seat."

The two men sat down at the table with their breakfast.

"Have you thought about running with me?" Will asked.

"I haven't thought about anything else," Kiel said. "I wasn't kidding about my health and about wanting to serve only four years."

"I'd rather have four years of your help than eight of a lot of other people's."

"Thanks, Will, I appreciate that."

"Tell me what your concerns are about running with me."

"I don't have any concerns at all about running; I look forward to it, in fact. My concern is that I don't want to be a wooden-Indian vice president."

"I don't want that, either," Will replied. "How do you see yourself operating in the vice presidency?"

"Two things," Kiel said. "I want to be a *deputy* president, as well as a vice president; I want to get the same briefings that you do, and I want unfettered access to you."

"All that goes without saying," Will said. "I wouldn't have it any other way."

"Good. The second thing is, I want to run foreign policy."

"Exactly what do you mean by running it?" Will asked. He had anticipated this, but he wanted to hear from Kiel.

"Will, I'm a lot more up on this than you are, just as you're a lot more up on domestic policy. I can help you a lot."

"I'm counting on it," Will replied. "How do you want to help?"

"I want to run foreign policy from top to bottom," Kiel said. "I want to choose the major appointees and give them their instructions."

"George, let's be perfectly clear on this," Will said. "The president runs foreign policy, and that's it. Of course, I'll want your advice on every move and on every appointment, but final judgment will have to rest with me. You know I can't delegate a major responsibility like foreign policy."

"Then I don't see how I can do it."

"You can do it, George. Tell you what, and this is just between you and me; I don't want to read about it in the papers: I'll give you a veto on the secretary of state appointment."

"Secretary of state and national security advisor," Kiel said.

"The national security advisor is more a member of the president's personal staff; I can't give you that. But I'll certainly want your opinion on my options for that post."

Kiel stared into his coffee.

"Come on, George; you're going to have to trust me."

"I suppose so," Kiel said.

"Listen, if you'd rather be secretary of state, I'll give you that."

Kiel shook his head. "No, I'd rather be over the secretary of state."

"And you will be."

"What if we disagree?"

"I'll bend over backward to see your point of view, but if there's a disagreement on a serious matter, I'll have to rely on my own judgment. It can't be any other way."

Kiel nodded. "All right; I don't guess I can get a better deal than that."

"Then let's announce it together," Will said, standing up. "One thing: I don't want you to say anything to anybody, except your wife, about serving only four years. First of all, you may change your mind. Second, I don't want a parade of other people lining up to go after the job in the second term."

"Okay," Kiel said. "Let's go."

The two men left the suite and walked down the path toward the waiting throng of press.

Zeke locked the cake in his locker and spun the cylinder on the combination lock. He was scheduled to work a double shift that day, most of it around the podium. He had arranged this so that the Secret Service, who already knew him, would be accustomed to his presence under the platform.

Will stepped up to the cluster of microphones that Kitty had set up. "Good morning," he said to the crowd of reporters. "A beautiful California morning." He waved a hand at the bright blue sky and the lush hotel gardens surrounding them. "You may have noticed that Senator George Kiel is standing by my side." Much laughter. "I'm delighted to tell you and the country that Senator Kiel has agreed to become my running mate in this election. His name will be placed in nomination at the convention tonight, and I trust he will be nominated.

"You all know of George's strengths in foreign policy. Before he became the Democratic leader in the Senate he was, for many years, chairman of the Senate Foreign Relations Committee, and he has had a hand in every important foreign-policy decision by every president, going back to Jimmy Carter and Ronald Reagan. His knowledge of people in government, the State Department, and academia who have credentials for foreign-policy work is unmatched, and I am going to rely heavily on him in choosing appointees— after we're elected. I promise you that George Kiel is going to be the most important vice president in this century. George, say a few words."

Kiel stepped up to the microphone. "Thank you, Will; I'm grateful for your confidence. I think you all know what an effort we're making to win back the Senate in this election, and I was certainly very interested in being the majority leader for a long time to come. But Will has offered me an opportunity that is even more important than being majority leader, and I am very happy to accept it. I have nothing but admiration for Will Lee and the way he has conducted himself in the Senate and as a candidate for the

Democratic nomination. I look forward to running with him."

Zeke closed the closet door behind him, took the cover off the voice-mail system, and began soldering. It took him less than ten minutes to run and conceal the wires. He replaced the plywood ceiling of the closet. Later in the day, it would take him even less time to place the explosives.

He began humming to himself, "Happy Days Are Here Again."

52

While the convention was nominating George Kiel for vice president, Zeke went to the employees' lounge and, after making sure that he was alone, opened his locker and removed the cake. Quickly, he dismembered it, put the gelignite and two detonators into his toolbox, and disposed of the remains of the cake in a nearby garbage can. Then he took the long walk to the front of the Coliseum, carrying his toolbox, and walked through the rear door under the platform. A Secret Service agent was on duty.

"What's up, Harry?" asked the agent, who knew him by sight.

"I've just got to run a final check on the sound system," Zeke replied. "We don't want any glitches during Lee's speech."

"Right," the agent said. "Go ahead."

Zeke walked toward the area under the podium, waving at another agent, who was guarding the front entrance to the area. He let himself into the electrical closet and went to work. He removed the screws from the ceiling he had built into the closet, set the gelignite on top of the plywood, and secured it in place with duct tape. Then he had only to connect the previously placed wires to the two detonators and stick them into the explosive, which had the consistency of modeling clay. He used two detonators, in case one might be defective. He screwed the plywood ceiling back into place and spent a moment checking the appearance of everything, then looked at his watch. Lee was scheduled to speak at nine o'clock, and it was 7:35. He closed his toolbox and left the closet.

"Everything okay?" the agent asked as Zeke departed the platform.

"Everything's just perfect," Zeke replied.

George Kiel, having been introduced to the convention, took the podium and made a rousing acceptance speech; then he introduced the vice president and stepped away from the podium.

Joe Adams stepped to the microphone amid thunderous applause. When he had finally quieted them, he began to speak. "Let me begin by telling you that if I had handpicked our candidates myself, the same two fellows would be on this platform tonight." More applause.

Zeke was already at Los Angeles International Airport. He parked his car in a dim corner of the long-term garage, removed his suitcase from the trunk, changed into a business suit, then found a bottle of Windex and a cloth and methodically sprayed and wiped every square inch of the Lexus, inside and out. Windex had been his friend at the Las Vegas apartment and at Rosa's house, and he had removed every trace of himself from both places. Now the car would be just as clean. He wiped the spray bottle clean, dropped it into the trunk with the cloth, and closed it with his elbow; then he picked up his suitcase and headed for the check-in counter.

On the way, he stopped in the shadows for a moment, removed an electric shaver from his bag, popped up the trimmer, and quickly shaved off his moustache. Then he put on a pair of horn-rimmed glasses. At the counter he presented his ticket, which he had bought at a travel agent's office the day before, then headed for the gate. He had plenty of time, so he checked in again, then took a seat at the bar across from his gate and ordered a scotch. Joe Adams was on the TV, and he had just begun his speech. He was running a little late and long, Zeke thought. His flight left at nine-thirty, and it was already ten minutes past. He had to make the call before he boarded, and it was going to be tight.

Joe Adams was winding up. "Now I present to you, and I say this with absolute certainty, the next president of the United States, Will Lee!"

Adams stepped back, and Will came forward. The crowd went wild. Will stood with Joe Adams as the cameras flashed and the crowd roared, then he waved George Kiel forward to join them.

The three men stood together on the podium and waved to the crowd.

Zeke stared at the television image. They had issued a last call for his flight, and he wanted Lee alone on the podium when he made the call, but why not take out the three of them all at once?

Under the platform, Hank Greenbaum, the crew foreman, stepped through the door and showed the agent in charge his ID badge. "Have you seen Harry Grant?" he asked. "He's one of my men, the one with the handlebar moustache."

"Yeah, he was in here, I don't know, maybe an hour ago, but I haven't seen him since."

"Funny," Greenbaum said, "I haven't been able to find him anywhere." He walked forward to the electrical closet and went inside. He picked up the wall-phone receiver, punched the button for the last line, and called the maintenance office. "This is Greenbaum," he said. "You seen anything of Harry Grant?"

"Last I heard of him, he was doing a final check on the sound system. I wanted to speak to him, too."

"Hang on a minute, and I'll look around for him," Greenbaum replied. He pressed the hold button and left the closet.

Zeke punched the number into his cell phone, staring at the TV screen and the three men. Busy signal. "What the hell?" he said aloud.

"Huh?" the man next to him said.

"Sorry," Zeke replied.

"Mr. Warren, Mr. Warren," a woman's voice said over a loudspeaker, "your flight has boarded and is about to depart. Please come to the boarding gate immediately."

Warren was the name on his ticket. Redialing the number, Zeke trotted toward the gate. Still busy. He walked down the ramp and into the airplane, redialing. Still busy.

"I'm sorry, sir," a flight attendant said, "you'll have to turn off your cell phone; FCC regulations."

Zeke punched off the phone and took his seat. "How soon can I use that?" he asked, pointing at the airphone on the bulkhead a few seats away.

"Not until we're at our cruising altitude and the seat-belt sign goes off," she replied.

"How long will that be?"

"We're pushing back now; shouldn't be too long."

Zeke buckled himself in, staring at the airphone.

Will stood alone on the podium. "My fellow Democrats," he said, "I am honored to accept your nomination."

The crowd roared.

Will quieted them and began his speech.

"Good evening, ladies and gentlemen; this is the first officer speaking; the captain is pretty busy. We're climbing through twenty-five thousand feet now, and we should be at our cruising altitude of thirty-three thousand feet shortly."

Relief swept over Zeke. He looked at his watch: 9:45. Lee should be right in the middle of his speech.

The first officer continued his spiel as Zeke stared at the airphone. He felt the airplane level off, and he looked up at the seat-belt sign, which was still on. The airplane began to buck and lurch.

"We're encountering some weather this evening," the first officer said, "so we'll be leaving the seat-belt sign on for a little longer, until things quiet down. We could be encountering some severe turbulence, so I must caution you to keep your seat belts tightly fastened until we're able to turn off the seat-belt light."

Zeke flagged down a flight attendant who was struggling up the aisle. "Miss, would you please hand me that telephone?" he asked, pointing at the airphone.

"I'm sorry," she replied, "but you'd need to place your credit card in the phone before the receiver will release, and I have to get to my own seat now; the turbulence is getting pretty bad."

Zeke fished a credit card out of his pocket. "Could you do it for me?"

"All right," she said, reaching for the card.

Zeke suddenly snatched it back. "Never mind," he said.

The woman went to her seat and buckled herself in.

He couldn't use a credit card. The name on it was Harry Grant, and the records would tell the cops which flight he had taken. "God damn it!" he spat.

"Sir," the woman next to him said sternly, "I know it's rough up here, but please watch your language!"

Zeke continued to swear, but only in his head.

Will wound up his speech and, once again, called Joe Adams and George Kiel to the podium to share in the ovation.

A little before two o'clock the following morning, a man named Walter Edmonds stood up in a bar on Melrose Avenue and, staggering a little, made his way to a nearby pay phone. He'd had too much to drink, and he already had one DUI on his driving record. He'd have to call his wife to come and get him, and she was not going to be happy about that.

He dropped a quarter into the phone and, bleary-eyed, began punching in numbers, hardly able to see the keypad. The phone began to ring. Suddenly a male voice said, "Welcome to the podium of the Democratic convention."

"What?" Edmonds said, outraged that he had gotten a wrong number. He reached into his pocket for another quarter, and as he did so, lost his balance, falling against the phone. His shoulder struck the keypad.

The Los Angeles Coliseum was lit only by emergency lighting at this time of night. The night watchman stopped in the high seats and inserted his key into the time clock. Before he could turn the key, a fireball rose from the platform at the other end of the building, and the shock wave in the enclosed space knocked him off his feet. He sat on the floor, his back against the wall, and tried to clear his head. His ears ached from the noise and the shock wave. Before he could get up, the sprinkler system came on, immediately soaking him. A moment later, from somewhere outside, he heard sirens, and they were coming his way.

53

The van drove slowly down the street, past the row of neat houses. The Secret Service agent in the front seat spotted the number first. "That's it," he said, "but keep going." He held his radio to his lips. "It's quiet at the house; the front door is open, but there's a screen door that might be latched. I want two vehicles in the alley behind the house; don't go in until you hear the word from me, and use maximum caution. No unnecessary radio traffic." He turned to the driver. "Make a U-turn and stop two doors short of the house." He buckled on his helmet and zipped up his flak jacket.

Sixteen men—four agents and twelve in the LAPD SWAT team—hit the house simultaneously from front and rear. They swarmed around the ground floor, kicking open doors. The agent led a group up the stairs. The two bedroom doors were open, and the agent could see a bare foot across the doorway to one.

"All clear!" someone shouted.

The agent went into the room and looked at the body of the naked woman. "I want an evidence team in here, and tell them to bring a rape kit. I want swabs from the woman." He looked around the bedroom. Except for the fact that there was a dead woman in the room and that the bed was bare of sheets, nothing seemed amiss.

The technician read from his notes: "The woman had sex, but I can't tell you even approximately when."

"I want semen samples for DNA."

"There aren't any," the tech said. "She was douched with something that may be window cleaner. The bedsheets were in the washing machine downstairs, still wet, reeking of bleach. This is one careful guy. We haven't been able to come up with a single fingerprint that doesn't belong to the woman."

"Shit!" the agent said.

Another agent came into the room. "Here's what we've got so far," he said, reading from a pad. "This Harry Grant rents an apartment in Vegas; it's empty and extremely clean. He has a bank account with less than a hundred dollars in it, a social security number, and two credit cards, and he owns a two-year-old Lexus ES300. Here are his driver's license and work ID photographs." He handed his chief the pictures.

The agent looked at them. "The big moustache will be the first to go, then he'll look like anybody. I want renderings of the photographs clean-shaven and bearded. My guess is his car is parked at a local airport, and it's just as clean as this house."

"The guy is a pro," the other agent said.

The chief shook his head. "Not just a pro, a fanatic. Run these photographs against our files on militias, white supremacist groups, antigovernment organizations. We've got to have *something* on him."

Will was lying in bed, spent and happy, having just made love to Kate. She was singing in the shower. He could not remember when he had felt so relaxed, so relieved, so unanxious. He flicked on the television.

". . . and the ATF is saying that the explosive used at the Coliseum was the same type that was stolen from a construction site less than a mile away. Police and the FBI are looking for this man." Two photographs of a sandy-haired man in his forties with a handlebar moustache flashed on the screen. "He is Harry Grant, of a Las Vegas address, who has been employed as a maintenance worker at the Los Angeles Coliseum. Police and Secret Service personnel raided the house where Grant rented a room early this morning. His landlady, Mrs. Rosa Rivera, forty-one, was found dead at the scene, having been strangled."

Coliseum? Will thought. *What was that about the Coliseum?*

Kate came into the room, wearing only a towel. "Why do you look so funny?" she asked.

"It's something about an explosion at the Coliseum," Will said, switching to MSNBC.

Anchorwoman Laurie Dhue came on. "Secret Service sources have told MSNBC that the explosives planted under the Democratic convention platform at the Los Angeles Coliseum were probably set to go off during the speeches last night, but somehow didn't detonate until the early hours of this morning. A Coliseum security guard was the only witness to the explosion."

Kate sat on the bed. "It's started," she said.

"Don't jump to conclusions," Will said, getting up.

"I will if I want to," she replied, staring at the television.

As he climbed into the shower, Will didn't doubt for a moment that he had been the target of the explosion.

Zeke got off the bus at a crossroads, and his son, Danny, was waiting for him in the pickup.

"Hey, Daddy," Danny said, kissing Zeke on the cheek.

"Hey, son," Zeke said, slapping the boy on the back.

"You want to go straight home?"

"That's good, but I won't be there long."

Danny put the truck into gear. "How'd your trip go?"

"Not so good," Zeke said.

The chief of Will's Secret Service detail sat across the coffee table, explaining what they knew. "We haven't been able to connect this man with any organization so far, but I have no doubt that he's a member of some group. He had a complete, verifiable identity established; that takes time and money, and Grant had no visible means of support, except a paper computer business."

"Do you know what flight he took last night?" Will asked.

"No. Half the people on airplanes are businessmen flying alone. We've run down every single person who bought a ticket with cash at the airport, but he was apparently too smart for that. We don't even know if he actually left the city. Leaving his car at the airport could have just been a decoy."

"Do you think he was the same man who was in Santa Fe?"

The agent nodded. "No doubt of it; he was registered at La Fonda under the Grant name. Our people are checking out the room, but it's been cleaned a couple of dozen times since he was there. The parking attendant at the hotel remembered his car."

"What's this about Santa Fe?" Kate demanded.

"There was a man on the roof of a hotel near the Plaza," Will said. "I didn't tell you about it, because it seemed so far-fetched."

"I don't want anything else kept from me," she said. "I hope that's perfectly clear."

Will nodded. "Is the airplane ready to leave?"

"It will be by the time we get to Van Nuys," the agent said. "We're putting you on the Kiel campaign airplane, which takes a longer runway than Santa Monica, and anyway, we now regard Santa Monica as insecure. Van Nuys has an eight-thousand-foot runway, which is plenty. We didn't think LAX was a good idea."

"All right," Will said. "We'd better get packed."

Zeke sat in his living room, drinking coffee, surrounded by the other men in his group. The women were in the kitchen.

"That's about it," he said. "Somebody used the telephone line I had the stuff connected to, so I kept getting busy signals. It's an incredibly long shot, but it happened."

"What made it go off in the middle of the night?" one of the men asked.

"I don't know. Maybe somebody called a wrong number. Who knows?"

"I like your technique," another man said. "We should use it again sometime."

"It didn't work," the first man pointed out.

"A fluke. I think it was brilliant, Zeke; it should have worked."

"Shoulda, woulda, coulda," Zeke said. "Next time, I'm going to have to use more direct means."

"That's gonna be dangerous, Zeke."

"I think it was Harry Truman who said that anybody could kill a president if he didn't mind dying himself. That goes for a candidate, too."

"Zeke, you're no good to us dead."

"Right now, I'm not much good to you alive, either," Zeke replied.

George Kiel's airplane was one of the new Boeing business jets. There were a bedroom and a shower aft, and an office adjacent. Up front there were seats for thirty-four staff and press. "Poor George," Kate said, settling into a comfortable armchair. "Now he'll have to fly in that fleapit you were using."

"You don't know George," Will said. "With his connections, he'll have something lined up in a hurry. I'll bet he was on the phone to Boeing before he made his acceptance speech."

The airplane was over Kansas on the flight to Washington when the news came that the president was dead. By the time they landed, the funeral had already been set for two days hence.

Will and Kate arrived at the house about dark.

"I'd hoped you could just rest while the Republicans hold their convention," Kate said.

"I'll rest," Will said. "The funeral is just one day."

Kate turned to the Secret Service detail chief. "I don't want my husband killed at that funeral," she said.

"Don't worry, Mrs. Lee," the man replied. "The senator's detail is of presidential proportions now, and that funeral is going to have the tightest security in the history of the world."

"You'd better be right," Kate replied.

54

Will and Kate were filing into the National Cathedral for the president's funeral. The organ was playing a prelude as the huge crowd moved toward the pews, and the echo of their murmurs mixed with the music to create a somber atmosphere. They were headed toward the seats reserved for senators when Will felt a hand on his shoulder and turned to find Freddie Wallace behind him.

"Morning, Will," the senator drawled. "A sad day."

"Yes, it is, Freddie. How are you?"

Wallace grinned a little. "I've been worse," he said. "I haven't had a chance to congratulate you on your nomination. Good going, boy."

"Thank you, Freddie," Will replied.

"Mind if I join you?" Wallace asked, sliding into a pew beside Will. "Good morning, Kate," he said, leaning forward to speak to her.

Kate gave him a tight little smile, then turned her attention to the pulpit.

"Kate's a little chilly this morning, isn't she?" Wallace said.

"It's a chilly time," Will said.

"Anything I can do to help you in the election?" Wallace asked.

Will turned and looked at him, astonished. "Freddie, that's quite an offer," he said. "Are you forgetting your party affiliation?"

"Friendship is more important than politics, son. Ben Carr and I were as close as you can get, and I've always admired you, helped you when I could, behind the scenes, of course."

"That's very generous of you, Freddie," Will said, not believing any of it. "I'll tell you what you could do that would be good for all of us."

"You name it, boy."

"Help Joe, instead of me. He's got precious little time left to serve, and I know he'd like to leave some substantive legislation behind. Help him get his package through."

"As much as I love Joe, Will, there's some pernicious stuff in that program."

"It was put together with serious consultation with Republicans, yourself among them."

Wallace shook his head. "I don't know, Will."

"Well, then, Freddie," Will admonished gently, "the very least you can do for him is to stop spreading nasty rumors about him."

Wallace looked shocked. "I have no idea what you're talking about."

"Freddie, leave him alone. Let him finish his term and retire gracefully."

"Will, I never said a word . . ."

"Listen to me, Freddie," Will said, and his voice was no longer gentle. "The odds are at least fair that I'm going to be elected in November. I'd like to think that, if I'm president of the United States, you and I could maintain the same warm relationship we've always had, rather than something more . . . contentious."

Wallace's eyes narrowed. "Are you threatening me, boy?"

Will lifted his eyes from the program in his hand and turned to face Wallace.

"Yes, Freddie, I am. Joe is my friend; if you want me for an enemy, then you have only to harm him."

Wallace was saved from replying by a sudden burst of organ music.

"Oh, look," Will said, glancing at the program. "The first hymn is one of my favorites: 'Standing on the Promises.'"

The audience plunged haphazardly into the rousing old Baptist hymn, and both men sang along without benefit of hymnbook.

At the reception for members of Congress that followed at the White House, Will was suddenly presented with a new attitude toward him from people of both parties; he was being treated more like a president than a senator. When it was his turn to present his condolences to the first widow in the reception line, he found himself standing next to Howard Efton. After they had both done their duty, Efton pulled him over to a window of the East Room.

"Congratulations on your nomination, Will," Efton said, shaking hands.

"And good luck to you at your convention, Eft. Actually, it looks as though you won't need much in the way of luck. You seem to have it just about sewn up."

"Well, we'll see," Efton said. "Will, I've been hearing disturbing rumors about Joe Adams."

"I've heard about those rumors," Will replied.

"Where are you in all this?"

"I'm between Joe and anyone who wants to hurt him," Will said.

"I hear at least one columnist has the story."

"It would be a grave error for any journalist to publish an unsubstantiated rumor of that sort, and it would be an even graver error for any public figure to lend credence to it."

"You could be right."

"Eft, we haven't gotten over the impeachment episode yet, and this business could have the effect of making things infinitely worse between the parties. I, for one, would take the same umbrage to some published report that I would to an attack on my wife." *Might as well kill two birds with one well-thrown stone*, Will thought.

"I'll do everything I can to see that neither of those things happens," Efton said.

"I'd appreciate that."

Efton smiled. "Of course, anything else is fair game."

Will smiled back. "I think we should both choose our weapons wisely, lest they cut both ways."

"That's good advice, Will," Efton said. "Now, we'd better get back to the ladies."

The two men returned to their wives, who were chatting woodenly. Will took Kate's elbow, and whispered. "Rumors about Joe are rife," he said. "I've done what I can to tamp them down."

"I've just heard that Joe is going to announce tomorrow that Jim Browner is his choice for VP. Maybe that will take some of the strain off the situation."

"I hope so," Will said, "but I'm not going to count on it."

55

Zeke logged on to the Internet and did a search for Senator Will Lee. Immediately, he found the campaign web site and, shortly, had the senator's travel schedule, which the site said was updated daily. He printed the schedule and logged off.

Later, at Harv's house, he met with his group. "Okay," he said, "I've got the senator's travel schedule for the rest of the campaign."

"Won't it change from time to time?" one of the men asked.

"Sure. So what I want to do is to pick an event that won't be changed, something the senator can't afford to miss."

"Any ideas?" Harv asked.

"The senator and Efton are debating three times," Zeke said. "I reckon the last one is the most important, and it's an event the senator wouldn't miss for anything. It's a week before the election."

"Where?"

Zeke permitted himself a small smile. "At Ford's Theatre."

Everybody burst out laughing.

"I love it!" Harv shouted, and everybody laughed again.

Finally, they quieted down. "How you want to do this?" Harv asked.

"I want to shoot him," Zeke replied. "From somewhere in the theater."

"It has a certain poetry about it."

"How you going to penetrate?" a man asked.

"I don't think the maintenance-worker thing will work again after L.A.," Zeke said. "I've thought about this, and I need an identity that's unlikely to be questioned at all. Anybody got any ideas?"

"Catholic priest?" somebody suggested.

"I don't think I know enough about being Catholic to fool anybody I got into a conversation with."

Harv leaned back in his chair. "So what do you know about?" he asked.

"Electrical, carpentry, construction, that's about it."

"You know about army," Harv said. "We all do."

"Good point," Zeke said. "Maybe I could move around in uniform without getting questioned too closely."

Harv turned to the youngest man in the group. "Benny, you're our hacker. Have you ever broken into a Pentagon computer?"

Benny nodded. "Yeah, but you can't do it repeatedly, and you have to do it from a remote location, not from home. The chances are too good of being backtracked."

"How about if you checked into a motel with a computer. Could you do it from somewhere like that?"

"What sort of files?"

"Personnel. I reckon we need an identity for Zeke that's so good it could only be real."

"I'll have a shot at it," Benny said.

"What do you need?"

"Nothing I haven't already got. I'll take a laptop, a modem, and a printer."

"You'll need an anonymous car with plates that can't be traced back to us."

"Yeah, I guess so."

"What will I be looking for?"

"We need a real army officer who's serving in the D.C. area—Virginia, Maryland, the Pentagon, maybe. He ought to be about Zeke's age, and it wouldn't hurt if they shared a general physical description. We'll need his jacket, basically, his personnel file."

"Okay, I'll have a shot at that. How soon?"

"As soon as possible; can you start today?"

"Sure. I'll steal a car this afternoon."

"Nah, too risky; buy one, something very ordinary."

"Okay."

Zeke spoke up. "Harv, you were a sergeant major; what else am I going to need?"

"An ID card," Harv replied. "I know a guy who can make you one. Then you'll need orders that will give you some freedom of movement, if you're questioned. I can cut those on my own computer; nothing to it."

"What about uniforms?" Zeke asked.

"Once we get you the ID card, you can walk onto any army base in the country, go to the PX, and buy whatever you want. We can pick up some insignia and ribbons at a gun show."

"What sort of rank?"

"Light colonel, maybe bird colonel. High enough that nobody will give you a hard time, but not a general; too many of them know each other. There's lots of colonels in the D.C. area. We'll put a chicken on your shoulder."

"I never got past buck sergeant," Zeke said. "Chicken colonel might be nice."

"You need any weapons?"

Zeke shook his head. "I've still got the Czech sniper rifle, and I'll load some special ammo, something that'll take his head off."

"Good. Okay, let's get to work on this."

Zeke was out back, working with the log splitter. He enjoyed the effort, and the growing pile of logs was a satisfying sight. Danny stacked them against the house as they came out of the splitter. When they were done, Zeke sat down on a bench and looked out across the mountains. It was a wonderful view.

Danny came and sat down beside him. "Daddy, I know I'm not supposed to ask about it, but I get the feeling you're leaving again soon."

"That's right, son," Zeke said. "And it's for your own good and your mother's and your sisters' good that you don't know too much."

"That's okay; I understand."

This is a good moment for it, Zeke thought. "Listen, son, there's a real good chance I won't be coming back from this one."

"Is it as dangerous as that?" Danny asked.

Zeke nodded. "I'm afraid there just isn't any other way to do it. I'm going to have to put myself on the line for this one."

"If you don't come back, will we know what happened?"

"Yeah, I expect you will. I don't think they'll be able to trace me back here, though; I don't think you'll be bothered."

"What do you want me to do, if you don't come back?"

"Run the place, take care of your mother and your sisters. You can always go to Harv for advice."

Danny nodded. "What about the movement? You've never let me have anything to do with that."

"You're not old enough to be of much use yet, Danny. It'll be all you can do to manage the place. After the girls are grown, it might be different. I'll tell Harv how I feel about this; he'll respect my wishes."

"Daddy, I was thinking I might like to go to college."

"What for?" Zeke asked sharply. "Haven't I taught you everything you need to know?"

"Sure, Daddy, but, you know, I thought it might be good to improve my mind. Later on, I'd like to travel some, see the world. I even thought about the navy."

"Let me tell you something, boy," Zeke said. "This country around here is all you need to know about. As long as you can run this place and take care of your family, you'll be a man, and college won't make you any better. Neither will the navy." Danny nodded, but Zeke wasn't sure he'd made a dent in that hard head. The boy had an independent streak.

"Okay, Daddy," Danny said, rising from the bench. "Whatever you say. You know I'll take care of the family and the place."

Zeke stood up. "Good man," he said, clapping the boy on the back. Zeke watched as he walked toward the barn. *Jesus,* he thought, *I'd sure like to be around to see how he turns out.*

56

Will stared out the window of the Boeing at the midwestern landscape and reflected on the past weeks. The United States Senate had met two days after the president's funeral and confirmed Joe Adams's nomination of Senator James A. Browner as vice president. A week later, the Republican National Convention had nominated Representative Howard Efton as its presidential candidate and Governor Robert Mallon of Arizona as its candidate for vice president. As a result of the attempt on Will's life, the security at the Republican convention was unprecedented, and Will's Secret Service detachment had tripled in size. Now there were four agents attendant on his person at all times, while others worked the crowds and did advance planning for the campaign. This had cramped Will's campaign's ability to make spontaneous changes in his schedule, and, in spite of the best efforts of the Secret Service, Will was beginning to find the agents' constant presence oppressive. Kate was being driven to and from work by agents, as well.

Now Will convened a meeting of his traveling staff around the conference table in the big jet. Moss Mallet, the campaign's pollster, had joined them at Kansas City, and they were bound for Chicago and the campaign's second debate. Tim Coleman and Kitty Conroy sat down.

"I'm dying to hear this, Moss," Tim said.

"Me, too," Will chipped in.

"Okay," Moss said, "here it is: Bottom line, we're in some trouble."

"Be specific," Will said.

"Specifically, although we're only a point or two behind, nationally, we've got the potential of a sizable deficit in electoral votes. Efton could win the popular vote very narrowly and still drub us in the electoral college."

"Where are the big electoral deficits?" Will asked.

"Illinois and California. We've got to win them both, or lose the election. It's as simple as that."

"Thank God the debate is in Chicago," Kitty said. "If you do well there, that could be a big, big help. Remember how the first debate helped us in the South."

"Yeah," Will replied, "and I'm beginning to wish the third debate were in California."

"That would be nice," Moss said. "I don't suppose we could arrange that."

"Not a chance," Kitty replied. "We're committed to the League of Women Voters for the Washington debate, and so is Efton. It's been hard enough to pin him down to these debates, without starting to ask for changes now."

The phone on the conference table rang, and Tim picked it up. "It's Sam Meriwether," he said, handing the phone to Will.

Will took the phone. "And how's my campaign director?" he asked. "Happy as a clam, I hope."

"Not exactly," Meriwether said. His voice was a little scratchy on the airphone.

"What's up?"

"Two things: First, Larry Eugene Moody's appeal has been rejected by the Supreme Court. He's scheduled to die on the Saturday night before the Tuesday election."

"And how do you think that's going to hurt us?" Will asked.

"I don't know that it's going to; it's just a distraction. The last debate is the night before the execution, and Efton is bound to try to use it against you in some way."

"Eft is a big supporter of the death penalty," Will replied. "He can't use this against me without coming off as a hypocrite."

"He's bound to harp on your competence at the trial," Sam said. "You'd better be ready for that."

"All right, we'll be ready for it. You said two things; what else is happening?"

"Eft has backed out of the Chicago debate."

"What?"

"He says he's too busy campaigning."

"Well, that's pretty lame. I'll give him hell about it."

"I think his people are prepared for that, or they wouldn't have pulled him out of the debate."

"Well, shit!" Will said. "Anything else?"

"Nope; I wish I had some good news."

"See you later, Sam." Will hung up the phone.

"What?" Tim asked.

"Eft has backed out of the Chicago debate."

Sounds of anger and outrage.

"I'll call a press conference at the airport," Kitty said. "We'll blow him out of the water."

"I think he's ready for that," Will said. "I guess we did too well in the Atlanta debate."

"He's scared," Kitty said.

"No," Moss interjected, "he's smart. He's obviously run the numbers and concluded that he'll lose fewer votes by pulling out than by debating you and seeming to lose."

"I think you're right," Will said, "and I think Eft is right, too."

"If that's the case, what's to prevent him from backing out of the Washington debate?" Tim asked.

Nobody spoke.

"Do you really think he'd risk doing that?" Kitty asked nobody in particular.

"He would," Moss said, "if his numbers supported the decision."

"We can't let him get out of the Washington debate," Kitty said. "We need that one bad."

"I have to agree," Moss said, "but we can't force him to appear."

Kitty suddenly brightened. "Maybe we can. Maybe we can force him to appear in Chicago, too."

"You going to put a gun to his head?" Moss asked.

"In a manner of speaking. Let's just go on with the Chicago debate."

Tim spoke up. "You mean have the senator debate an empty chair? That's kind of hollow, isn't it?"

"No, I mean a real debate—well, *nearly* real."

"You mean debate a substitute? Hire an actor to play Eft?"

"No, I mean have Eft play Eft."

"What are you talking about, Kitty?" Will asked.

"I mean, we go right ahead as planned. We show up at the hall, and we rent a really big TV set and put it on the stage with you. Then we put together a series of Eft's statements during the campaign, and play them back as his part of the debate. Then you answer them."

Will's eyebrows went up. "Debate a TV set?"

"It'll get a lot of play," Kitty said, "and, of course, you'd have the advantage of knowing what Eft is going to say."

"The networks would never give us the time for a one-sided debate," Will said, "and I don't want to see Eft's clips in advance, not that that would change their minds."

"Then we'll buy it," Kitty said, "and quick, since the networks already have it scheduled. And, if we can make this work against Eft, he won't dare back out of the Washington debate."

"I think it's a brilliant idea," Moss said. "It has

the additional advantage of making Eft look like a fool for backing out."

"Have we got the money to buy the time?" Will asked Tim.

"We'd have to cancel a lot of other television time," Tim replied. "Unless you and Sam can raise a lot more money in a hurry. And it only makes sense to buy one network, not all three. All the others will pick up excerpts for their newscasts."

"How much airtime do we have to buy?" Will asked.

"They've scheduled ninety minutes," Kitty said, "but let's buy only thirty. I don't think anybody would sit still for an hour and a half to watch you debate a TV set, but they would for half an hour."

"The debate is scheduled for the day after tomorrow," Will pointed out. "Have you got enough time to assemble the tape clips of Eft?"

"It'll be tight, but we can do it."

"Call Tom Black and get him on it, too," Will said. "Get him to Chicago, if necessary."

Kitty picked up the phone and started dialing.

"Was that all Sam had to say?" Tim asked.

"Well, no," Will replied. "Larry Moody is going to die in the electric chair three days before the election. The Supreme Court turned down his appeal."

"Oh, shit," Tim said.

"We need to think about how this can hurt us," Will said. "I'm not really sure that it will. Sam thinks Eft will try to find a way to use it against me in the Washington debate."

"We'll be ready for that," Tim said. "But there's something else I'm not sure we can be ready for."

"What's that?" Will asked.

"Charlene Joiner," Tim said.

"I hadn't thought about Charlene," Will admitted. "What do you think she'll do?"

"God only knows, but you know how hot she is to save Moody's life. I have a feeling it could be noisy. I'm not sure how we can plan for that."

"Neither am I," Will said.

57

Zeke Tennant was driving north through Virginia toward Washington when flashing lights popped on in his rearview mirror. He pulled the Ford Taurus over to the shoulder of the interstate and watched in his side mirror as a state trooper approached.

Zeke took a couple of deep breaths and lowered the window. His weapons were in the trunk; he'd have to handle this with his hands, if it came to that. "Morning," he said.

"Good morning, Colonel," the trooper replied, seeing the eagles on the collar of Zeke's starched and pressed camouflage fatigues. "Can I see your license, registration, and proof of insurance, please?"

"Sure," Zeke replied. He dug his license out of a pocket and reached into the glove compartment for the other documents. He handed them over. "Mind if I get out?" he asked. "I'd like to stretch my legs." He couldn't handle the man while sitting in the car.

The trooper looked at him carefully, then at his license. "Go ahead, Colonel."

Zeke opened the door, got out, and made a show of stretching.

"Come back here and take a look at something," the trooper said, beckoning him toward the rear of the car.

Zeke followed him.

The trooper pointed at the place where the license plate should be. "See the problem?"

Zeke grimaced. "Damn dealer," he said. "I only bought the car this morning."

"Maybe the plate is in the trunk," the trooper said. "Shall we take a look?"

The sniper's rifle was in the trunk, and Zeke had no intention of opening it. "Sure; let me get the keys," he said, walking back toward the driver's door. He was about to kick back at the trooper when he saw a brown envelope lying on the backseat. "This must be it," he said. He opened the door, retrieved the envelope, and took out the plate. "I thought they had put it on the car."

"You'd better put it on now," the trooper said.

"I don't have any tools; I'll stop at the next service station and get it done." He wanted to get away from this guy before he was recognized.

"I've got a screwdriver in the car," the trooper said. "Just a minute." He walked back to his patrol car, got in, and began looking for something then he picked up a microphone and began speaking into it.

Zeke walked slowly toward the patrol car; he'd

move as the trooper got out. Then a hand came out of the car with a screwdriver in it.

"Here you go," he said. "Be with you in a minute; I've got a radio call."

He's recognized me, Zeke thought as he walked toward the rear of his car. He knelt and began removing the screws from the empty license-plate frame. In a moment, he had the plate attached, and as he rose, the trooper approached. Zeke was ready for the fight.

"Sorry to trouble you about that, Colonel," the trooper said, "but somebody else would have stopped you eventually." His hand came toward Zeke. "Can I have my screwdriver back?"

"Oh, sure," Zeke replied. "And thanks for letting me know about the plate."

"Not at all," the trooper said. "Drive carefully."

Zeke got back into the car, sweating. "Fucking car salesman," he muttered to himself. "I damn near killed that trooper."

Zeke crossed the Potomac and drove to the Fairfax Hotel, where he had booked a room. He changed into his first-class uniform, then enjoyed a good lunch in the Jockey Club restaurant. When he had finished and signed the check, he went to the concierge's desk.

"Good afternoon, Colonel Waldron," the man said, glancing at the name tag on his uniform. "How can I help you?"

"I'm interested in Ford's Theatre, where Abraham Lincoln was assassinated," Zeke replied.

The concierge dug out a brochure. "Of course.

They have tours there twice a day; you can still make the afternoon one." He gave Zeke a map of the city and showed him how to get to the theater.

"Thanks very much," Zeke said. He went to the front door and asked the doorman for his car. He found the theater, on 10th Street NW, and parked the car, removing the briefcase containing the sniper's rifle from the trunk. He arrived in the lobby just as the tour was starting.

"Good afternoon," the elderly lady who was the tour guide began, "and welcome to Ford's Theatre. Before we start the tour, I'd like to give you a little of the rather odd history of the building. The theater opened its doors in 1862, having been converted from a former Baptist church. Some of the church members were disturbed that such a secular use was being made of what had been a holy building, and someone predicted that no good would come of it. The theater, which was originally the Athenaeum, burned to the ground within a few months.

"Mr. John T. Ford, who owned the theater, rebuilt it, named it after himself, and reopened the doors on August 27, 1863. After the assassination of Mr. Lincoln, the War Department closed the theater with the intention of never reopening it. The government bought the property and turned it into a warehouse. In 1893 the upper floors of the building collapsed, and twenty-two government employees were killed and many others injured. The building was again rebuilt and used as a warehouse.

"It was not until the nineteen-fifties that Congress appropriated the funds to restore the theater, and in 1968, it finally became a theater again. Now, if you'll follow me, I'll show you the box where Mr. Lincoln was shot, then we'll go backstage, after which you can see the little museum in the basement. Then you may wish to visit the Peterson House, across the street, where Mr. Lincoln died of his injuries."

The woman led the little group of people upstairs. Zeke hung back at the rear and allowed the group to leave him behind. He walked back to the rear of the theater, checking sight lines, and then he saw a small sign pointing up another flight of stairs. It read PROJECTION BOOTH. He followed the stairs and came to a door, which was ajar. Across the little hallway was a men's room.

He pushed the projection-room door open and found a light switch. Two large 35mm projectors filled most of the room. There was also a table with two cranks mounted for rewinding reels, and next to the projector was a single theater seat, where the projectionist could sit and watch a movie through his own window. Zeke looked carefully at the ceiling and found a large air-conditioning duct. He stood on a chair, took out a Swiss Army knife, and unfolded a screwdriver blade. In a moment he had the grating off; then he took the briefcase and slid it into the duct, where it fit very nicely. He replaced the grate, switched off the light, and left the room. As he departed, he noted a ladder fixed to the wall. He climbed and pushed open a trapdoor in the ceiling. He stuck his head up and looked around the roof. Maybe he wouldn't have to die after all.

He rejoined the group, which was just leaving Lincoln's box.

"Oh, did we lose you?" the guide asked.

"I was just looking for the men's room," he replied. As the group walked back toward the stairs, Zeke stepped into Lincoln's box and stood, looking over the theater. John Wilkes Booth, he knew, had slipped into the box as Lincoln watched a performance of a comedy, *Our American Cousin*. He had crept behind Lincoln and fired a single bullet into the back of his head from close range.

Soon, Zeke mused, he would add another interesting page to the history of Ford's Theatre. He'd give the tour guides something new to talk about.

58

THE WILL & EFT SHOW
Part Two
By our political editor

Last night, a national audience was treated to the second of two debates between the presidential candidates, but with a difference. This time, Representative Howard "Eft" Efton didn't show. Well, not exactly, anyway. Mr. Efton, after taking a bit of a drubbing in the Atlanta debate three weeks ago, backed out, citing a campaign schedule that was too busy to include the city of Chicago, his advisors having apparently told him that he had less to lose from canceling than from showing up.

But Senator Will Lee seems to have gotten better advice from his people. Not only did he show up, he dragged Eft Efton in by the scruff of the neck, as it were, and debated him whether he liked it or not. The audience arrived for the telecast to find a big-screen TV set up on one side of the stage (Efton's), and a lectern on the other (Lee's). A moderator introduced both candidates, and the debate began. Lee's staff had assembled a series of Efton's statements from campaign appearances, speeches on the House floor, and from Efton's acceptance speech at the Republican convention. When Efton was called on to speak, he appeared on the TV screen and made his statement; then Senator Lee was allowed to rebut. When the process was reversed, Efton clips were chosen to state the opposite position.

But if the audience was surprised by this turn of events, the biggest surprise came in the way this spectacle was conducted. The Lee campaign could have chosen Efton clips to make him look bad or to set him up for Lee's punch lines, but they didn't do that. Instead, they treated the Republican candidate respectfully, showing clips that Efton might have chosen himself. The result was not just a political stunt, but something very close to a real debate. Furthermore, the Lee staff issued a statement claiming that Senator Lee had not been told in advance which Efton clips would be used, so that his responses would be spontaneous.

Although Efton himself had no comment on any of this, his advisors were incensed. "This just shows how low Will Lee will stoop to win political points. This was an unethical, unfair, and un-American carnival sideshow," Efton's campaign manager said to reporters, conveniently ignoring the fact that Efton could have made it fair simply by showing up, as he had promised to do.

Who won? Far be it from me to offer an opinion, but an unscientific telephone call-in poll on the eleven o'clock news gave Lee the nod by a twenty-point margin. We'll have to wait a day or two for the national pollsters to do their work and tell us how much Lee really benefited, if at all.

But one thing Will Lee seems to have accomplished is to pretty much guarantee that Eft Efton will not duck out of the final debate from Ford's Theatre in Washington next week. And that may have been his intention all along.

Kitty put down the newspaper, from which she had been reading aloud. "And what's more," she said, grinning, "we've pulled in more than a dozen editorials from major newspapers around the country, saying pretty much the same thing."

Will smiled and sipped his coffee. "You're a very smart woman, Kitty," he said.

"We're redoing the schedule for the last week," Tim Coleman said. "All your appearances are going to be in Illinois and California, with one or two others on the way to or from. It's driving the Secret Service advance men crazy, but they're getting with the program."

Will turned to Moss, his pollster. "You think this is the right thing to do, then?"

"Will, it's the *only* thing to do. My newest numbers project that Efton can win if he takes either Illinois or California, but for you to win, you have to take both."

Will shrugged. "Let's do it, then."

Zeke was at the office of the League of Women Voters two hours before it opened, and a line had already formed. He cursed himself for not getting up earlier. His plan was all worked out, but in order to make it happen, he had to get inside the theater on the night of the debate, and that meant getting a ticket.

The doors opened, and the line inched forward. Finally, there was only one person ahead of him, a small woman with a child in tow.

"This is the absolutely last one?" she asked, holding aloft the ticket.

"The very last," the woman behind the counter responded. "You're very lucky."

"But what about my husband?" the woman demanded. "My husband has to be there, too."

"I'm sorry, ma'am," the woman replied, "but you're holding the very last ticket available to the public. The rest have already been issued to the two campaigns and the press."

Zeke wanted to strangle the woman and take her ticket.

"Why does this always happen to me?" the woman wailed.

"I don't know," the woman behind the counter said. "Do you want it, or not?"

The woman turned and faced Zeke. "Here, soldier," she said, holding out the ticket. "You take it."

Zeke accepted the ticket with a big smile.

"Congratulations, Colonel," the woman behind the counter said. "Now if you'll just step over there and give the Secret Service agent some information." She pointed to a man behind the desk.

Zeke walked over. "The lady told me to see you," he said to the man.

"Right," the agent replied. "I'll need your name, your date of birth, and your social security number. You'd better give me your military serial number, too."

Zeke was happy to give the man all of that.

59

As the Boeing set down at Van Nuys airport, Will braced himself against the shower wall. There was something very strange, he thought, about a shower that moved around. Plumbing was supposed to be in a fixed position. As the airplane taxied toward the FBO, Will got into trousers and a shirt and toweled his hair as dry as he could get it. There was a knock at his cabin door. "Come in."

Tim Coleman walked in. "Senator, we've got a little problem," he said.

"How little?"

"I'm not sure. Charlene Joiner is standing at the bottom of the boarding steps, and she insists on seeing you."

Will winced. "Tell the Secret Service to shoot her."

"I'd like nothing better, but I think you'll have to let her on board."

"And let her be photographed here?"

"She's already been photographed," Tim said.

"There's the usual media greeting party outside; she's chatting them up and getting interviewed now."

Will thought for a moment. "All right, get all the traveling press off the airplane, then show her into the office area. After three minutes, interrupt us with the greatest possible urgency, and get me off the airplane. Tell the crew to keep her on until we've driven away and the press has followed us."

"Got it," Tim replied, then left.

Will was tying his necktie when Charlene arrived, so she was unable to embrace him. She looked sensational in a tailored suit that still managed to show a considerable amount of creamy cleavage. "Hi, there," Will said. "What brings you to Van Nuys? It's a long way from Malibu."

"Will, I've got to talk to you," she said, leaning against a desk and giving him a better view of the cleavage.

"Better hurry; I've got to be out of here in just a minute. I've got sixteen campaign stops in the L.A. area before noon tomorrow, and I have to be back in Washington for the debate tomorrow night."

"It's about Larry Moody."

He'd thought it would be. "Oh?"

"His appeal has been turned down by the Supreme Court."

"Oh? They didn't think I was incompetent?"

"Apparently not. Now Larry's only hope of living is a commutation of his death sentence to life by the governor of Georgia."

"Hmmm," Will said.

"I've got a plan to get the governor to change his mind," Charlene said, "but I need your help."

"Charlene," Will said, getting into his jacket, "Bill Mackey is a Republican; I have zero influence with him."

"Just call him, Will; it might help."

"Charlene, if I get elected, Bill Mackey is going to take the greatest delight in appointing someone I despise to my Senate seat, possibly even himself. He and I have absolutely nothing to say to each other."

Charlene put her hands on her knees and pushed her shoulders forward, turning what had been cleavage into an inspiring view of her breasts. "Will, I read that there's a bed on this airplane; any truth to that?" She kept her chin down and raised her eyes to his, evoking in Will a memory of a photograph of Grace Kelly with John F. Kennedy many years before.

"Ah, now." Will laughed. "*That* could work."

"Huh?"

"That look, that angle on the boobs, that invitation. Bill Mackey reputedly has a Clintonesque weakness for women, and he's not accustomed to encountering many as beautiful as you. That's your best shot, Charlene, believe me."

Tim Coleman burst into the office. "Senator, you've got to leave right now! The Secret Service say there's some sort of threat against you!"

"Good God!" Will said. "I'm sorry, Charlene, but I have to go. You stay aboard the airplane until we're gone, and the crew says it's okay to leave; I don't want you to get shot at. Bye." He sprinted up the aisle, and Tim closed in behind him, leaving Charlene staring after them.

Will dived into the car. "Very good, Tim," he said. "Or was there really a threat?"

"The threat is still on the airplane," Tim said as the motorcade sped away.

60

THE VIEW FROM HERE
By Hogan Parks

It's been one hell of a run. Not since the Nixon-Humphrey contest in '68 has a presidential race been so tight. As we come down to the final of the three campaign debates (well, two and a half) tonight, Howard "Eft" Efton still seems to have a razor-thin margin, but it could go either way.

My sources in both campaigns agree that the race is going to be won or lost in Illinois and California. For some weeks it has been clear to pollsters that either state could give Efton the margin of victory, while Lee would need to win both, but since Efton stumbled by pulling out of the Chicago debate, and Lee so masterfully capitalized on his nonappearance, Illinois seems to have shifted narrowly in Lee's favor. Which means that California, with its fifty-four electoral votes, is now the 400-pound gorilla in this race.

If any further evidence of that fact were

necessary, one need only look at the campaign schedules of the two opponents. Neither has drawn a breath outside California for the past four days.

Perhaps the most interesting aspect of this race is how Eft Efton, at a time when the Democrats seem likely to win at least the House, and maybe the Senate, has managed to run so strongly nationally. He has done it by seeming less a Republican than a centrist independent, co-opting Democratic positions wherever he could and downplaying the traditional Republican rhetoric on tax cuts and abortion.

Efton has touted a plan to save Social Security that is almost indistinguishable from one proposed by the Democrats more than a year ago; he has rejected an across-the-board tax cut and opted, instead, for targeted reductions, mostly to the middle class; he's come out for new expenditures on education, although he wants school districts to spend it as they see fit, instead of being made to use the money to build and repair schools. And, most un-Eft-like, he has restrained himself from personal attacks on Lee and, especially, on Lee's wife, an important CIA official, something voters seem to appreciate.

Lee, whose political positions have often been undercut by Efton's sidestep toward the center, has chosen to campaign almost as though Efton didn't exist, touting his New Center as the way to go for the 21st century and ignoring Efton's attempts to join him in the middle of the road. Lee's great strength has been his personal charm, which, although it falls short of the kind of animal magnetism Bill Clinton projected, has done much to make him stick in the minds of voters. He has also proved an agile wiggler. When some right-wing Republicans tried to hang movie diva Charlene Joiner around his neck like a latter-day Gennifer Flowers, he managed to tap-dance his way around their insinuations by the simple device of being innocent of the charges, except for a single dalliance when they were both single. I'm told there is even some polling evidence to indicate that white males' opinion of Lee was lifted by the fact that he once slept with someone who is now a movie star.

All of which brings us back to Ford's Theatre tonight and the debate that Lee supporters hope will give him the final push he needs, especially in California, to edge past Efton and into the presidency. Look for Efton to give us more of the same, and for Lee, perhaps, to inject some fireworks into the proceedings. And look for both to offer some special incentives for California voters.

Kitty put down the *Washington Post.* "Well, that's depressingly close to the truth, isn't it?"

"We can always rely on Hogan Parks to state the obvious, can't we?" Will sighed. "Now let's get back to work on these debating points. We either blow Eft out of the water tonight, or we sink trying."

Charlene Joiner got off the Centurion Studios G-V jet at Atlanta's DeKalb Peachtree airport, and, unspotted by the press, got into a waiting limousine. "Take me to the governor's mansion," she said to the driver.

61

Zeke prepared carefully. First, he dressed in civilian clothing and went out and bought a car, a late-model Toyota Camry, metallic beige in color, using another well-prepared identity. He parked it near Ford's Theatre, then took a taxi back to his hotel. He showered, shaved, and packed, then went over the hotel room, wiping every surface with window cleaner, after which he dressed in a pair of lightweight black trousers and a long-sleeved, navy blue T-shirt. Over that he put on the freshly pressed first-class army uniform, with its ribbons, insignia, and name tag. Finally, he packed all the uniforms into a single B-4 bag and his civilian clothes in another bag, then checked out of the hotel, mentioning to the desk clerk that he had a plane to catch at Reagan National.

He drove to Ford's Theatre and parked the Taurus in a parking lot nearby. Leaving the bag containing the uniforms in the trunk, he walked to the new Toyota and put his civilian clothes into that car's trunk. Finally, with everything ready and half an hour to spare, he walked to Ford's Theatre and got into the ticket holders' line. Secret Service agents were everywhere, watching everything. They walked down the line of waiting people and cut several people out of the group for a chat, checking tickets and IDs. A deranged-looking man was taken away in a car. Zeke noticed that the people getting the most attention from the agents were unaccompanied men, but when they came to him, the agents simply nodded and went on. The uniform worked.

At twenty minutes before the hour the doors were opened and the crowd admitted. Zeke immediately made for the stairs to the balcony and found a seat on an aisle, only a few steps from the staircase to the men's room and the projection booth. Now he had only to wait.

Will sat in his dressing room and tried to hold still for the makeup lady, while continuing to go over debating points with Tim and Kitty. A television set was tuned to MSNBC, and the mention of Larry Moody's name stopped all conversation. Everyone turned to watch.

"In just a minute we'll be going live to the Georgia governor's mansion, where the governor is about to make a statement on the Larry Moody case. Moody is scheduled to go to the electric chair at Reidsville State Prison tomorrow night. We've had a report that the actress Charlene Joiner visited with the governor last night and again this afternoon, leaving the mansion around five o'clock. Our reporter caught up to her at a local airport as she was boarding a private jet."

Charlene appeared on camera at the door of the Centurion Studios airplane. "I visited with the governor last evening and again today and talked with him about Larry's case. I believe he spent the day alone at the mansion, reviewing the case in detail, and I hope for a favorable announcement soon. This is Larry's last chance to live." She turned and boarded the airplane, and a steward closed the door.

The camera moved from the taxiing jet to the reporter. "Sources tell MSNBC that, after her arrival last night, Ms. Joiner was not seen to leave the governor's mansion until late this afternoon. The governor's wife is out of town, and his staff was kept at arm's length all day as he and Ms. Joiner discussed the case. Back to the studio."

Anchorwoman Laurie Dhue came on screen. "We go now to the governor's mansion for the governor's statement."

The governor was seen to approach a cluster of microphones.

"You think Charlene was with him all night and all day?" Tim Coleman asked.

"He looks pretty tired to me," Kitty replied.

The governor began to speak. "I have been reviewing in great detail the clemency request of Larry Eugene Moody, whose final appeal was recently turned down by the Supreme Court. I have concluded after much study and thought that, although Mr. Moody is certainly guilty of the crime with which he was charged, his defense by then senatorial candidate Will Lee with regard to the death penalty was a thoroughly incompetent one. I have therefore decided to commute Mr. Moody's death sentence to life in prison, and I signed the appropriate papers a few minutes ago. That's all; thank you." The governor turned to go as the gathered reporters shouted questions.

"Did the visit by Charlene Joiner have anything to do with your decision?" one yelled.

The governor turned. "Ms. Joiner is one of the people I talked with about this."

"How long did you spend with her?" another reporter demanded.

"Is your wife still out of town?" a woman's voice shouted.

"Good night, ladies and gentlemen," the governor said, then walked back into the mansion and closed the door.

Will turned to the makeup lady. "All finished?"

"All finished," she said.

"Then would you excuse us, please?" He waited until the door had been closed. "I don't believe it," he said. "I actually suggested this to Charlene."

"Suggested *what?*" Kitty asked.

"She was aboard the airplane in Van Nuys, looking all sexy, and I said, why don't you turn that on the governor? I'm damned if she didn't!"

Tim's mouth dropped open. "You mean you think that Charlene spent all night and all day screwing the governor?"

"Didn't you see the bags under his eyes?" Kitty asked.

"She's certainly capable of that," Will said, "and you heard that his wife was out of town."

"And that he spent the day alone," Kitty added, "but Charlene didn't leave until this afternoon. This has got to be a first in the administration of justice."

"You just have to wonder," Tim said, "what Charlene was administering."

"You notice he got in a good punch at you, Senator," Kitty said. "Two to one, Eft is going to come at you on this."

"Let him come," Will replied.

There was a knock at the door, and a Secret Service agent came in. "They're ready for you, Senator," he said. "You're on the air in five minutes."

"Let's do it," Will said.

62

Will followed a young woman to the wings at stage left. Looking across the stage, he could see Eft Efton, and they exchanged a wave. Will thought Efton was smiling rather smugly.

Zeke had to stand up to let a man into his row of seats; the man took the seat next to him, then glanced at Zeke's ribbons.

"You were in 'Nam, were you?"

"Right," Zeke replied.

"My name's Dave Waters," the man said, offering his hand.

"Henry Waldron," Zeke replied, shaking the man's hand.

"What outfit were you in?"

Zeke told him.

"You guys saw a lot of fighting at Da Nang, didn't you?"

"You better believe it," Zeke said.

"I never got out of Saigon, myself," Waters replied.

Zeke was relieved when the lights went down and a voice came from the PA system.

"Good evening, ladies and gentlemen, and to our national television audience. Please welcome your moderator for the debate, Jim Lehrer of PBS." There was a round of applause.

Lehrer took the stage. "Good evening," he said. "Our format tonight provides for a three-minute opening statement from each candidate, followed by a series of questions from me. After that, the candidates will be allowed to ask each other questions, and each will have two minutes to answer them. Finally, each candidate will have three minutes for a closing statement. We flipped a coin earlier to decide who would speak first, so Representative Efton will go first with the opening statement, and Senator Lee will be first with the closing statement. Gentlemen?"

Will came from the left wings as Efton came from the right, and they took their positions at the lecterns, to considerable applause.

"Mr. Efton, you may begin," Lehrer said. "I will warn you when you have thirty seconds left, and I will cut you off sharply after three minutes, if you are still talking."

Efton cleared his throat and began to speak.

Zeke found himself to be nervous. He didn't want to sit through all this; he wanted to get on with it. He stood up and walked toward the staircase to the men's room and projection room. A Secret Service agent stopped him.

"Where are you going, sir?" he asked.

Zeke placed a hand on his lower abdomen. "To the men's room, up the stairs, there."

"You'll have to use the one downstairs in the lobby," the agent said.

Zeke frowned as though in pain. "I'm having an intestinal problem," he said. "I don't think I can make it that far."

"All right," the agent said, "go ahead."

Zeke began walking up the stairs, and as he did, the agent moved away, apparently continuing on his rounds. At the top of the stairs Zeke looked back to be sure no one was observing him, then opened the door to the projection room and went inside, pulling on a pair of latex surgical gloves. There was no lock on the door, so Zeke braced a chair under the doorknob. First, he emptied his pockets, shucked off the army uniform, and wrapped it into a ball, tying the shirtsleeves in a knot. Then he put the pocket contents into his black trousers, switched on a small flashlight, and, holding it in his mouth, took his Swiss Army knife and began unscrewing the grille over the air-conditioning duct. He removed the briefcase containing the rifle, then shoved the bundled army uniform into the duct and replaced the grille.

Will listened patiently as Efton made his three-minute speech. The first two minutes were bland enough; then Efton changed tack. "As you may have heard, the governor of Georgia last night felt he had to commute the death sentence of a murderer and rapist, because the man's lawyer had given him an incompetent defense. That lawyer was none other than Will Lee, and I think he should explain to us tonight why his incompetence as a lawyer allowed a killer to escape the death penalty, and why we should expect him to be any more competent as president."

Will hadn't expected this so early in the debate. Now he was going to have to spend at least part of his opening statement defending himself, putting him at an immediate disadvantage.

Dave Waters, who had been sitting next to Zeke in the balcony, was worried, and he felt he had to do something. He got up and began looking up and down the aisles, but he didn't see what he was looking for, so he walked down the stairs to the lobby, where he spotted a man with a small medallion in his lapel. "Excuse me," he said to the man, "are you Secret Service?"

"Yes," the man replied, "what can I do for you, sir?"

"I need to speak to the agent in charge, and right away."

"What about, sir?"

Waters produced a military ID card. "I'm General David Waters, and I want to speak to him *right now*."

"Yes, sir," the agent said. He raised his cupped left hand to his lips and spoke briefly into it, then seemed to listen. "He'll be here in just a minute, sir."

"Ten years ago I was called into a judge's office in Greenville, Georgia, the seat of my home county, and asked to defend a young man accused of murder. I was reluctant to do so, but the judge pressed me, and I agreed. At my first meeting with the defendant, he told me that he was innocent of the charges and that he had never had any problems with the law. I defended him—well, I think—then, near the end of the trial, a witness blurted out that the defendant had once been accused of rape. This shocked the courtroom, the prosecution took full advantage of the situation, and the defendant was convicted as charged. Had he not lied to me, he would probably have been acquitted. During the trial, I received a cash fee from an anonymous supporter of the defendant. Later, I learned that the money had come from a right-wing militia group, the kind which has so often supported Representative Efton in his campaigns, so I donated the fee to an organization of African-American lawyers. The defendant later claimed, in his appeals, that he received an incompetent defense, a claim that was thrown out by every state and federal court that heard it, including the Supreme Court of the United States. I think that is all the vindication I need, even if it isn't enough for Mr. Efton."

A middle-aged man in a dark suit approached Dave Waters. "General Waters? I'm Charles West, the agent in charge of the Secret Service detail here. What can I do for you?"

"Agent West, just before the debate began I sat down next to an army officer, a Colonel Waldron, in the balcony. I introduced myself and, noticing his ribbons and insignia, I asked him what outfit he had been with in Vietnam. He said his name was Henry Waldron, and that he had been with *my* outfit. I said that I had heard the unit had been at Da Nang, and he confirmed this. My outfit was never at Da Nang, and the officer I knew as Henry Waldron was not the man sitting next to me. I believe he is impersonating an army officer, and considering the circumstances, I thought you should know about it."

"Thank you, General," the agent said. He brought a fist to his lips. "Attention all agents," he said. "Suspicious person in the theater, dressed as an army colonel. Locate immediately and detain." He turned back to Waters. "Thank you, General," he said. "I'd appreciate it if you'd remain here to identify the man when we find him."

"He got up and left his seat in the balcony about five minutes ago," Waters said, "but I didn't see where he went."

Will finished his statement, compressing his opening remarks in order to stay under the time limit. As he finished, he saw a small flash of light somewhere high up at the rear of the theater.

63

Zeke quickly assembled the rifle, then, judging the distance between the projection booth and the stage, adjusted the sight. The projectionist's window was hinged in the middle; he opened it, rested the tip of the rifle's barrel on the sill, and brought the stock to his shoulder.

Agent West stood in the open doorway between the lobby of the theater and the orchestra seats, only a few seconds after broadcasting the first warning to his agents. "Chief, this is Robbins," a voice said through his earpiece. "Five minutes ago, I allowed an army colonel to use the men's room at the top of the theater. I'm on my way there now."

"Roger," West replied, then something occurred to him. "Is that the one opposite the projection booth?"

"Affirmative," Robbins replied.

West brought the microphone concealed in his

left palm to his lips. "Maximum alert! Maximum alert! All agents on the upper level converge on the men's room and projection booth at the top rear of the theater! Consider suspect an assassin, armed and dangerous!" He began running for the stairs.

Zeke brought the crosshairs to bear on the head of Will Lee. As he focused the telescopic sight, a movement at stage right caught his attention, and he swung the rifle toward it. To his astonishment, Howard Efton was lying on the floor behind his lectern, and a man was lying on top of him. He swung the rifle back toward Lee, and as he did, a man appeared from the wings and began reaching for the senator.

Zeke fired without resighting, and there was an explosion at the lectern. Then Zeke heard the sound of running feet on the upper level of the theater. He dropped the rifle, kicked the chair away from the doorknob, ran into the hallway outside, and started up the ladder, throwing open the trapdoor to the roof. As he turned to slam it behind him he saw a man with a gun running up the stairs toward the projection room.

Zeke sprinted across the roof, surprised that a Secret Service agent was not waiting for him. Probably any agents on the roof had been called inside the theater when the debate began, he reckoned. He reached the parapet and ran along it, looking for a fire escape or a drainpipe. Nothing. He jumped to the roof next door and, staying low, continued along the row of buildings.

Glancing back, he saw lights playing around the roof of the theater.

On the third roof he found a drainpipe, and it took only seconds to slide down it into the alley below. He ran down the alley toward the street, shucking off the latex surgical gloves he had been wearing, and as he turned the corner, he stopped running and started walking, taking deep breaths, calming himself, trying to look like an ordinary citizen. He turned toward where he had parked the Toyota and realized that would take him directly past the entrance to Ford's Theatre. What the hell, he thought, they wouldn't expect him to be there.

He blended in with the other pedestrians headed in that direction, and as he approached the theater, the front doors burst open and armed men ran onto the sidewalk, looking in every direction. They were looking for an army colonel, he reminded himself, and he had left the uniform in the air-conditioning duct where he had stored the rifle. He stopped with the other pedestrians and stared at the commotion. Then the man who had sat next to him in the balcony came out of the theater with a Secret Service agent. Zeke walked to the curb, waited for traffic to ease, and, walking as casually as he could, crossed the street. It was another block to the car, and it was going to be a very long block.

Will sat in his dressing room, surrounded by staff and Secret Service agents. Kitty was holding a cloth to his forehead while an agent rummaged in a first-aid kit. "What happened?" he asked.

"Somebody took a shot at you," an agent said. "I already had hold of you and was pulling you toward the wings. Apparently, the bullet hit the microphone on the lectern, and the thing exploded. You caught some shrapnel, but it's not serious. You may need a stitch or two, though, and as soon as the area is secure, we're going to get you to a hospital to get looked at."

"You think it's the same guy from L.A.?" Kitty asked.

"It's gotta be," the agent replied. "Either him, or another member of his group, if there is a group."

"Have you caught him?" Kitty asked.

The agent held a finger to his ear, pressing on the earpiece. "He's out of the building," he said. "They're searching the streets for him now. Apparently, a member of the audience can ID him."

"My wife is in the audience," Will said.

"We've already got her in a car," the agent replied. "She'll meet you at the hospital."

Zeke got into the car, started it, and pulled into traffic. He made the first turn possible, and he could see police halting traffic ahead of him. He drove around the block and headed for the Beltway; he had already memorized the route.

Will lay on a table in the ER while a surgeon who had been on call for the Secret Service stitched the wound in his forehead. Kate sat next to him, watching closely.

"Maybe I'd better learn to do this," she said, "if people are going to keep trying to kill you."

"Maybe the guy was trying to kill Eft," Will said. "If he did, I'd probably win California."

"You should wish he had hit you," she said. "Being shot is a sure vote-getter. Look at Reagan."

The following morning, Zeke drove west along the interstate at the speed limit. He was a happy man, considering that he'd failed. He hadn't really expected to be alive at this moment, and he found the condition pleasing. Home lay a thousand miles ahead of him. They still didn't know who he was. They'd never find him. He'd go home and wait for another opportunity.

64

Will looked out the window of the Boeing as it lifted off from Oakland airport and turned east, toward Georgia. The lights of the city passed under him, then vanished as the airplane climbed toward the Sierras. It was just after 1 A.M., Tuesday morning, election day. It was over.

He had made more than seventy campaign stops around California during the past three days. His campaign and the party had poured every possible cent into television advertising all over the country, but especially in California. Efton had done the same thing, he reflected.

"What do you think?" he asked Kitty Conroy, who was sitting next to him.

"I think we're going to win, of course."

"Does Moss still think it's too close to call?"

"Yes, but he plans to do exit polling tomorrow—I mean, today."

"Tell him not to waste the money. What's the point of polling when we'll have the answer by midnight, anyway."

"I'll tell him," she said. She got up and walked forward.

Will got out of his chair and followed her. He might as well have a last word with the press. He passed Moss and Kitty, deep in conversation, and opened the door to the forward compartment, summoning up a last bit of energy. To his surprise, the cabin was dark; bodies lay under blankets on the reclining seats; snoring could be heard. He'd thought there'd at least be a late poker game, or people writing their last campaign stories.

He closed the door and walked aft to his private cabin and the flying bed that awaited him. He had one more stop, a morning appearance to thank the campaign workers in Atlanta, then to Delano, to vote, then back to Washington. For a while, he replayed the campaign in his mind. There was nothing more he could do. He fell asleep.

When he finally reached the Georgetown house, Kate was already home from work, watching CNN.

"You look exhausted," she said, kissing him and drawing him onto the sofa next to her.

"I think that's a fair assessment of my condition," he said. "The strange thing is, I'm not sleepy. I got a few hours on the airplane last night, and a good nap on the way from Georgia to D.C. What does the news say?"

"A good turnout, but not a huge one," she replied.

"Oh." They had been hoping for a large turnout, usually better for Democrats. "Did you vote?"

"You bet."

"Dare I ask for whom?"

"Don't push your luck, kiddo."

Will held up his hands in a defensive posture. "I guess it's too late now."

"What time are we due this evening?" she asked.

"Ten o'clock," he replied. His campaign had taken a hotel ballroom and a suite and had rented a lot of TV sets for election night. "We can have a nice quiet dinner here."

"Who's cooking?" she asked. "I had a tough day, too."

"Let's order a pizza."

Kate laughed. "The next president of the United States orders a pizza on election day."

Their attention was suddenly drawn to the TV set by the mention of Will's name, and they turned to watch.

"The Secret Service and the FBI have identified a suspect in the assassination attempt last Friday night at Ford's Theatre in Washington," the anchorwoman was saying. A photograph of a bearded man flashed onto the screen. "He was identified from a fingerprint on the outside doorknob of the projection room at the theater. He is William Ezekiel Tennant, formerly of an address near Atlanta. Tennant disappeared from his home some ten years ago, after he failed to make a federal court appearance in Atlanta, and a warrant for his arrest dates from that time. Tennant was a member of a right-wing militia group headquartered in the Atlanta area, a member of which made an attempt on the life of Will Lee, who was at that time a candidate for the Senate. Tennant is rumored to be somewhere in the northwestern United States, and authorities are already searching for him there.

"In another breaking story, CNN has learned that a South Carolina newspaper is running a front-page story tomorrow, alleging that Senator Frederick Wallace of that state has for many years kept an African-American mistress, and that he has two grown sons by her. We're attempting to locate Senator Wallace now for comment, and we'll keep you up to date on this story."

Kate and Will burst out laughing. "I don't know which story I like better," she said.

"Neither do I," Will agreed.

65

Will, Kate, Peter, and Will's parents walked into the hotel ballroom and stood for a moment, taking in the scene. A big band was playing swing tunes, and many of the campaign workers were dancing to the music. A movie-theater-sized television screen had been erected, and other TV sets were scattered around the ballroom.

Will and Kate made their way to the stage, were introduced, and Will stepped to a microphone as the band stopped playing.

"I just wanted to speak to you for a moment," he said. "Although we don't know the outcome yet, I'm optimistic. I want to take this opportunity to thank you all for the hard work you've put into this campaign. If we don't win tonight, it won't be your fault. I don't think any candidate has ever had such an enthusiastic group of people working for his election, and I'm very grateful to each and every one of you. Kate and I are going to go upstairs, now, and wait for the final returns. I'll speak to you again, after we know the result of the election. In the meantime, have a great evening. You've earned it!"

The five of them were whisked backstage and to an elevator that took them to a large suite on the highest floor of the hotel. There waiting for them were Will's closest staff and a lot of big contributors to his campaign and to the party.

Kitty ran over. "The polls have just closed in Illinois," she said, "and the networks, based on their exit polling, are giving it to us by two points."

"We can all thank you for that, Kitty," Will said, hugging her. "Your idea for the debate against the TV set gave us the state."

"I hope that turns out to be true," Kitty said. "I'll never get tired of taking credit for it."

Will deposited his parents on a comfortable sofa with drinks; then he and Kate wandered around the huge suite, shaking hands and talking to supporters, while the voting results mounted from around the nation.

Tim Coleman came over to Will. "It's going pretty much the way Moss predicted: We're neck and neck in electoral votes; California is going to decide the election."

"Is there anything we didn't do in California?" Will asked.

"Not that I can think of," Tim replied.

"I don't think there's a hand in the state I didn't shake," Will said. "My arm is sore to the shoulder."

"That's the way it ought to be," Tim said, laughing.

Midnight was approaching, 9 P.M. in California, when the polls would close and the networks could announce the results of their exit polling. The crowd in the suite were all sitting down, occupying all the furniture and much of the carpeted floor, facing the big TV screen, which was divided into quarters, one each for NBC, CBS, ABC, and CNN. Kitty was switching the sound from network to network. More coffee than champagne was being served at that hour.

"Quiet!" Kitty yelled, switching to NBC, where Tom Brokaw was speaking.

". . . the closest presidential race in American history," Brokaw was saying, "closer than Kennedy-Nixon, in 1960, closer than Nixon-Humphrey, in 1968. The polls have just closed in California, and we can now talk about the exit polling we've been doing in that state all day, right up to a couple of hours ago. Based on that polling we can now call the California race. Although no more than one percentage point separates the candidates, we can now say that California has gone to Congressman Howard Efton. And that means that Efton takes all fifty-four of California's electoral votes and the election. Howard Efton is going to be the next president of the United States."

The crowd sat in shocked silence. "Switch to ABC," Tim Coleman shouted.

". . . California gives the election to Eft Efton," Peter Jennings was saying.

Kitty switched to CBS and Dan Rather. "It looks as though Efton has won this election," Rather said.

Kitty switched to CNN. More of the same.

Nobody said much of anything.

Will beckoned Moss Mallet over. "What do you make of this?" he asked.

"No other kind of polling is as accurate as exit polling," Moss said. "They talked to people who had already voted, as they left the polling places. Quite frankly, if even one of the networks had disagreed, I'd say we have a chance, but they're all coming up with the same result. I'm sorry, Will, but we've lost it."

Will stood up. "Listen up, everybody. I'm not going to say anything now, except to thank you for being here tonight and for your support during the campaign. Certainly, it doesn't look good at the moment. Kate and I are going to go home and get some sleep, now, and I suggest you do the same. Kitty, schedule a press conference for noon tomorrow, on the Capitol steps, and I'll make a statement then." Will took Kate's arm and started for the door, shaking hands along the way.

Kitty appeared at his elbow. "I'll call you if anything changes," she said.

"Don't," Will said. "I'm going to go home and sleep the sleep of the dead, and I don't want to be disturbed by *anybody*. Please see to that." He hugged her. "I'm sorry, Kitty; I know how hard you worked and how much you wanted this. Set up a dinner tomorrow night with just you, Tim, Moss, and Sam Meriwether and my folks, and we'll pick over the bones and talk about what we might have done. I'll be in the office by eleven-thirty. Have a statement ready for me to look at."

"All right, Senator," Kitty said, and there were tears in her eyes.

Will and Kate were quiet on the ride to George-town, but Billy seemed to want to talk.

"You know," he said, "you ran one hell of a campaign, and if there were any justice, you'd have won. But we both know there's precious little justice in politics."

"I guess you're right, Dad," Will replied.

"I had an awful good time, though."

"So did I," Patricia echoed. "You've got a lot to be proud of, Will."

When they got out of the car, the head of the Secret Service detail approached Will. "Senator," he said, "we've just had word that the FBI has tracked down Zeke Tennant. He's in a mountain cabin in Idaho, and they're planning to take him tomorrow morning. They're not releasing this to the media; they don't want to alert him."

"That's good news," Will said. "I want to thank you and all your people for your great work during the campaign," he said. "You saved my life more than once. I'd appreciate it if you'd put together a list of the name of every man and woman who worked on the detail. I'd like to write to them."

"Of course, Senator," the agent said. "I've had your cars brought back; they're in the garage.

Our people are already out of the house, and I'll leave a couple of men on the front door to see that no one disturbs you tonight; in the morning, we'll be gone."

Will let them into the house and began closing blinds. "God, I'm tired," he said.

Kate walked to the rear hallway, switched off the telephones, then came back. "The agents are already gone," she said. "They left everything as neat as a pin. Would you like something to eat? There's still some pizza in the oven."

"No, I just want to sleep," Will said. He took her hand, and they walked upstairs together.

"Do you folks need anything?" Kate asked Patricia.

"I might have a glass of milk after a while," Patricia replied, "but right now I just want to get Billy to bed. He's very tired. Don't worry, I know where the kitchen is."

"Good night, then," Kate said, kissing her.

Kate switched off the upstairs phones. "How do you feel?" she asked.

"Numb," Will replied. "Let's talk about it tomorrow."

They got undressed and into bed.

"You know," she said, "life will be simpler now, but I had started looking forward to your being president. I think I'm more disappointed than you are."

"I'll catch up with you tomorrow," he said.

Will fell asleep with Kate's head on his shoulder.

66

Will came awake very slowly in the darkened room. Kate wasn't there, and he could smell coffee brewing downstairs. He rolled over and looked at the bedside clock. Nearly seven o'clock. He'd slept through the night without even turning over.

He got up, went to the bathroom, and brushed his teeth, using his left hand. His right was too sore and swollen from shaking hands to make a fist. He put on a robe over his nightshirt, got into his slippers, and walked downstairs.

Kate looked over her shoulder from the kitchen. "Morning. Your folks are still asleep; you want some eggs?"

"Don't mind if I do," he said, looking around. "Did you bring in the papers?"

"Nope."

"Do we have any sausage?"

"Some in the freezer, I think. I'll nuke it."

It suddenly occurred to Will that he had lost the election, and he felt momentarily nauseated.

He drank some orange juice and felt better. "I'll get the papers," he said.

He walked through the darkened living room, undid the latch on the front door, opened it, and stepped out onto the porch. Suddenly, he was blinded by a hundred flashes, and a roar of voices washed over him. Blinking, shielding his eyes from the continuing flashes, Will looked around him. Except for his block, the street was full of people, press, and cameras, held at the cross street by police, and the sudden din was amazing. The police removed the barricades, and the crowd rushed toward the house, stopped only by another cordon of barricades at the foot of the steps.

Kate came to the door. "What the hell is going on?" she asked.

Kitty Conroy, Tim Coleman, Moss Mallet, and Sam Meriwether broke through a cordon of police and rushed up the front steps of the house. "You won!" Kitty shouted over the noise.

"What?" Will yelled back.

Kitty shouted into his ear, "There was a huge rush of after-work voters in California, and most of the absentee ballots were for you; those two things put us over the top. Efton is conceding even as we speak!" She handed him a copy of the national edition of the *New York Times*. "This edition went to bed at midnight." EFTON DEFEATS LEE, the banner headline read.

Will stood, dumbfounded, staring at the newspaper. His parents joined him on the porch, and Kate slipped an arm around him.

"Wave at the people, dear," she said. "Try not to look semiconscious."

Will waved at the crowd and held up the newspaper, to the crowd's delight.

"Smile," Kate said. "Presidents have to smile a lot."

Will smiled, showing all the teeth he had.

At first light, Zeke was eating a bowl of homemade granola when his son, Danny, came down the stairs from the log cupola carrying an assault rifle, a 9mm pistol strapped to his side. The boy was pale. "What is it, son?" he asked.

"They're coming through the trees," Danny said, and his voice trembled.

"Wake up your mother and your sisters and get them armed," Zeke said, "then come upstairs with me." Zeke ran up to the cupola and looked down the hill. Men in camouflage suits were creeping up the incline in squads, one group taking shelter and covering, while another group ran ahead a few more yards. They were three hundred yards away, Zeke calculated, using the distance markers he had placed. He checked the wind sock and adjusted the telescopic sight on his rifle for distance and windage. He heard Danny coming slowly up the steps behind him. "Hurry up, goddammit!" he yelled. "We've got to pick off as many as we can before they get any closer."

"No, sir," the boy said quietly. He sounded very shaky.

Zeke turned and looked at Danny. He was

holding the Glock pistol out in front of him. "What's the matter with you?" he demanded.

"I'm not going to let you get Mama and the girls killed," Danny said. "Nor me, neither."

"You holster that weapon and get to a gun port," Zeke commanded. "We've spent two years preparing for this, and we're not going to screw it up now."

"You brought this on us," Danny said, "and you're not going to stop until we're all dead." His voice was stronger, now. "And I'm not going to have it."

"You'll do as you're told, boy, and you'll do it right now!" Zeke yelled at him.

"No, sir, I won't," Danny said, pointing the pistol at Zeke's head.

"Have you completely lost your mind?" Zeke shouted.

"No, sir," Danny replied, "but you have." He pulled the trigger.

It was the loudest noise Zeke had ever heard.

Down the mountainside, the FBI agent in charge heard two shots. He picked up a handheld radio. "Shots from the house," he said. "Everybody hold your positions." He trained his binoculars on the house and waited. Nothing happened for a good two minutes, then the front door opened, and a teenage boy walked out, his hands in the air, followed by a woman and two girls. "Hold your fire," the agent said into the radio. He stood up and walked up the hill, motioning a squad of agents to follow him.

He stopped ten feet short of the little group. "Stand still, son, while my people search you," he said.

The boy and the women were quickly frisked. "Everybody's clean," an agent said.

The agent relaxed a little. "Good morning, folks," he said. "Who are you?"

"My name is Danny Tennant," the boy said, "and this is my mama and my sisters."

"Where's your father, Danny?" the agent asked.

"He's up in the cupola," Danny replied, pointing to the top of the house.

"Is he going to give us any trouble?" the agent asked.

"No, sir; he's dead. I shot him."

The agent took a quick breath, then motioned to his men. "Take a look inside," he said, "and be careful."

Three minutes later they returned. "Tennant's upstairs," an agent said. "He's dead, like the boy said. There's nobody else in the house."

The agent took Danny's arm and walked him toward the front porch. "You want to tell me what happened, son?"

"Yes, sir, I do," Danny replied, "but it's gonna take a while."

"We've got all the time in the world," the agent said.

67

Will Lee stood coatless in the bright January sunshine on the steps of the United States Capitol and tried not to shiver in the stiff breeze that snapped at the numerous American flags in his immediate vicinity. Only Kate knew he was wearing his ski underwear.

He had been president for less than sixty seconds, and as he waited for the roar of applause to die, he considered his position. He had a twenty-two-vote majority in the House of Representatives, a result, he knew, of the reaction of voters to the disgraceful Republican conduct of the Clinton impeachment proceedings. He had cleverly reduced the two-vote Republican majority in the Senate to one, by, with George Kiel's consent, appointing as secretary of state a Republican senator whose home-state Democratic governor had appointed a Democrat to the remainder of his term. Having worked for many years to befriend Senate Republicans, he had no doubt he could swing a couple of their votes when it counted.

He had, after a select committee had recommended her, appointed his wife to the position of Director of Central Intelligence, and he fully expected her to win confirmation by the Senate, on the grounds that she had earned the job by means other than sleeping with the president. As a result, he reckoned, he had a better-than-even chance of discovering who had really killed Jack Kennedy and if a spaceship had actually crashed at Roswell, New Mexico.

He glanced over his shoulder at Joe Adams, who was beaming broadly at him as he pounded his hands together, and who looked greatly relieved no longer to be president.

He looked at his parents, who had stopped applauding and, instead, had their arms around each other.

He looked at Peter and, finally, at Kate, and he thought that she had never looked happier, when sex was not involved.

All was as right with the world as it would ever again likely be, unless he could, by force of his long experience and personal leadership, make it even better. He was determined to do so.

He looked into the crowd of one hundred thousand inauguration attendees and into the lenses that connected him with a hundred million other of his countrymen.

"My fellow Americans," he began. . . .

Acknowledgments

I want to express my deep gratitude to Gladys Justin Carr, my editor for many books, who is retiring. During our work together she has always been very supportive, and her acute editorial judgment has improved every manuscript I have sent her. I wish her the happiest of retirements. Her assistant, Dierdre O'Brien, who manages a thousand details, also has my sincere thanks.

I would also like to thank Carolyn Marino, who has taken over from Gladys during the production and promotion stages, for her hard work on my behalf.

My agents, Morton Janklow and Anne Sibbald, and all the people at Janklow & Nesbit, continue to labor on my behalf, always with excellent results, and they, as always, have my gratitude.

I want to thank Melody Miller, Deputy Press Secretary to Senator Edward M. Kennedy of Massachusetts, who has always been there to supply the political background and verisimilitude so necessary for novels like this. I am grateful for her help and her continuing friendship.

My wife, Chris, is always my first reader and most fearless critic, and I thank her for her candor and her love.

Author's Note

I am happy to hear from readers, but you should know that if you write to me in care of my publisher, three to six months will pass before I receive your letter, and when it finally arrives it will be one among many, and I will not be able to reply.

However, if you have access to the Internet, you may visit my website at *www.stuartwoods.com*, where there is a button for sending me e-mail. So far, I have been able to reply to all of my e-mail, and I will continue to try to do so.

If you send me an e-mail and do not receive a reply, it is because you are among an alarming number of people who have entered their e-mail address incorrectly in their mail software. I have many of my replies returned as undeliverable.

Remember: e-mail, reply; snail mail, no reply.

When you e-mail, please do not send attachments, as I *never* open these. They can take twenty minutes to download, and they often contain viruses.

Please do not place me on your mailing lists for funny stories, prayers, political causes, charitable fund-raising, petitions, or sentimental claptrap. I get enough of that from people I already know. Generally speaking, when I get e-mail addressed to a large number of people, I immediately delete it without reading it.

Please do not send me your ideas for a book, as I have a policy of writing only what I myself invent. If you send me story ideas, I will immediately delete them without reading them. If you have a good idea for a book, write it yourself, but I will not be able to advise you on how to get it published. Buy a copy of *Writer's Market* at any bookstore; that will tell you how.

Anyone with a request concerning events or appearances may e-mail it to me or send it to: Publicity Department, Penguin Group (USA) Inc., 375 Hudson Street, New York, NY 10014.

Those ambitious folk who wish to buy film, dramatic, or television rights to my books should contact Matthew Snyder, Creative Artists Agency, 2000 Avenue of the Stars, Los Angeles, CA 90067.

Those who wish to make offers for rights of a literary nature should contact Anne Sibbald, Janklow & Nesbit, 445 Park Avenue, New York, NY 10022. (Note: This is not an invitation for you to send her your manuscript or to solicit her to be your agent.)

If you want to know if I will be signing books in your city, please visit my website, *www.stuart woods.com*, where the tour schedule will be published a month or so in advance. If you wish me to do a book signing in your locality, ask your

favorite bookseller to contact his Penguin representative or the Penguin publicity department
with the request.

If you find typographical or editorial errors in
my book and feel an irresistible urge to tell someone, please write to David Highfill at HarperCollins Publishers, 10 East 53rd Street, New York, NY
10022. Do not e-mail your discoveries to me, as I
will already have learned about them from others.

A list of my published works appears in the
front of this book and on my website. All the
novels are still in print in paperback and can be
found at or ordered from any bookstore. If you
wish to obtain hardcover copies of earlier novels
or of the two nonfiction books, a good used-book
store or one of the online bookstores can help
you find them. Otherwise, you will have to go to
a great many garage sales.